STALKER'S REVENGE

LINDA HALES

Paperback ISBN 979-8-9909989-0-2

Hardcover ISBN 979-8-9909989-1-9

To my dear, sweet mother, Betty, my support system and treasured friend. I miss you and will love you always.

Stalker's Revenge

Chapter 1

Despite the blistering Arizona heat, Kaylee shivered, and chills ran down her back. Sitting on the leather recliner, she was surrounded by its billowy cushions. Her black funeral dress accentuated her shimmering-blond hair and slender figure, but felt tight and constricting. As she watched the minister shake hands with Jeff's friends and coworkers, she couldn't help but picture her fiancé lying on the ground–blood pooling around his mangled body. Jeff had tried to help her cope with the loss of her mom, but now he was gone, and she had no one, not even her father. Kaylee knew her father's business needed his constant attention, but she had only asked for two hours. She should have known better. Her father had never shown any compassion before, especially not to her; why would he come to her fiancé's funeral? Sitting in Jeff's living room and watching the other mourners hug and console each other, she never felt so alone.

Kaylee's future, the one she had been planning since she was sixteen, the one that had included Jeff, a fast-paced career, and eventually, kids, was gone. They'd met in high school and had become best friends. Jeff could make her laugh, even during the saddest times, but now he was gone, and she had many unanswered questions.

She inspected Jeff's décor to help pass the time and distract her from the inevitable, but it left her feeling lost and empty. When Kaylee glanced toward the terrace, she noticed a tall man with thick black hair and a dark suit. He looked familiar, and she recognized his posture. She hadn't seen or heard from Kyle in months, and he hadn't contacted her after Jeff died. Kaylee watched him intently; he headed

1

straight toward her. His strides were long and determined, and he quickly covered the ground between them. She stood to leave, but he stopped, and his coal-black eyes stared down at her.

Kaylee met his unflappable gaze and asked, "What are you doing here?"

"I'm here to pay my respects and to warn you about a potential threat."

"What? That's ridiculous." Kaylee laughed.

"I know it sounds bizarre, but it's true. You could be at risk. Let's go somewhere private and discuss it."

She couldn't believe what she was hearing. Kyle had some nerve to show up and try to convince her she could be in danger. Jeff had been the one to fall to his death—he had been the victim of tragic circumstances.

"I'll tell you what I know. Jeff didn't deserve to die all alone, and he didn't deserve to be abandoned by his best friend. So, if I were you, I'd leave."

"He was my friend, too. I have every right to be here." Kyle insisted.

Kaylee shook her head no. "You betrayed him."

Kyle loomed over her. "No. I didn't."

"You took advantage of me, of our friendship. Just go."

"That's not true, and you know it." Kyle stepped back, widening the space between them. "Maybe this isn't the best place to discuss this, but it's urgent, and I need to speak with you as soon as possible."

"You're right. It's not a good time."

Kaylee turned on her heel and quickly strode to the living room; no one noticed she had gone, which added to her overwhelming isolation. She needed her father's support, but he couldn't be bothered. Her father, Michael Chambers, was respected and even feared by some. His financial prowess earned him the admiration of Arizona's business leaders. He expected nothing less than perfection from everyone, including her. Since childhood, she had wanted nothing but to please him. It was a daunting task, one she took seriously. While in high school, she had been an Honors student with a perfect GPA, an award-winning athlete, and a community volunteer. When she had received acceptance letters from three Ivy League universities, she had rushed to her father's office to tell him the good news, and, even after telling his receptionist it was a family emergency, he had refused to see her. She suspected then that her accomplishments had meant nothing to him, and neither did she. She couldn't understand why a man who valued success above all else would be indifferent to his only child's efforts to be successful.

Another storm brewed high in the sky as the last mourners hurried to their cars. Kaylee quickened her pace, but the rain pelted her before she could reach her Shelby. She shook off the excess water and slid into her Mustang. She loved the rain, and Arizona needed it desperately, but today, it only added to her frustration. Attending Jeff's funeral alone upset her, but her run-in with Kyle angered her. It had been five months since she saw him last, and after Jeff had died, he hadn't called to offer support or his condolences. Instead, Kyle had decided to ambush her when she had felt raw and exposed.

The Kyle she had met and had dated in ninth-grade Algebra class, the one she had trusted in high school and college, had been solid as a rock, and he would've dropped everything to help his friends. But after Jeff announced their engagement, Kyle made excuses to avoid being around them. And that hurt. Their friendship had meant everything to her, and his spot-on advice had helped her through many difficult situations.

Her chest felt heavy, and her outlook for the future felt as gloomy as the gray, clouded heavens. She knew the sky would eventually clear up, but right now, she couldn't be sure which direction her life would take. And that worried her. She had no hope of salvaging any relationship with her father. Still, she had hoped Jeff's untimely demise would bring her and Kyle closer together. But it didn't. They were further apart than ever, and his accusations were offensive and unfounded. What makes him think she could be in danger? Jeff fell. It was an accident, end of story.

While driving home, her stomach grumbled. A quick mental checklist of her pantry confirmed that she had nothing to eat. She weaved in and out of the lanes, trying to beat the unpredictable showers. She pulled into Barrington's Fine Foods shopping center and was forced to park in the back. The rain pummeled the ground; her long, blond hair stuck to her dress and dripped water down her back. Water splashed on her shoes and legs as she tried to dodge the deep puddles. If her boss could see her now, she would never hear the end of it.

Once inside, Kaylee laughed at her ridiculous reflection, and curious shoppers glanced her way and continued shopping. She stuffed the essentials, bread, milk, eggs, and coffee, into the top part of the cart. She loaded the rest with candy, cake, whipped cream, and strawberries. She relied heavily on sugar to get through crises, and she needed it now more than ever.

She had eaten a lot of ice cream after her mom had died. Her father hadn't been there for her, and she had been drowning in grief. If Jeff hadn't entered her life, she would have sunk into a dark abyss, never to return. Now, her head and heart were reeling from Jeff's sudden death, and Kyle's betrayal and odd behavior only made matters worse.

She shook her head, dispelling the painful memories, at least for now, and headed to the freezer section. Kaylee took in the vast selection; several ice cream flavors caught her eye. She debated on which to try first. Her stomach rumbled in anticipation. Her eyes were glued to the newest flavor, Death by Chocolate. Her stomach tightened; Kaylee tore herself away from the chocolate and

4

chose the butter pecan. She heard a familiar voice and dropped the ice cream into the cart. She twirled around. Kyle was speaking with one of the clerks.

She watched him intently. Kaylee's eyes moved from his leather shoes to his raincoat and coal-black hair. He looked like a model she had seen on the cover of a fashion magazine, not a hair out of place, and his smile plastered on as if with glue. His shoes were the only indication that a violent storm had ravaged the city.

She had been shopping here for years and never once ran into him. Why today? Kaylee watched as he smiled at the clerk and disappeared down the nearest aisle. She pushed the cart slowly and turned down the same aisle; he stopped and stood in front of the meat counter.

As she continued to observe him, he placed an order with the butcher. Her stomach clenched again. She looked down into her cart. Maybe she should get some meat and cheese. Kaylee didn't eat much meat. However, she enjoyed fillet mignon paired with the right wine and grilled asparagus. When she looked toward the meat counter again, Kyle moved on. Relief and disappointment overwhelmed her.

Kaylee skipped the deli section and headed toward the registers. The cashier rang up her items, probably calculating the calories as she went or wondering if Kaylee was trying to put herself into a sugar coma. Kaylee just smiled and swiped her card.

*****

At home, she relaxed in her favorite chair, in front of the seldom-used fireplace, and combed her wet hair. Surrounded by her favorite possessions, she felt safe and let out a sigh of relief. The Savannah-styled wing chair, with its regal high back and decorative arms, added a touch of simple elegance to the room, but the British rosewood cane-top coffee table was the centerpiece. The rich color and ornate legs instantly appealed to Kaylee, and she had to have it. With its luxurious feel and comfortable cushions, the Zanzibar sofa enveloped her in warmth. It perfectly complemented the coffee table and wing chair.

The hypnotic flickering of the flames and the crackling of the logs held Kaylee captive. She glanced up at the clock above the mantel. Time ticked by as she watched the hands meticulously move from one number to the next. It felt as if everything she loved had vanished, and a storm had swept through her life, leaving only devastation and pain in its wake.

She sat motionless for hours, shifting when her joints cramped. The fire warmed Kaylee's body but not her soul. Two pivotal people in her life had passed, but life would go on, and life meant there was hope. Healing would take time, and she knew her whole life might change again in a split second. She wondered if she could accomplish the one thing that mattered the most: prove worthy of her father's love.

Throughout high school and college, she excelled in academics and athletics, trying to earn her father's love and respect, but nothing she did made any difference. His beloved empire had, and always would be, his only reason for living. He couldn't even spare two hours for Jeff's funeral, but what did she expect? At her mom's funeral, he behaved like the grieving husband, but didn't offer Kaylee one moment of empathy or support. As far as he was concerned, she didn't exist.

She pushed the memories of her father's continued rejection out of her mind and let her thoughts drift back to Kyle. Why did he show up at the funeral and the grocery store? Kaylee's curiosity piqued, and she wondered what Kyle wanted to tell her about Jeff. She thought the investigation into Jeff's accident had been closed, and she could put this upsetting portion of her past behind her.

Apparently, that wasn't going to happen. If Kyle had information, had he shared it with the police, and if so, would she be subjected to the pain all over again? If that happened, her secrets might come to light. Nothing good would come from that. Jeff and their secrets were dead and buried, and if there were any justice in the world, they would stay that way.

Memories of kissing Kyle invaded Kaylee's thoughts. Her arms had wrapped around his neck, and her tongue had danced with his. She had pressed up close and had clung to his muscular body. His lips had been warm and soft. Her head had spun, and her knees had buckled. Kissing Kyle had been exhilarating. She couldn't remember which of them pulled away first. It had been wrong, and later, she had been consumed with guilt. Kaylee's relationship with Jeff had been on a slow decline, but from then on, it only worsened. She couldn't change the past, so she had promised to stop reliving it and move forward.

Getting ready for bed, she searched for the blue nightgown her best friend and college roommate, Sara, had given her. Kaylee's methodical, organized behavior kept her sane amid the world's chaos, and her closet was no exception. She arranged her clothes by purpose and color. The nightgowns were kept on the shorter rack next to the door, but her favorite gown had been moved. She shrugged it off and chalked it up to grief. Kaylee left the light on and crawled into bed. Her eyelids were heavy and started to close, but she knew this would be another long, restless night.

The nightmare had replayed over and over, and the following morning, Kaylee woke with a pounding headache. In her dream, she found Jeff on the sidewalk, lying in a pool of blood, his eyes staring up at her. No matter what Kaylee did in the dream, he died, and she felt trapped by overwhelming guilt. Did she try hard enough to save him, or was Jeff's death her fault?

The morning sunlight flooded the kitchen and warmed Kaylee's face. Her stomach growled nonstop; it felt like ages since she'd eaten. She smothered warm toast with butter and powdered sugar and downed some aspirin. She pulled on the freezer door; the carton of ice cream remained unopened, and the thought of eating it revolted her. She added more sugar and creamer to the coffee and took a bite of toast. Excess sugar floated down, leaving traces of feather-soft powder on the counter. She stirred the coffee and watched it turn a smooth caramel color. She took a sip and enjoyed the hot, sweet liquid. She really missed her mother, especially during times like these.

Her mother had been a great cook. She would always prepare something new and different. If Kaylee had refused to eat a new dish, her mother would coax her into trying it, and more often than not, Kaylee had been glad she did. After eating, they'd sit at the large island, talk, and finish their drinks, coffee for her mother and hot chocolate for Kaylee. She really missed those talks. Her mother had been a great listener, and she had known just the right time to interject some of her motherly wisdom. Kaylee wondered what her mother would say to her now. Would she be disappointed in Kaylee's behavior and choices, or would she do as she always did, support and love her daughter?

While sipping coffee and answering emails, she heard the phone ring and hurried to answer it. Commander Blanchard from the Violent Crimes Bureau at the Central City Precinct requested she come to the station immediately. He said it was urgent, but refused to say anything else.

She dressed, grabbed her purse, and jumped into her Shelby.

Chapter 2

At the police station, the desk sergeant directed Kaylee to take a seat. Each second ticked by slowly and painfully. She crossed and uncrossed her legs. Why was she here; did this have anything to do with her father? Had his business affairs finally crossed the line? His empire meant everything to him. It wouldn't be a stretch to assume he would do everything, even something illegal, to protect it. A familiar sound floated down the hallway, and she focused on his voice. What was Kyle doing here?

A tall, muscular man with short brown hair and hazel eyes extended his hand. "Miss Chambers, I'm Detective Randy Jensen. Please come with me."

He spoke confidently and carefully, enunciating each word. His soothing tone helped relax her. He seemed capable of diffusing difficult situations and putting people at ease. Kaylee flashed a quick smile and shook his hand. She followed him down the hall to his office. She walked past Kyle, who waited near the door, and sat down. Kyle took the seat to her left but didn't say a word. Kaylee wondered why she had been summoned to the station and why Kyle sat beside her, tall and rigid. His expression lacked emotion, and he stared straight ahead. He didn't look like the Kyle with whom she had gone to high school and college. The fun-loving guy she remembered was not in the room.

She turned to face the detective. "I thought Commander Blanchard would be meeting me? And what's so important that I had to come down here on a Saturday?"

"Commander Blanchard oversees the violent crimes unit; he called you on my behalf. I appreciate you coming in today. I have some important questions for you, but it shouldn't take long. Would you like a cup of coffee, maybe some water?"

"No, thank you." Kaylee sat tall and focused on the detective. "If you don't mind, I'd like to start."

Detective Jensen nodded. "You were engaged to Mr. Jeff Swanson at the time of his death; is that correct?"

She swallowed. "Yes."

"How long were you two engaged?"

"Almost one year."

"When and how did you meet Mr. Swanson?"

"I met him in high school about eight years ago." She met Detective Jensen's questioning gaze. "I thought you wanted to speak to me about my father, Michael Chambers."

"What gave you that idea?"

"Jeff's dead."

"Miss Chambers, to my knowledge, your father is not in danger or needs a criminal attorney. Do you have reason to believe he is?"

"No, but I buried Jeff yesterday. Nothing you ask me will change that, so why am I here, on a Saturday, answering questions about him?"

Detective Jensen glanced at an open folder, "I apologize for the inopportune timing. You're still grieving, but I have a few loose ends to tie up."

Kaylee shifted. "Your investigators said it was an accident. Why did you wait until his funeral to speak with me?"

"New information is now available, and I am responsible for looking into and processing it. I need some background information on Mr. Swanson and his relationships."

"What information did you receive?" Kaylee asked.

"I can't discuss it with you, but I would appreciate your cooperation. Anything you can tell me will help me put this matter to rest once and for all."

No one wanted that more than her.

"Can you think of anyone who wanted to hurt Mr. Swanson?"

"Hurt him? No."

"What about an old girlfriend? Or a college rival? Did he get along with his neighbors? How about someone from work, a business partner, or a disgruntled client? Was he ever the victim of road rage? No one is without enemies. Are you sure you can't think of anyone? Anyone at all?"

She wasn't prepared for the barrage of questions, and the smell of stale cologne made her nauseous.

"I don't know of anyone who wanted to harm him."

"What about the guy from high school, Greg Goldman," Kyle asked?

"Why would Greg want to hurt Jeff?"

"Remember the bruises on Jeff's face, which he told you were from football practice?"

She turned to face Kyle. "What about them?"

"Greg gave him those."

"Why would he do that," Kaylee asked?

"The kid had it bad for you. That's why he followed you from class and waited at your locker. Greg constantly told Jeff he wasn't good enough for you, and one day, Jeff got tired of it, and they fought."

"Why would—"

"Do you know where Mr. Goldman works or lives," Jensen asked?

Kyle shook his head no, "I haven't seen him since high school, but I think he works for his father's law office somewhere in Phoenix, maybe Scottsdale."

"Mr. Masters, what makes you think Mr. Goldman would want to hurt Mr. Swanson after all these years?"

"You asked if we knew anyone who would want to hurt Jeff, and even though it was back in high school, Greg was the only one I know of who publicly had an issue with Jeff."

"Do you know why Mr. Swanson and Mr. Goldman fought?"

"After the fight, Jeff told me someone had put a note in his locker. I'd assumed it had been Greg since he and Greg fought."

"Did Mr. Swanson tell you the content of the note?"

"No, but he was angry for weeks."

"Miss Chambers, do you know anything about a note?"

She examined the detective. He appeared to be in his thirties, well-dressed, clean-shaven, and intelligent, but why was he wasting everyone's time by rehashing stupid high school pranks?

"Miss Chambers, did you hear me?"

"Yes, but I'm not going to answer any more of your questions until you tell me what's going on."

Detective Jensen met Kaylee's defiant glare, "Miss Chambers, new evidence has surfaced, and we now believe Mr. Swanson was murdered. We are investigating his death as a homicide."

She leaned forward. "Murdered?"

Detective Jensen moved his gaze from Kaylee to Kyle and then back to Kaylee. "I'm trying to find someone with a motive who had the means and opportunity to end Mr. Swanson's life."

Kaylee couldn't believe it. The police think that someone murdered Jeff? What information do they have now that they didn't have a week ago?

"I'm trying to process all of this, but it's a hard concept to wrap my mind around. The man I chose to marry, the man who I called best friend, was murdered, and no one knows why."

"If you just bear with me, I'll try to resolve this issue as quickly as possible."

Kaylee answered the detective's questions about her relationship with Jeff and their plans for the future. She gave straightforward responses. Some of the questions were sensitive, and Kaylee hesitated to answer. She didn't want to bare her soul to Kyle or a stranger. So, she deftly side-stepped questions about the note, her relationship with Kyle, and her love life with Jeff. No one needed to know Kaylee had attended Senior Prom with Kyle because Jeff had been in a car accident that left him scarred both physically and mentally. She also failed to mention that while dating Jeff, they hadn't had sex. Who would believe that a couple who had dated for eight years hadn't engaged in any sexual activity?

Jeff had been disappointed when Kaylee had told him she wouldn't make love to him, but he had agreed to respect her wishes. After a while, he had insisted that they have sex to solidify their future. When she had stood her ground, he had become angry and had stormed out of her apartment. She didn't want to give Detective Jensen any reason to believe she had been involved in Jeff's death, so she kept quiet. If Kaylee told him about her abstinence, she might reveal the actual reason, and she couldn't do that, at least not now.

When he asked where she was on the night Jeff died, Kaylee realized he suspected everyone, including her. She told him she had to finish a project and stayed in her office until ten. When he asked if anyone could corroborate her whereabouts, she said no. He asked her about her clients, coworkers, and their relationships, as well as her boss, James Canon, and his fall. He asked about Jeff's family, and Kaylee told him about his stepdad, David Swanson. The detective was the epitome of thoroughness. He asked some of the questions repeatedly. Did he want to trip her up so Kaylee would give him the answers he wanted, or did he hope she would confess to murder? She was exhausted and relieved when he turned his attention to Kyle.

The detective's questions were direct and evoked painful memories, especially when she knew Jeff had been robbed of a future. Kaylee regretted not making the last year of his life more enjoyable, but their relationship had been falling apart. Kissing Kyle had been a pivotal moment in her life, making her rethink her situation with Jeff. Since the detective didn't ask her about her relationship with Kyle, she kept their kiss a secret and hoped Kyle would, too.

When Detective Jensen asked Kyle if he had an alibi for the night of June first, the night Jeff died, Kaylee turned to face Kyle. He was sitting tall and looking bored.

Kyle answered matter-of-factly, "I met with a potential client."

"I will need your client's name and contact information."

"We had dinner at the Top of the Rock; if you speak to the executive chef, he will verify I left at ten o'clock."

"I'll do that, but I need your client's name."

Kyle refused to answer.

"Mr. Masters, I'm going to have to insist. What is your client's name?"

"Stephanie Ortiz. She is a former high school classmate."

Kaylee turned toward Kyle. "You know Stephanie?"

"Miss Chambers, please let me ask the questions. Why were you meeting Ms. Ortiz?"

"She needed help finding a second location for a workout salon and had other investment questions."

"Investment questions," Detective Jensen asked?

"Real Estate is my primary interest, but I offer services for other long and short-term investments."

"Mr. Masters, have you ever had an intimate relationship with Ms. Ortiz?"

"No."

"Did she know Mr. Swanson?"

"You'll have to ask her."

"I'll need her number and any other contact information you have for her."

Kyle's admission surprised her. She knew most of Kyle's friends but didn't know that he knew Stephanie or that he had kept in touch with her. Why did she choose to meet Kyle on the night that Jeff was murdered?

Kyle flipped through his phone and gave the number to Detective Jensen.

"Do you know of anyone else who had a physical altercation with Mr. Swanson?"

When Kyle didn't respond, Detective Jensen asked again.

"Do you know of anyone else who might have wanted to hurt the deceased?" Jensen waited. "Mr. Masters, I can see something is bothering you. Do you want Miss Chambers to leave?"

"Why would he want me to leave," Kaylee asked?

"Did you ever hit or fight with the deceased," Jensen asked?

"Once."

Kaylee tightened her grip on the armrest.

"When and where did this happen?"

"I attended a pool party about four months before Jeff died. When I saw Jeff hitting on some girls, it made me angry, and I punched him."

"Are you sure he was flirting with them? Do you know who they are?"

"Yes, but I don't know their names. One of the girls seemed to enjoy his attention more than the others."

"And you're sure you don't know her or where I can reach her?"

"Yes."

"Did he hit you back?"

"No, he'd wiped the blood from his lip and started laughing."

"Why would he do that?"

"At the time, he appeared to be high; maybe he had too much to drink."

"Did the deceased ever use drugs or abuse alcohol?"

"Not to my knowledge."

"Other than the time at the pool party, had you ever seen him with any woman, other than Miss Chambers, while they were dating?"

"No."

Kyle had hit Jeff, and neither one had mentioned it; Kaylee should have been mad, but she wasn't. Kyle didn't bring up their kiss. She dodged a bullet. Chivalry wasn't dead after all.

"Do you have any more questions for me?" Kaylee interrupted.

"Just one more. Do you have anything else you'd like to tell me that might help me find Mr. Swanson's killer? No detail is too small or insignificant."

"Not right now. I need some time to process."

"Of course. I'm sorry for your loss."

"What's going to happen now?"

"I will verify the information you gave me and interview your high school classmates; I need to speak to the guests who attended the party. Do you have the host's contact information?"

Kaylee gave him the number and stepped toward the door, but stopped.

"Can you tell me who supplied you with the new information?"

"I did."

Her head whipped toward Kyle. "You? Why didn't you tell me you thought Jeff had been murdered?"

"I had no proof, so I asked the police to investigate it."

Not only did Kyle betray Jeff and their friendship, but he also kept vital information from her. She didn't know if she could ever trust him again. She pressed her lips tightly together and, at the sound of wood scraping on the floor, glanced toward the detective.

Jensen pushed away from his desk and offered her his hand. "Thank you for your cooperation. I know this has been a trying time for you."

She shook his hand. "Thank you."

She took long strides and searched for her keys in her purse. She found them tangled in her hairbrush and worked to free them. She heard footsteps following close behind; it had to be Kyle. Abandoning her after Jeff died hurt her, but she couldn't forgive this. Their friendship was over.

She disarmed her car and reached for the door handle.

"Kaylee, can we talk?"

She tossed her purse onto the passenger seat. "No."

"It's important."

She whipped around to face him. "You hit Jeff and didn't tell me, then you sneak around behind my back and start an investigation into his death. What else aren't you telling me, and why didn't you warn me that the police would contact me?"

Kyle exhaled. "I couldn't discuss it with anyone, not even you."

"You should've come to me first; if needed, we could have gone to the police together."

"It's not that simple."

"Loyalty and friendship are simple concepts."

"I never meant to hurt you or keep secrets. It just turned out that way. I'll come by your house tonight and tell you everything I know about Jeff's death."

"I've had enough of your lies–don't bother."

17

"I didn't lie; I had to wait until I had concrete evidence."

She moved closer to the car. "What evidence?"

"After Jeff died, I asked my father to audit Jeff's finances, and he found that Jeff had made several large deposits that were traced back to a mortgage company, Reality Title Mortgage Inc. The company had been buying mortgages and illegally evicting the homeowners."

Kaylee shook her head. "Jeff had nothing to do with that."

"Jeff owned the company, and Jeff's signature had been on all the contracts."

"I don't believe you. Why would he evict anyone?"

"I'm not sure, but all evictions were in the same neighborhood."

"None of this makes any sense."

"Kaylee, Jeff bought your mortgage from the original lender."

She drooped against the car. "Why would he do that?"

As soon as she asked it, she knew why. Jeff must have discovered that she had purchased a new house and kept it a secret. She hadn't dared tell him she wanted time to reconsider marrying him. But how did he find out?

The sun pounded her face, so she put on her sunglasses.

"How do I get my mortgage back?"

"Call Tim Barnes, the attorney general; he'll tell you what you need to do."

"Do the police know about Jeff's company?"

"Yes, that information prompted them to reopen the case."

"Great, I just became their number one suspect. They'll say I killed Jeff to get my house back."

"Even if it were true, at least a dozen other homeowners have that same motive."

"We were engaged to be married. The police always look at family and friends first."

"They have to prove you knew about it. Did you?"

"No."

"Then don't worry about it."

Kaylee chewed her bottom lip; she wondered why Detective Jensen hadn't drilled her about her mortgage. Why would he wait to ask her?

"It probably doesn't matter now; what's done is done, but why did you start looking into Jeff's death," Kaylee asked?

Kyle leaned against the car, "The moment I received the call that Jeff died, I knew something was wrong. That area is crawling with people, even at night. Why didn't anyone see him, and what could he have been doing at the building so late?"

"The police didn't think anything of it, or they would've said something before he was buried."

"They couldn't rush in and upset everyone, especially your dad, with no evidence or probable cause. But now that they have the right information, they'll find out who killed Jeff, and you'll be safe."

"Safe?" She rubbed her temple; massive pain took hold of her, crushing her ability to think.

"Are you alright?"

"My head is going to explode."

"Go home; it's been an exhausting morning."

She waited for Kyle to drive away and thought back to what he had said about the police, trying not to upset her father. Kaylee knew all about that. She had spent every waking moment devising ways to make him proud, but he never noticed her efforts. It only took one time to make him mad, and she would never forget it.

Kaylee had just finished a full day of high school, homework, and volunteering at a daycare center when a friend called to meet at the mall. She had met with her friend and lost track of time. When Kaylee pulled into the driveway and heard the front door bang, she watched her father head straight for her car. His lips were turned down, and his brows pinched together. It surprised Kaylee to see him because he never left work before ten. He yanked open the car door and ordered her out.

"Where have you been?"

"I—"

"Your mother was worried sick. Give me your keys."

She had dropped them into his hand. Her heart pounded. She had apologized profusely for worrying her mother and promised never to do it again. Kaylee wondered what had made her father so mad. She had worked hard to impress her father; she didn't want one miscommunication to ruin it. She planned to tell him about a volunteer award she had received and hoped the news would lighten his mood.

"I'm sorry. Time got away from me." She continued to ramble as his scowl deepened. "I forgot to tell you... I won an award—"

"You're not getting the keys back." He stated flatly. "Go to bed."

Her father had glared at her. Kaylee had received his icy stare before and wondered if anyone was competent enough to please him. Had she been wasting her time? Had it been pride that motivated him to act with such disdain? When he diminished her achievements, she felt as if loving her was a duty he felt obligated to perform.

What if being a lousy father had been his only flaw, and he blamed Kaylee for it? It must have been hard for him to fail at anything. Maybe he hadn't wanted children, but to appease her mother, he had compromised. That could explain why he had seemed indifferent, or perhaps he had wanted a boy to carry on his legacy. Did she do something wrong, or was he simply incapable of caring for any child?

20

She watched Kyle's Lincoln pull out of the parking lot, and then she started her car. Kyle seemed convinced that Jeff had been involved in some nefarious scheme. Kaylee couldn't believe it and had a hard time accepting it, but Jeff's strange behavior right before he died had frightened her. He might still be alive if she had had the courage to tell someone.

Chapter 3

Most people hated Mondays, but not Kaylee. She would wake up anticipating a great week, take a hot shower, regardless of the outside temperature, and have a cup of hot coffee. She would read some articles from *Money* magazine and then go to the office. She stuck to her morning ritual but didn't enjoy it. She worried about what the investigation would reveal. She had to make certain that no one, not the police or Kyle, dragged Jeff's memory through the mud. He had lived a hard life, and she wanted people to remember him as the fun-loving, hard-working man he had been; she owed him that much.

Arizona's summers were brutal; morning temperatures could soar over one hundred degrees. And today was no exception. Kaylee leaned back in her office chair and stared out the two-story window. Sunlight reflected off the glass, and the low-hanging clouds hovered over the summer landscape. The unpredictable weather kept everyone on their toes; one calm moment could lead to a vicious storm that could devastate the city.

Kaylee stared at the folders piled high on her desk. She should make some calls to check on her clients, but couldn't muster enough motivation to pick up the phone. Instead, she rolled her pen between her index finger and thumb and watched the gold shimmer in the light. The pen was a gift from her mother, Kaylee's biggest supporter. She bought it to celebrate Kaylee's new position at Lawson and Canon's consulting firm. It represented Kaylee's first opportunity to shine rather than stay hidden in the shadow of her father's accomplishments.

Breaking free from the mindset that she had it made because she was a Chambers proved to be more difficult than she had realized. Her father, the unparalleled Michael Chambers, had left his mark everywhere she went. Even if she wanted to pursue a career in real estate, she would've been at a disadvantage. She didn't possess the right body parts. The old Boys' Club was an exclusive network of men who formed social and business connections in college. Her father never wanted her around as a child, and she doubted he would appreciate her trying to make a name for herself in his domain, only to disappoint him at every turn. She had chosen consulting, not real estate, for that precise reason.

As a process consultant, she must scrutinize every aspect of the work environment, including gauging relationships between employees and employers, evaluating the office layout and functionality, and fine-tuning the procedures and methods by which her clients handle their customers and office policies. She hated to admit it, but her father had influenced her career path, and she couldn't be happier.

Kaylee rearranged the items on her desk, took a look, and moved them back. She tapped her pen, twirled it between her fingers like a baton, and began tapping again. She wasn't accustomed to doing nothing or letting someone else take charge. Detective Jensen said he would resolve the issue as quickly as possible. Still, she knew Jeff better than anyone else, so it seemed reasonable that she could assist in the investigation. She wasn't sold on the idea that Jeff was killed, but if he was, and she could help bring the killer to justice, it might diminish the soul-piercing pain and guilt that overwhelmed her.

She grabbed her purse, took the elevator to the main floor, and crossed the lobby to the parking garage. She waved goodbye to Manara.

Manara sat at the circular desk in the center of the lobby, where the mirrored doors allowed her to see everyone entering or exiting the elevators. During the day, she worked as an office receptionist but modeled for local retail and cosmetic companies at night.

Before entering the parking garage, Kaylee glanced out the window toward Camelback Road. The bushes and trees ruffled as the wind blew, and large, dark spots speckled the sky. Kaylee quickened her pace and pulled out her keys.

The Ford Shelby Cobra, her pride and joy, waited for her, strong and familiar. The guys in the office, including her boss, teased her about her choice of cars. It wasn't what most women of her age and background would have chosen. Her coworkers assumed she would buy a Lexus or Mercedes. Kyle had introduced her to fast cars, but after her mom told her that her father had a secret love for Mustangs, Kaylee made them her passion, too. She researched and then purchased her Mustang based on her father's favorite color, blue, hoping to use it to connect with him.

She remembered how her heart had pounded when she had driven off the lot. The Cobra was Vista Blue with white Lemans stripes, had a V8 engine with a six-speed manual transmission, and sports leather bucket seats. She had savored the power and control it gave her as if she could overcome any obstacle. She had called her father and arranged to meet at his office. She had been elated and couldn't wait to show him her new car. She had thought today would be the day her father would be proud and say he loved her. She recalled thinking it was odd to feel that she had to earn his love, but strange or not, she had to try.

She had pulled up next to his car in the parking garage. She thought seeing his reaction to his luxury car and her muscle car side by side might be interesting. She had hurried across the lobby and up to the seventh floor. Her hands had been sweating, and she had felt as if she had a hundred butterflies fluttering in her stomach. She had walked past the receptionist's desk, knocked on his door, and entered. She took a seat and waited for him to finish his call.

He placed the phone in its cradle and asked harshly, "What's so important it couldn't wait until later?"

It felt like the wind had been knocked out of her. Michael had agreed to see her; she assumed he would be glad to see her. "I know you're busy, but I've made a major purchase, an investment, and I'd like to show it to you."

"You bought a home or some land?"

"I bought a Shelby Cobra. I thought you might like to drive—"

"Why on earth would you do that? You would be better suited in a Lexus or maybe a BMW—"

She swallowed hard. "Kyle passed on his love of fast cars to me, and I thought it would be fun to—"

"You should think more about servicing your clients and less about having fun. College is over." He had picked up the phone and dialed.

Kaylee had spent seventy thousand dollars and numerous hours of research to impress him, and he couldn't be bothered to take a look. She had leaned over the desk and had disconnected his call. "I thought you'd be interested—"

His voice had quaked with anger. "Let go of my phone and stop wasting my time."

She had recoiled. "Don't worry. We're done!"

Her father had shot her down again. She should have been used to it. That was one of the last times Kaylee had made a conscious effort to bond with him.

While in her office, before Kaylee impulsively decided to visit her father, she had devised a plan to research Jeff's business activities, and if she didn't hurry, she might change her mind. Jeff made his living in real estate, and so did her father. The last time she had seen her father, she had told him they were finished. Kaylee had meant then; she had been furious but regretted it ever since. They were family; how could they be through? She wondered if she would be allowed back in the building. Her

25

father may have ordered his staff to keep her off the premises. If he did see her again, she would be subjected to his contempt.

Kaylee stopped for a light; in just a few minutes, she would come face-to-face with her father. Would he see her or send her away? She had only seen him once since he rejected her at her mom's funeral–when she tried to show off her car. That hadn't gone as planned. And now, moments away from asking him, of all people, for help, she wondered if he would be willing or if he even cared. He wasn't her first choice, but he had powerful friends like the governor and other high-ranking officials; having them on her side couldn't hurt. Maybe she should call to see if he was busy. If she did call, he would have his watchdog secretary give her some line of bull and try to put her off. It had to be a surprise visit.

Her father owned a fifteen-story building in Phoenix, located on Central Avenue in the Central Corridor district. Corporate offices from all over the world lined the corridor, and three of Arizona's tallest buildings were visible from there. Chambers Towers was the grandest building on Central Avenue. A prominent architect and a college buddy of her father's had spent six months designing it. Her father had paid a fortune for the finest stone and glass. It was a masterpiece, one that her father would come to love more than his family.

She tapped her fingers on the steering wheel, thankful for the delay, and her mind drifted back to Saturday night, to Kyle and his theories about Jeff. Did Kyle tell her everything, or did he withhold information like before? Did Jeff have money problems, or did something else cause his sudden anger and nervousness?

Her search might uncover criminal activity, but her deepest fear would be that intimate details of her relationship with Jeff would be revealed. After Jeff died, Kaylee finally accepted responsibility for her part in their relationship's demise, but she hadn't learned to forgive herself. Perhaps that would come later. If only Kaylee could find a way to keep her secret, she would save everyone a lot of pain.

At Chambers Towers, everyone wore the usual professional garb, and even in her Anne Klein suit and Prada shoes, Kaylee felt like a lone fish in a vast aquarium. While her stomach did somersaults, she approached the elevator with confident strides. Seeing her father again after all this time might prove to be more painful than her mother's death.

After her mother had died, Kaylee had plummeted into a deep depression. An all-consuming emptiness had threatened to devour her. Feelings of despair haunted her waking moments and kept her from sleeping or eating. Kaylee grieved the loss of a friend, an ally, and a mother. She felt lost and didn't know what her future held. How could she succeed when her most trusted advisor was gone?

She hoped her mother and her mother's twin were peacefully reunited because, without that hope, her mother was just gone, and that would be too much for Kaylee to bear. She wondered if her mom had ever felt guilty when she had realized her twin would never get the chance to fall in love or start a family. It must have been difficult living with that. Her mother had tried to express the pain and loss that she had felt as a result of losing her sibling, but Kaylee never fully understood until she lost her mom. Kaylee had wandered aimlessly, trying to make sense of it all. Planning the memorial service had been a daunting task. When she wavered, her father stepped up and finished the arrangements.

During her mother's service, Kaylee's father sat beside her in the front pew. He stared straight ahead and listened intently to the minister. When she leaned closer, and her shoulder touched his, he pulled away; the mere touch of her repulsed him. Kaylee had choked back the tears and had squashed down the feeling to run and never return. Kaylee had never felt more alone than she did that day, and she had vowed she would never see her father again.

She squeezed into the crowded elevator, pushed the button, and waited for the elevator to climb to the seventh floor. Her father didn't believe in luck and never gambled, but he swore by the number seven. In one of his rare family moments, he had told her a story about how he had come to depend on it, but as hard as she tried, she couldn't remember it.

The door opened, and Kaylee waited until the last person exited the elevator before heading toward the reception desk.

"I'm here to see Mr. Chambers."

The impeccably dressed and perfectly manicured receptionist eyed her up and down, "Do you have an appointment?"

"No, but it's an urgent family matter. Is he in?"

The platinum-blonde smiled. "No, I'm sorry, he's out on an appointment."

"When will he be back?" Kaylee asked.

"I'm not sure," The blonde paused. "Would you like to leave a message?"

"No message. Thank you."

Kaylee walked back to the elevator and pushed the down button. The receptionist didn't know Michael had a daughter. Why would she? Why would he tell anyone she existed? Kaylee was a huge disappointment to him, and even if he agreed to see her, the chances of getting him to help were slim to none. She knew this was the possible outcome, but the optimist in her refused to believe it.

A deep, hearty laugh echoed down the hall. Kaylee scanned the area for Kyle. Her heart pounded as she passed the receptionist to her father's office. She pushed open the door. Kyle leaned against the wall next to the window,

28

looking down. Her father reclined back in his chair, his feet crossed and resting on his desk. They turned as she entered.

"Father, I need to speak with you—alone."

Her father walked over to Kyle and slapped him on the back. "It was great seeing you again."

Kyle shook hands with her father and nodded to her as he left.

Kaylee stared at the closed door for several painstaking minutes.

"What's he doing here?"

"He dropped in to say hello."

"Why," Kaylee asked?

"Just a social call. "

She shook her head in denial.

"We were just catching up."

She didn't buy that, not for one minute. Why was Kyle really meeting with her father?

Father. How could a single word be the source of so much heartache? Michael had been one of the final words her mother spoke before she passed away.

Michael had been the love of her mother's life. When she spoke of him, you could hear how much she cherished him. Before Kathryn died, she had tried, to no avail, to get Kaylee to forgive him, but the wound cut too deep. She had been losing her mom at the time, and forgiving her father had been out of the question. All of his wealth and connections couldn't stop the cancer from ravaging her mother's body; what good was money if it couldn't save the one person Kaylee loved more than life?

At the sound of her name, Kaylee looked up. If only her father knew how hard it was for her to come here. She had swallowed her pride, had broken her vow never to see him, and had, at least momentarily, put aside her animosity for him and his choices. Still, his nonchalant, disinterested gaze proved he had more important things to do than deal with her or her problems.

"Father, I need your help. I know it's been a long time since we last spoke, and I wouldn't be here if it weren't a life-or-death situation. But I need you to use your connections to find out if Jeff had a business partner and, if he did, what kind of trouble he was in."

"This is about Jeff," Michael asked.

"Yes, why else would I come?"

"I thought you were here because today is the first anniversary of your mother's death."

A sharp pain shot through Kaylee. How did she forget that one year ago today, her mom had passed away, and she had been left with the knowledge that her father would never love her?

The pain and sorrow that had consumed her then came flooding back. Jeff had promised to help Kaylee overcome that sadness and emptiness. Now they were both gone, and here she stood in front of the man who gave her life but couldn't give her what she needed most: his love.

She met her father's questioning gaze. "I'm not here because of mom. I'm here because the police are investigating Jeff's death."

"I thought the police ruled it an accident."

"They did, but now they have evidence that might prove otherwise and are looking into it."

"What makes you think I can help?" Michael asked.

"You have money and power. You sacrificed your family to get it, so I'm asking you to help me find out what happened to Jeff."

"I think the police would be better equipped to handle a murder investigation—"

"Are you turning your back on your family again?"

Michael remained silent. Kaylee wondered if he thought her question was rhetorical. After what felt like an eternity, he responded.

"What would you like me to do?"

That was too easy. Maybe the anniversary of Mom's death made him feel some empathy toward her. It would be temporary, and she would probably never see this side of him again. Kaylee didn't care. She needed his help and would take full advantage of the situation.

"I need you to find out who Jeff worked with and what they planned to do with the mortgages they bought."

"I will make some calls."

Kaylee took a moment to look at her father; fine lines were visible around his eyes, and his usual vigor was gone. She wanted to believe he would keep his promise, but couldn't be sure. He was her best hope of finding out what happened to Jeff. So, for now, she would have to trust him. She mumbled a weak thank you and headed for the door. Kaylee grabbed the handle and turned back. She wanted to remember him this way, compassionate and humane.

Michael had turned toward the portrait of his wife and daughter and said, "I miss her too."

Chapter 4

Detective Randy Jensen had been with the Violent Crimes Bureau for eight years, and no case had ever been reopened. When Jeff Swanson's case was initially investigated, he was out of town, on his only vacation since becoming a detective. Jensen hated how things had ended with his girlfriend, Bridget, so his mother suggested he get away. She had been concerned he would turn out like his father and grandfather, obsessed with the job at the expense of a personal life, and then burn out young. Violence had worn them down, and she hoped Jensen would distance himself from his work whenever possible.

Jensen's best friend had loaned him a cabin near the Grand Canyon so he could spend time exploring and hiking away from the bustle of downtown Phoenix. He needed time to think, quiet time without his phone or laptop, but instead, his vacation had been wrought with car problems, weather issues, and self-doubt. Jensen wished he had been more considerate of Bridget's feelings. He had an important and demanding job, and any woman he dated who truly cared for him would be understanding and supportive.

Upon his return, he was briefed on the Swanson case and immediately was filled with anger and shame. He had purposely avoided all media outlets to unwind and reflect on his relationship. Jeff Swanson's fatal fall occurred after Jensen had already left for the Canyon, and he had been off the grid and unavailable when Commander Blanchard tried to reach him. Jensen was entitled to life outside the precinct, and for a brief moment, he had put personal needs above all else; due process paid the price. His colleagues were capable and, under normal circumstances, could handle any case, but, due to the victim's connections, Blanchard had hoped that Jensen could use his finely tuned finesse on Chambers and his power-wielding friends.

Jensen's calling as a police officer had chosen him, and he had to make the commitment necessary to see it through. He vowed not to let his civilian life jeopardize it again. Jensen hoped to move forward with this investigation without interference or pressure from Michael Chambers and to resolve the case quickly and quietly. Since the evidence was new to him, his fresh, untainted perspective might be what it takes to close the case for good.

After the interview with Kaylee and Kyle, Jensen compiled a list of leads and compared it to the list in the file. Kaylee had been the only one interviewed, and her statement had been brief and vague. Commander Blanchard had warned him that the file was incomplete and that the previous investigation had been cut short at the request of Michael Chambers.

Michael Chambers, a wealthy and well-connected real estate magnate, was the father of the victim's fiancée; his one call had changed the direction of the investigation. Blanchard had mentioned potential witnesses, but he couldn't find a list or any statements in the file. The consensus seemed to be that the victim had fallen, and when the investigation didn't show otherwise, the case had been closed.

Since Saturday, Jensen had made significant progress in tracking down potential leads. Most of the victim's classmates were still in town and held highly visible jobs, making them easier to find. He couldn't locate the victim's stepfather, David Swanson.

Kaylee had told Jensen that David left town after his business tanked twelve years ago. Records show his business had been thriving for years, but for no apparent reason, profits plummeted one year, and the company never recovered. He searched for other family members, but that was a bust, too. The victim's mother had passed away a few years ago, and the only family he had, or would have had, was the Chambers. Jensen had his work cut out for him, but he loved a challenge.

He flipped through the crime scene photos. The ten-story building should have been completed in late August, but construction had ceased due to a lack of funding and the pending investigation. Jensen sorted through the photos of the victim, who had sustained multiple facial and head injuries. Head trauma from the fall had been listed as the cause of death. Jensen couldn't believe the pile of mangled flesh and bone had once been human; it was, even to the trained eye, unrecognizable. The victim had visited the construction site late at night, but no one knew why. What an odd and unsafe thing to do. He would check into that.

The light on his phone flashed.

"Send him in." Jensen requested.

The tall, thin man's hair hung past his ears but was trimmed and shaped for his square face. His light red hair emphasized his pale skin. He sat with shoulders high, chin jutted out, and dark hazel eyes stared across the desk. Detective Jensen extended his hand. The man took it and squeezed.

"Mr. Goldman, I appreciate you taking the time to meet with me."

"I didn't have a choice."

"You ignored my numerous requests, so I had to make it official. Your attorney could have accompanied you."

"I am a lawyer," Greg stated.

"You know what they say about a man who represents himself."

"Yes, he has a fool for a client," Greg leaned forward. "I assure you, Detective Jensen, I'm no fool."

Jensen met Greg's menacing stare. "I appreciate your time and didn't mean to imply you were incapable."

34

"Is my father here?"

"Yes, he's in the interview room."

Greg's brows arched. "You mean the interrogation room."

"You and your father may have pertinent information that leads us to closing the Swanson case."

"I thought it had been ruled an accident."

"New information prompted us to reopen the case, and we are treating it as a homicide."

"It's a shame that Kaylee is suffering, but it doesn't surprise me that someone may have killed Jeff."

"So, you remember Mr. Swanson and Miss Chambers," Jensen asked?

"Everyone knew Kaylee and her loser boyfriend, Jeff."

"Please tell me about your feelings for Miss Chambers while attending school together."

"We were friends. We never dated."

"I need you to be more specific. Were you interested in her romantically?"

Greg drummed his fingers on the armrest. "How I may have felt for someone in high school is irrelevant today."

"Any information, no matter how trivial it seems to you, may be the key to getting a killer off the streets."

"Very well, I wanted to date her; her dad is filthy rich, and she is grounded and sincere. It didn't hurt; she came in a hot package."

Jensen nodded.

"Kaylee only had eyes for Jeff. She couldn't see that Kyle loved her or that Jeff would one day be the end of her."

"Are you referring to Kyle Masters?"

"Yes, and I don't know why Kyle tolerated Jeff. I'm guessing Kyle remained loyal to him because they'd been friends since grade school."

Jensen scribbled down some notes. "Tell me about Mr. Swanson being the end of Miss Chambers."

"It wasn't any one thing or a specific event. I just had a nagging feeling. Somehow, I knew Jeff would drag her down to his level."

"Drag her down," Jensen asked?

"Some people are just cool. Other people try hard to be, but they never will be."

"Would you say there was a status difference between Mr. Swanson and Miss Chambers?"

"Kaylee had class and money, and Jeff didn't, but she liked him, and nothing else mattered."

"Did the other students treat Mr. Swanson differently? It must have been torture to know he would never fit in."

"Jeff thought he fit in. And as long as he had Kaylee, he did, at least on the surface."

"Do you think Mr. Swanson cared about Miss Chambers?"

Greg rolled his neck. "Who knows? He probably thought he did."

"If Mr. Swanson was wrong for Miss Chambers, why do you think Mr. Masters never did anything about it?"

"I guess he didn't see what the rest of us saw."

"What did you see," Jensen asked?

"He was a gold digger."

"Even after all these years, you sound bitter," Jensen stated matter-of-factly.

"It's regret. Honestly, until a few weeks ago, I didn't think about Kaylee or Jeff."

"What happened to remind you of Miss Chambers?"

"Jeff's fall popped up on every news channel, and one of your detectives came to my father's firm and harassed me."

36

"I'm sure Detective Stone used discretion. Interviewing is one of her specialties." Jensen referred to his notes. "While attending school, did you ever wait for Miss Chambers at her locker and follow her to class?"

"Wow…Kyle has a great memory."

"Mr. Goldman, please answer the question."

"This is getting old. Fast."

Jensen met Greg's stare. "I understand this is a tedious process, and I appreciate your cooperation and honesty. This shouldn't take much longer."

"I need a break, and I could use some water."

"I'll be back in a few minutes."

"Take your time."

Jensen closed the door and headed to the lounge. He grabbed a water bottle, went to the interrogation room, and knocked. Detective Olivia Stone stepped out.

"How's it going, Stone?"

"As to be expected. If Goldman's son is involved in the Swanson's case, his dad doesn't know or isn't talking, at least not yet."

Jensen rubbed his neck. "Depending on how Junior plays it, I should be done in an hour."

"Is he giving you problems?"

"When he's not being evasive, he's off on some wild tangent."

Stone smirked. "Typical lawyer."

"I'd better get back to the drama queen; I don't want him sneaking out of here. When you're done with Senior, finish your notes and put them, along with the Canon file, on my desk. I'll go over them when I'm done with Junior."

Jensen closed his office door and handed Greg the bottle.

Greg glanced at the label, took a sip, and scrunched his nose.

Jensen ignored Greg's distaste for the working man's water and sat.

"I asked if you ever followed Miss Chambers or waited at her locker."

"Obviously, you know the answer to that."

Jensen's lips thinned as he waited for a response.

"I wanted to keep her safe and convince her to dump Jeff."

"Why did you feel the need to protect her?"

"I told you. Jeff only wanted her money. He didn't care about her, and I wanted to make sure he didn't hurt her."

"So, you had no motive but to shield Miss Chambers from her boyfriend."

"Of course, I had other reasons. I wanted to date her."

"You wanted to date her because she was a sweet girl, or did the Chambers' money have anything to do with it?"

"I already told you she had a great figure. That's what a teenage boy sees first. Her dad's money only sweetened the deal."

"Is that why you fought Jeff, to be the victor and to win the spoils?"

"I never knew Kyle to be a chatterbox, but he seems to be dredging up irrelevant events."

"Mr. Masters was forthcoming, as I hope you will be."

Greg threw the bottle in the wastebasket. "Jeff and Kaylee were fighting, and he made her cry. After she left, I got in Jeff's face. He punched me, and we wailed on each other until Kyle pulled me off."

"Do you know why they were fighting?"

"Someone started a rumor that a note had been left in Jeff's locker, implying that Kyle loved Kaylee and vice versa."

"Did you ever see Mr. Swanson hit or threaten to strike Miss Chambers?"

38

Greg jolted forward. "He hit her?"

"I can't discuss an ongoing case. You know that. Do you know firsthand about any violence between Mr. Swanson and Miss Chambers?"

"No, he wouldn't have dared hit her."

"How can you be so sure?"

"Kaylee has a myriad of friends; if he hit her, someone would have known and stopped it. Besides, he'd never do anything that would upset her dad–he's the one with the money."

"Were you or Mr. Swanson injured in the fight?"

"We both sustained some physical bruising, but Jeff's pride was crushed. I came out on top."

"You're proud of that, aren't you?" Jensen observed.

"You're making me sound like a pompous ass."

"Are you?"

Greg's light skin darkened with a reddish hue. "No, I am not. You're questioning me about a specific person, and I am answering accurately and truthfully."

Jensen nodded. "Fair enough. Are you sure there were no other physical confrontations between you and Mr. Swanson?"

"As I said, it's the only one I remember."

"We interviewed some of your former football teammates. They said you were intentionally brutal toward Mr. Swanson. Is that true?"

"I played hard and treated everyone the same. If you can't take the heat, get off the field."

"So, your answer is no."

"Yes."

"Your law firm specializes in criminal cases, is that correct?"

"Yes, but we cater to a wealthier clientele. You think one of my clients is involved in Jeff's murder?"

"At this point, I'm examining everyone. Money doesn't exempt someone from committing crimes, even dangerous ones. Do you know if any of your clients have done business with the Chambers or Mr. Swanson?"

"That's privileged information."

"If you have information regarding the death of Mr. Swanson, I need to know," Jensen demanded.

"If I've had a discussion regarding the Swanson murder case with any of my clients, I can't tell you. It's covered under attorney-client privilege. And if you don't have probable cause, no judge will issue a warrant, especially where my clients are concerned."

"No one is above the law, not even you."

"Are you suggesting I killed Jeff to have Kaylee all to myself? Don't be ridiculous."

"It's not as outlandish as you might think."

Greg tapped his foot loudly on the tiled floor. "I don't have time to play games with former high school crushes, and I'm not compelled to participate in illegal activities. My career is my only priority."

"I'm just doing my job."

"You're wasting my time and taxpayers' money."

Greg glanced at his right wrist; his Rolex shimmered as he checked the time.

"I have court in an hour, so if you have any more questions, you have to ask them later."

"Nice watch."

"Yes, it is."

Chapter 5

Were her father's feelings real, or were they just for show? Kaylee drove home and wondered if she could trust them. Was he starting to, after all this time, yearn to build a relationship with her, his only heir? Or were his feelings just for his dead wife?

Kaylee's father had never been home much while she was growing up and never supported her academic or athletic endeavors. The only contribution he made to the family had been financial. She had often wondered what it would be like to have a 'real' dad who would love her unconditionally and forever.

At home in her den, Kaylee realized that she would likely have to find out what happened to Jeff on her own. She needed someone on her side, someone she trusted completely. Only one person fit that description: Sara.

As college roommates and best friends, Sara and Kaylee shared their clothes, secrets, and a love of chocolate. They knew each other so well that most times, they didn't need to speak; a nod or a smile confirmed they were thinking the same thing. Remembering how close they were, Kaylee felt guilty. She had one secret she never told anyone, not even Sara. She had kept it to herself and would, if necessary, take it to her grave. After graduation, they talked daily until life and work, and Jeff monopolized her time. And when Sara took a position at a California law firm, staying in touch became even more complicated.

Kaylee searched for Sara's number on her cell phone but couldn't find it; she wondered why it wasn't on her new phone. Weeks earlier, when the police had called to say Jeff had died, she had thrown her phone against the wall. Her mother's death had left her with a gut-wrenching pain, but when Kaylee had learned of Jeff's untimely demise, an unfamiliar and frightening emotion had taken control.

Kaylee had thrown the phone and had watched it shatter into a dozen pieces. Kaylee stared at it and recognized this time was different; this time, she would have to look inside herself and consider her role in Jeff's death.

Her new phone appeared to have all her other contacts. Did Kaylee delete Sara's number in a bout of despair? Was she trying to erase everything from the past and move forward with a clean slate? Had her recent tragedies diminished her ability to stay focused and organized? Kaylee hoped not. She considered her inherent strength to maintain a level head, even in the most stressful situations, one of her most precious gifts. Without it, Kaylee would feel lost and exposed.

While searching her contact list for Sara's number, Kaylee ran across a few numbers she hadn't called in a while. Most of them were high school friends she only spoke with once a year or so, and some had known Jeff.

She dialed the first number and waited.

"Brenda Simons."

"Hey, Brenda, it's Kaylee Chambers. How are you?"

"I'm well. " Thank you." Brenda hesitated. "I haven't heard from you in a while." How are you doing?"

"I guess you've seen it on the news, Jeff died recently. I'm still coming to terms with that."

"Can I help you with anything?"

"I hope so. I'm reaching out to former classmates to get information. Have you, or do you know of anyone who had contact with Jeff after we graduated?"

"I haven't, and the only person I know of that ever mentioned him to me was Greg Goldman."

"Do you think Greg and Jeff had a good relationship?"

"Not that I know of. Jeff may have been a part of your life, but most of us, your friends, didn't like to be around him."

Kaylee realized Brenda hadn't offered her condolences when she mentioned Jeff had died.

"What did he do to make you dislike him?"

"Does it matter?" Brenda sighed. "He's dead."

"I'd like to know why my friends didn't tell me back then how much they didn't like him."

"We wanted to stay friends with you, and you'd made it clear that he was your friend and, in your life, and that was that."

Peer pressure could be challenging, and Kaylee knew her name carried a lot of weight in the popular circles. No wonder her friends kept quiet.

"Is there anything you can tell me?"

"Ask Greg Goldman."

Brenda disconnected the call, leaving Kaylee feeling frustrated and disappointed. She wondered if she would receive the same attitude toward Jeff from her other friends.

The persistent ringing of the doorbell interrupted her thoughts. Kaylee hoped it would be Kyle. She wanted to confront him about meeting with her father. And ask him why he kept popping up everywhere she went. Kaylee yanked open the door, ready to blast Kyle, but instead, let out a sigh of relief. She couldn't believe it. It had been such a long time. The woman standing in front of her was just what Kaylee needed. She stepped forward, wrapped her arms around Sara, and hugged her tight.

Kaylee dragged in the overstuffed suitcase and motioned for Sara to come in. "I couldn't find your number, and I've looked everywhere. How have you been? Are you still in California? What are you doing here?"

Kaylee took a breath, and Sara laughed.

"I'm fine. I'm still in San Diego and love my job at the firm. If I'm lucky, I'll be a partner in a year or two."

"That's great. And…"

"Kyle asked me to come down for a visit."

"He did," Kaylee asked?

"Yes, he told me you needed a friend, so here I am."

"What exactly did he tell you?"

"He told me Jeff's death wasn't an accident, and the police are looking into it."

"Did he tell you anything else?" Kaylee heaved the suitcase to the stairs and leaned it against the railing.

"Like what?"

"That he betrayed Jeff and kept his murder a secret from me?"

"No, he didn't, but he did mention he's worried about you."

"I bet. Something's going on, and Kyle seems to be in the middle of it."

Kaylee motioned for Sara to sit in the living room and went to the kitchen for something to drink.

As Kaylee handed her a water bottle, Sara said, "I forgot how hot it is here."

"Yeah, but it's a dry heat, and I'll take that over humidity any day."

Sara sank onto the sofa and took a long drink.

"You've known Kyle a long time. He's one of your closest friends. Do you really think he's involved in something as heinous as murder?"

"I didn't mean to imply he killed Jeff, but he knows more than he's telling me. Whatever it is, he feels guilty about it and is trying to hide it. And we haven't been friends for a while."

"I always thought Kyle was one of the good guys."

"He's keeping secrets from me, so no matter how close we were before, he's not to be trusted."

While Kaylee lugged the suitcase upstairs, she remembered the day she met Sara.

It had been the Fall of her freshman year at Arizona State. Kaylee had been in the Memorial Union and had decided to get a snack from a vending machine. Her bag of peanut M&Ms had gotten stuck, and Sara had helped her tip the machine forward to free her chocolate. They hung out together for the next three hours. They realized their tastes in music and clothes, and their goals, were almost identical, but Sara's determination impressed Kaylee the most. She had left her entire life in New York and moved to Arizona alone to finish her education and start a new life. They had become best friends and had spent the next three years as confidants and roommates.

She headed toward the kitchen and found Sara sitting with her head hanging low and eyes focused on the table. Kaylee sat and waited for Sara to look up.

"I'm a horrible friend. I should have come out after Jeff died, but Ben and I were in the middle of a messy breakup, and I couldn't find the time to get away. I know it sounds really lame. I should have tried harder."

"Just because we've been busy and out of touch for a while doesn't mean we're bad friends. You're here now, and that's all that matters."

"So, you forgive me?"

"There's nothing to forgive." Kaylee would forgive Sara anything.

She checked the time; it was eleven. The meeting with her father had only lasted twenty minutes, so Kaylee had the rest of the day to spend with Sara. "Go freshen up, and we'll go for a ride in my Shelby."

Kaylee opened all the windows and turned on the AC full blast. As they drove down the road, they laughed and sang off-key to Maroon 5, No Doubt, and Queen. The music opened a floodgate of memories, and they reminisced about college, dorm life, and dating. For the first time in months, the weight on Kaylee's shoulders was lifted.

After lunch at the Olive Garden, they headed north. Kaylee didn't realize it, but she headed straight to work. She parked in the employee garage at Lawson and Canon's Consulting Firm next to the employee elevator, then punched in the private code.

"Did you forget something in your office," Sara asked?

"No, we're in the neighborhood, so I thought I'd stop by. Besides, I want you to meet my friend and boss, Larry Lawson."

"What about Mr. Canon?"

"James passed away several months ago, and Larry still gets angry and upset when any of us mention James or the accident, so we don't."

In the lobby, Manara, who stood five feet eleven inches, towered over the reception desk even while seated, answered the multi-line phone, and updated customer files.

They approached the desk, and Kaylee asked Manara if she had heard back from the modeling agency. Manara parted her lips, tilted her head, and ran her fingers through her thick black mane.

Kaylee went around the desk and hugged her. "When do you start?"

"Next week," Manara smiled, "I can't believe it. It's really happening."

"I'm so happy for you. Are you going to tell your mother?"

"I can't. I'm not ready to be the one to disgrace our family name, so for now, I have to keep it a secret."

"What a shame—"

"I'm just glad my dad is on my side. It really helps."

"You're lucky to have a supportive father—"

Sara cleared her throat.

"I'm sorry." Kaylee motioned toward Sara. "Sara, this is Manara Thompson, our in-house celebrity, and Manara, this is my best friend, Sara Hill."

Sara reached over the counter and shook Manara's hand. "Congratulations."

"Thanks."

"Manara, I would love to meet your new man; do you know when he can come by the office," Kaylee asked?

"I'll ask, but he's busy right now. He's in charge while his boss is out of town."

"Every time he comes in, I'm not here. I'd like to meet him before you two get married."

Manara laughed and picked up the receiver. "Lawson and Canon."

Sara asked, "Why can't she tell her mom she's a model?"

"Her mother is from the Middle East and is devout in her religion and culture. She would be mortified if Manara exposed herself to the world."

Kaylee and Sara rode the elevator to the third floor, which consisted of two equal-sized offices. One was for Larry, and the other a shrine to the late James Cannon. Kaylee directed Sara to the left, to Larry's office.

"Wow." Sara marveled.

"I know. Wait until you see inside." Kaylee knocked, then entered.

Larry's desk was in the center of the office, facing east. The south and west windows spanned from floor to ceiling and wall to wall, giving Larry a sweeping, unobstructed view of Camelback Road and 32nd Street. Pictures of the Seven Wonders of the World, photos of Phoenix as it grew, and a birds-eye view of James and Larry's favorite fishing holes were proudly displayed along the north wall.

Larry had dedicated the east wall to James and his family. When Larry got tired or stressed, he would lean back in his chair with his arms behind his head and gaze at the collection of pictures of his best friend's children. Larry had actively participated in their upbringing. Now that James was gone, Larry quickly stepped into a father-like role.

Larry walked around his desk, hugged Kaylee, and extended his hand to Sara. His white, thinning hair was combed over, and dark lines marked his weathered skin.

"Larry, this is my friend Sara Hill."

Larry smiled at Sara. "Nice to meet you."

In her four-inch heels, Sara towered over him. "Thank you. I've heard a lot about you."

He laughed, displaying his sunken jawline. "All good, I hope."

"Mostly." Sara laughed and looked out the west window. "The sun must pound you in the afternoon; don't you get hot?"

"No, my old bones enjoy it," he smiled and returned to his seat. "What are you two girls up to?"

Kaylee pounced on the opportunity to share her plight with Larry. "The police are looking into Jeff's death as a homicide, but they won't tell me anything, and they want me to stay out of the investigation."

Larry gazed pensively out the window. "It's a shame they waited so long; the healing process had begun, and now they're ripping open the wound." He turned to Kaylee. "Don't you think it would be best to leave murder to those who are better equipped to handle it?"

"My father seems to think so, but I haven't accepted Jeff's death as a murder; the police have no proof to back up their claim. If there's no murder, then there's no danger."

"Kaylee, you know how I feel about you. You're the daughter I never had, and I don't feel comfortable with you getting involved in this. If Jeff *were* killed, a murderer is on the loose."

"I'm just trying to find information to help the police and give me a better understanding of why Jeff died."

Larry's phone rang, and he answered it.

Kaylee walked over to the west window and looked out over Camelback Road. What a great location. If she needed a snack or a shot of caffeine, she would walk across 32nd Street, and she was set. Both sides of the street were lined with thirty-foot palm trees. As a child, Kaylee had wondered how palm trees could grow in the desert, and her mom had told her that anything could grow with enough love.

Just as Kaylee started to dream about her mom, Larry covered the mouthpiece with his hand and said, "I need to take this. Please be careful."

In the car, Kaylee glanced at Sara, who leaned back in the seat with closed eyes. "What's on your mind?"

Sara opened her eyes. "I love my job in California, but miss the weather here and my Arizona friends. I wish I could move back."

The thought of having Sara back in Arizona made Kaylee's heart pound. "Why don't you?"

"I can't."

"You're smart; you could get a job anywhere."

Sara lowered her lashes. "It wouldn't work. It's complicated."

"No situation is ever perfect. Every day is a gift, and you must live life to the fullest–you never know what direction it will take or when it will end. It won't be easy, but you could make the move."

Sara adjusted her seatbelt, played with her hair, and refused to answer.

Kaylee tapped her finger on the steering wheel. She debated whether to ask; it was personal, and Sara might not want to talk about it yet.

"Why did you and Ben split? Did he cheat on you?"

"No, why would you think that?"

"Most people, when in love, can forgive just about anything, so I figured he committed the ultimate sin and had an affair."

Sara mused. "No, we just grew apart."

"If he had cheated, would you have been able to forgive him?"

"I think so, I loved him so much. It ripped me apart when we couldn't work it out."

"But if he had slept with another woman, how would you put that behind you and move forward?"

"If you truly love someone, you find a way—"

"Damn," Kaylee muttered.

"What's wrong," Sara asked?

"I missed my turn."

Kaylee hit the brakes, and after circling back, she made a sharp right and pulled into a deserted construction site. A lone structure stood erect amid dirt and concrete. The equipment hadn't been used in months; it was covered in soot and grime. Tree branches, tumbleweeds, and trash were scattered across the site from the recent storm. The immense scaffolding stood ominously. Several emotions swept across Kaylee's face, and she headed toward the elevator. She didn't want to be here, the place where Jeff's life ended, but she had to see it and maybe piece together why.

"It's not safe. We're not supposed to be here…"

Sara's strained voice faded, but Kaylee's strides were deliberate and confident.

Sara rushed to Kaylee's side. They ducked under the crime scene tape and stepped into the elevator. Kaylee pushed the fourth-floor button. The elevator started its slow, shaky ascent. Dried-up concrete and dirt covered the sides and fell to the ground.

Sara glanced around. "This is creepy."

"You can wait in the car, but I must do this."

The elevator jerked. Sara gasped, squeezed Kaylee's arm, and didn't let go until they reached the fourth story. The wind blew, stirring up soot on the floor. A few strands of Kaylee's hair slipped out of the French twist, and white-powdery dust stuck to her navy suit. The wind didn't deter her. She walked across the grimy floor toward the railing.

"You're too close," Sara warned as Kaylee moved nearer.

Kaylee leaned over the rail. Jeff must have known his assailant, or he wouldn't have been so close to the edge. A muffled moan and a thud startled Kaylee; she stepped away from the edge. Sara was on the ground. Kaylee hurried to her side and dusted off her face. She cradled her friend's head in her lap. Kaylee clung to her friend for several fearful moments. Her heart pounded while she waited for Sara to move or smile, but her eyes remained closed. She tapped Sara's face, trying to revive her. "Sara!"

Kaylee tapped her face again. Nothing. She shook her shoulders.

Sara moved her head and moaned. She struggled to get up, but Kaylee held her down.

"What happened?" Kaylee asked.

Sara's words were strained. "It's too high up here. I should've reminded you and stayed in the car."

"Are you okay?"

"I will be, but I need coffee."

Kaylee helped Sara to her feet, and they made their way across the slippery floor, leaving a trail of dust swirling around their ankles.

Chapter 6

Detective Jensen pulled into the Tempe Wellness and Life Center near Arizona State University. Undergrads and graduate students hung out using free Wi-Fi, munching on spinach and tofu wraps, and sipping fruit smoothies. Jensen parked and headed to Sophia's Body Sculpting Salon. It was nestled between a reflexology shop and an apothecary shop. Students were huddled under the armada, taking advantage of the misters, and a thick, lightweight material covered the shop's door handles.

Jensen closed the door to reduce the sun's glare and to minimize the escape of the cold air. He approached the reception desk and took in the scantily clad women in brightly colored leotards. The music had a slow, continuous beat. He scanned the room for her, but he only had a driver's license picture to go by, and if she lost weight and toned up, she might not look like her picture.

He stopped at the unattended desk, looked over and down at the appointment book, and tapped the bell with his index finger. Jensen rested his elbow on the counter and waited. Women stretched upward and forward, baring their behinds for all to see. Two college co-eds giggled as they walked down the hall. They dropped their towels to their shoulders, just enough to flash skin. It was harmless flirting and reminded him of Bridget.

He had met Bridget while hiking Camelback Mountain, and they'd dated for three years. She was sexy, full of energy, and had a big heart. On their last night together, he had snapped at her for quoting one of her favorite books, and she had told him that she couldn't wait around for him to show up for dates and hated it when he ran out on a moment's notice.

Looking back, Jensen realized not everyone had the right temperament to date a law enforcement officer. It took courage, love, and a lot of patience. He had high hopes for Bridget, who was intelligent and independent. Still, she didn't understand his dedication to his job, which drove her away.

Jensen tapped the bell again, and a petite woman with large, soft eyes emerged from down the hall.

"May I help you?"

"I'm Detective Randy Jensen. Is Ms. Ortiz finished with her class?"

"Stephanie will be out in a few minutes; she blocked off thirty minutes for you. She must like you."

Jensen shook his head from side to side. "I'm here to speak to Ms. Ortiz about an investigation I'm working on. It's not personal."

Her brows arched. "Thirty minutes is an entire session; it's a lot of money to give up to speak to someone she doesn't even know."

"I appreciate Ms. Ortiz taking time out of her busy schedule to meet with me, but it is important."

"I hope it is Detective Jensen."

Jensen pivoted around.

"Thirty minutes will pay for my car payment this month."

He extended his right hand. "Thank you for meeting with me on such short notice."

Stephanie's grip was soft but firm and lingered before she pulled away. Her dark, mocha eyes widened, and her glimmering lips curved up. "You did say it was urgent."

"Can we speak in private?"

Stephanie stepped closer.

Jensen inhaled. Stephanie's perfume, a light floral blend, made it difficult to concentrate.

She gestured, "This way."

Jensen straightened his jacket lapel and followed behind.

She led him down the hall to a large office and motioned for him to sit.

She sat and met his gaze, "Now, what can I do for you?"

"I have a few questions about some of your high school classmates."

"I'm not sure I'll be much help. I've only stayed in touch with one or two people."

"Have you ever had any contact with Kaylee Chambers or Jeff Swanson?

"Not that I remember."

"While in high school, you never once spoke to or bumped into either of them?"

Stephanie shook her head, sending her curls flying across her face. "We weren't friends, so even if I did bump into one of them, I probably wouldn't remember."

"Was there something about them you didn't like," Jensen asked?

"No, they had their friends, and I had mine. I didn't know enough about her to like or dislike her."

"You knew she had a wealthy father and had access to an unlimited amount of money. Didn't that bother you?"

"We went to school in Scottsdale. Everybody's parents had money, some just more than others. Jeff and a few other students didn't have much money. I heard Jeff's dad ran off and left his mom penniless. Jeff was lucky to have what he did."

"What else do you know about Mr. Swanson and his family?"

"Everybody at school knew he mooched off Kaylee, and she probably did too. Like I told you. I didn't hang around them."

"Did you ever, on any occasion, go near or put something in Miss Chambers or Mr. Swanson's school locker?"

"Like what?" Stephanie asked.

"A note."

She shrugged. "I may have, but you can't expect me to remember everything I did as a teenager. Most people spend half their adult lives trying to forget high school."

"That doesn't answer my question."

"Fine. On a dare, I put a poem in Jeff's locker. He didn't take it too well, so I stayed away from him."

"Who gave you that challenge?"

"I don't recall. It could've been almost anyone at the school."

Jensen watched Stephanie rearrange the items on her desk. "Are you sure you don't remember?"

"Yes, I'm sure."

"Did you ever date Greg Goldman?"

"Bridget said you could go from sweet and kind to cold and professional, all in one breath."

"What?" Jensen stiffened.

"Bridget Carter, your ex-girlfriend."

"You know Bridget?"

"Yeah, she takes my morning Zumba classes."

Jensen smelled a trap. "When did you see her last?"

"Bridget came in this morning."

"Why were you talking about me," Jensen asked?

"I mentioned I had an appointment with a detective today, and she told me she used to date one. She didn't tell me about your sex life or anything like that, but she did say she missed you and wished you could have worked things out."

Jensen excused himself and went outside. He leaned against a pillar and called Commander Blanchard, but he wasn't in. Jensen left a message about the possible conflict of interest. He clarified that he hadn't contacted Bridget in over a year, so there shouldn't be an issue. Jensen refused to let Stephanie Ortiz muddy the waters by name-dropping. He knew she lied about the note, and when he asked about Goldman, she deftly changed the subject–turning the tables

55

in her favor. He would return, turn up the heat, and see if she would crack.

Jensen walked past the receptionist and straight into Stephanie's office. She hung up the phone and smiled.

"Are we done? Your thirty minutes are almost up?"

"That all depends on you. Are you going to give me honest answers?"

"I have."

"Let's try this again," he suggested. "Did you ever date Greg Goldman?"

"We went out a few times, but he was stuck on Kaylee."

"Why did you lie?"

"I didn't want to admit that Greg liked her."

"Did that make you mad?"

"It upset me, but what could I do?"

"Put a note in Mr. Swanson's locker and start a fight," Jensen suggested.

Stephanie shrugged. "If Jeff and Kaylee broke up, Greg would jump at the opportunity to date her, and I didn't want that."

"Then, why do it?"

"She made me angry. Kaylee could have any guy she wanted, and she chose Jeff, and she didn't realize how much trouble she caused."

"Trouble?" Jensen echoed.

"We had to put on an act to indulge her. I hated it."

"Why didn't you like Mr. Swanson?"

"I was forced, like the rest of my friends, to pretend to like Jeff. If we didn't, we would have been excluded from the inner circle, and to survive high school, that's where we needed to be."

"Did you ever date or have intimate relations with Mr. Swanson?"

Stephanie burst out laughing. "Sleep with Jeff–are you crazy? The only person who wanted to be around him was Kaylee."

"If, as you stated, everyone tolerated Mr. Swanson, why do you think Miss Chambers liked him? He must have had some redeeming qualities."

"I can't speak for Kaylee, but everyone at school considered Jeff an underdog. His stepdad bailed on him, and his mom worked hard to give him what little he had, which must have thrilled Kaylee. She devoted her time to pet projects."

"Pet projects?"

"You know a 'worthy' cause. Kaylee couldn't help herself. She constantly joined one club or another to raise awareness for something: save the animals, the trees, or the drama club. It never stopped, but none of us could figure out why she settled for Jeff when she could be with Kyle. He was head over heels in love with her."

"The entire class knew Mr. Masters had feelings for Miss Chambers?"

"Not just the class, the entire school. We nicknamed them K-squared."

"Why?"

"Kyle loves Kaylee; Kaylee loves Kyle. It infuriated Jeff; that's why we called them that."

"But they weren't a couple?"

"No, but we knew they would be."

"How," Jensen asked?

"Jeff was a poser; we knew Kaylee would eventually realize that."

"Mr. Swanson had no father figure, and his mom struggled to support them. Don't you think he deserved a break?"

"As an adult, I know we treated him badly, but as a kid, I had to fit in to survive and to find my own way.

Besides, his mom didn't work that hard but seemed to have more than enough money."

"What type of job did she have?"

"Some cushy office job, but she only worked part-time. How could she afford a big house in Scottsdale and buy Jeff a slightly used Mercedes?"

Jensen leaned against the back of the chair, and while Stephanie shifted, he stared straight across at her.

"You stated earlier that you weren't friends with Miss Chambers, yet you seem to know quite a bit about her. Why is that?"

"High school is a gossip breeding ground; it's where we learned to communicate. Besides, everything Kaylee did was news. So, you see, things haven't changed much. She's still the center of attention."

"Sounds like it still bothers you."

"Not really. Kaylee's just like the rest of us; she has her good and bad days. But the Chambers name and money, that's what sets her apart from the pack, and she knows it."

"So, it's not Miss Chambers you hold a grudge against; it's her father?"

"I didn't say anything about harboring ill feelings for anyone; I told it like it is, nothing more and nothing less."

"From your perspective," Jensen pointed out.

"Yes, but you can speak to anyone; they'll say the same thing."

"Have you ever threatened Miss Chambers or Mr. Swanson?"

"Just because I didn't have the money she did–no one did–that doesn't mean I want to hurt her.

"And yet, you put a note in Mr. Swanson's locker that you knew would start trouble. Maybe you became incensed because the poem didn't work, and you plotted and waited until the right time to—"

"Kill Jeff?" She shook her head. "I'm a lover, not a fighter."

"Is that why you went after Mr. Masters?"

"What?" She faltered. "Oh, you mean the dinner. Did Kyle say I came on to him?"

Jensen's cell phone vibrated. "Excuse me."

He read the text from Commander Blanchard: Finish with Ms. Ortiz and see me when you're done.

"Anything important?" Stephanie asked.

"Just business."

"Maybe if you had managed your time better, you and Bridget would've worked out. She really liked you, and based on what she told me, she was falling in love with you."

Jensen shoved the phone into his pocket—time to put an end to this.

"Ms. Ortiz, we both have jobs to do. My job is to ask pertinent questions relating to this investigation. Your job is to answer my questions directly and honestly. My personal life is none of your business. I don't want you to mention Bridget's name or anything she may have said. Is that clear?"

"Is it?"

"Yes."

"Because if it's not, I will escort you downtown, and we'll finish this at police headquarters."

Stephanie nodded.

"Good. What day did you meet Mr. Masters?"

"We had dinner on June first."

"Was that the first time you contacted him since high school?"

"Yes."

"Were you two friends?"

"No."

"Tell me why, after six years, you decided to meet Mr. Masters on the night that Mr. Swanson was killed?"

"I had no idea Jeff was going to be killed that night or any other night. I chose the date because it worked for both of us. I needed advice on a piece of property I wanted to buy."

"With all of the real estate companies in the state, why is it that you chose Mr. Masters, one of the men who loves your nemesis, to get advice?"

"He's smart and successful. He seemed like the logical choice."

"I don't believe you. I think you wanted to get back at Miss Chambers. You invited him to dinner to seduce him. But it didn't work; he rejected you, too. Didn't he?"

"This is ridiculous. Jeff's dead, not Kyle."

He leaned in close. "So, he did reject you, and it made you angry, made you mad enough to kill."

"I didn't say that. I wouldn't have killed Kyle."

"You wouldn't have killed Mr. Masters? What about Mr. Swanson?"

"Don't twist my words."

"Mr. Swanson was the root of all your problems. If Miss Chambers dated Mr. Masters, you could have Mr. Goldman all to yourself. So, you killed the man who ruined your life."

"Are you serious?"

"People have been killed for a lot less," Jensen leaned forward. "You tried once before to break up Miss Chambers and Mr. Swanson, but you failed. You wanted the man who destroyed your chances with Mr. Goldman dead. So, you followed him to his building and pushed him to his death. Didn't you?"

"NO."

"He made your life a living hell. He made you cower down to the woman you hated. He had to die—"

"Stop it!"

"Why did you meet Mr. Masters on the day Mr. Swanson was murdered?"

"I already told you."

"In a homicide investigation, there are no coincidences. Even though you have an alibi, you had the strongest motive to want Mr. Swanson dead."

"Motive?"

"He stole your one chance at true happiness."

"You're wrong."

"I may need to speak to your boyfriend; what's his name?"

She exhaled. "I don't have one."

"So, six years after high school, you're still alone?"

"Get out!"

"I have a few more questions," Jensen interjected.

"Here's my attorney's card. Call him."

*****

Jensen headed back to headquarters. The downtown streets were congested, and the never-ending construction only frustrated him. He pushed Ms. Ortiz too far. He should have conducted the interview downtown. Her livelihood depended on her ability to teach classes and to manage the salon, so he had decided to meet her there. That was a miscalculation on his part, one that would never be repeated. Their voices had carried all the way down the hall, and his private interview with a person of interest had turned into a sideshow.

Jensen drummed his fingers on his thigh as he responded to Commander Blanchard's question.

"I haven't seen Bridget in over a year, and I didn't know Ms. Ortiz knew her. If I did, I would have sent Stone. She's the epitome of professionalism. I would never jeopardize any case, especially not this one."

Blanchard scowled. "Ms. Ortiz called and said she thought your behavior was unprofessional and inappropriate."

"She's lying. I pushed her hard so she would tell the truth."

"She said you were gawking at her and her clients and making lewd comments."

"Sure, I looked. I was in a room with barely dressed women bending and moving in suggestive ways, but I was there to work, and she waited until the end before mentioning she knew Bridget. She planned it, don't you think?"

"I do, and you're lucky, and if she weren't a person of interest, you'd be stuck on paid leave until we sorted this mess out. I bet she intended to throw doubt on you and this department. It didn't work; Michael Chambers likes you, so you're the Golden Boy for now. The previous investigation had already been tainted, and I don't want it to happen again. Until this is over, stay away from Ms. Ortiz and your ex-girlfriend."

Blanchard seemed to imply that Jensen's absence caused the botched investigation, or did Jensen's guilt allow Blanchard to get the best of him?

"What did you find in the Canon File," Blanchard asked?

"Canon appeared to be in the throes of a heart attack when he fell down his private stairs, so he had multiple lacerations and injuries consistent with a fall. The coroner could not definitively determine the COD. It could've been the heart attack or the fall that killed him. So, the cause of death was listed as undetermined."

"Do you think it's related to the Swanson Case?"

"He died two months ago and was Miss Chambers' boss. Anything's possible, but I'll have a better idea after interviewing his partner, Larry Lawson."

"I want you to finish interviewing Goldman Junior and get his alibi."

"He's in court for the rest of the day; I'll call and make an appointment for tomorrow. I haven't been able to reach anyone from the pool party to verify Master's version of the events from the day he fought with the vic, so I'll be in my office making calls if anything comes up. I'll start early tomorrow, beginning with Goldman."

Chapter 7

The aroma of caramel floated through the house, and Kaylee's stomach grumbled. She was always hungry in the morning, but coffee laced with something sweet satisfied her hunger until lunch. She shrugged into her robe and jogged down the stairs, anticipating the sugary drink. Kaylee peeked into Sara's room, expecting to find Sara still sleeping, but she saw a darkened room with no Sara. So when she entered the kitchen, she presumed Sara would be there sipping coffee and reading the newspaper, but she wasn't.

Kaylee poured a cup of the hot liquid, added a double splash of creamer, went to the front window, and peered out. Sara and her rental car were gone. Why didn't Sara tell Kaylee she had plans? Sara didn't need a babysitter or tour guide, but Kaylee had planned their day out to the last detail and was disappointed Sara had left.

She sipped the creamy coffee from her favorite chair, recalled the past year's events, and considered how they had shaped her life. It had all started when Kaylee had lost her mom.

After her mom died, Jeff's demeanor changed. At first, he had been supportive and compassionate, but then one day their relationship soured. Jeff started questioning Kaylee's every move and demanded she call him every hour. He had acted like she had been cheating on him, and when she had confronted him about it, he had screamed at her and thrown the TV remote. Kaylee had tried to calm him down, but it hadn't worked. His anger had increased, and his mood had darkened. His lack of trust and uncontrollable anger had killed their future and friendship.

Kaylee had considered going to a therapist to help her cope with the loss of her mother and possibly save her relationship with Jeff, but her pride wouldn't let her. She had been worried about what her father would think. Would the invincible Michael Chambers look down on her? Would he be angry if Kaylee had shared her private pain outside of the family? But she had no family. Both sets of grandparents were dead; her mother's twin brother had passed away in the neonatal ward at the tender age of two days, and her father was an only child. Jeff had tried to help, but she knew he had his own demons to fight.

In college, Kaylee and Sara had been teammates on the track team, and Sara still loved to run. Kaylee had given up running but admired Sara's continued dedication to the sport. Kaylee showered, dressed, and planned to drive by the park near her home. It was the best place to run in the neighborhood, and she hoped to find Sara finishing up. Kaylee stood at the top of the stairs when the front door opened and closed. She hurried down to see Sara in the entryway. Her chest heaved up and down, and her damp shirt clung to her curves.

"Where have you been?"

"I ran to clear my head; I guess I lost track of the time."

"You've been gone for hours."

"I could really use a swim; it helps me cool down. Why don't you have a pool?"

Kaylee's stomach turned, and her throat tightened. "Pools require a lot of maintenance and time. Besides, almost everyone in Arizona has a pool, so if I want to swim, I can go to a friend's house."

Sara shrugged. "What's the plan for today?

"We're going to my father's office, and then we'll regroup."

"Michael? You're going to see Michael?" Sara stuttered.

"No, *we're* going to see him."

From the rearview mirror, Kaylee could see the worried look on Sara's face. "You look as if you're going in front of a firing squad."

Sara looked out the side window. "For years, you've told me nothing but what an awful person your father is. Now you're going to see him. I can't help but wonder how desperate things are and how he will behave in front of me, a stranger?"

"Don't worry," Kaylee said dismissively, "He's charming and kind to strangers. He only rejects and ignores his family. Kyle knows."

"What does Kyle have to do with Michael?"

"That's what I'd like to know. Kyle paid Michael a visit at his office yesterday, and Michael said it was just a social visit."

"You spoke to him yesterday?"

"Yes, in his office. But when I arrived, Kyle acted like he owned the place."

Sara's gaze fixed on Kaylee's face. "You saw him yesterday?"

"Why are you repeating everything I say?"

"I thought you two never talked."

"Our relationship has changed a little since Jeff died."

"Are you on good terms then?"

"Definitely not." Kaylee shook her head to dispel that thought. "I need help finding out what happened to Jeff; unfortunately, he is the only person that I can get the information from."

"What about Kyle? Can't he help?" Sara implored.

"Kyle and I aren't friends anymore. Maybe he knew Jeff was in trouble and didn't help him, but now Jeff's dead, and he feels guilty. I don't know what it is, but I will find out." Kaylee glanced sideways at Sara. "For a lawyer, you sure are trusting."

"I work with Fortune 500 corporations, not criminals."

"Everyone lies, even wealthy tycoons."

Sara's strange behavior surprised Kaylee. They used to share the same thoughts and jokes without even speaking, but Sara didn't appear to be listening to anything she said. Kaylee hoped Sara would be glad that her relationship with her father had improved. Still, Sara's reaction showed that nothing could be further from the truth. Michael was her only living relative, and even though their past had been wrought with pain and disillusionment, it only seemed natural to Kaylee, under these dire circumstances, that she would seek help from him.

She parked in the private garage and took the elevator to the seventh floor. Kaylee hated thrusting her father on Sara, but she needed moral support. They stepped out of the elevator. Kaylee glanced around to see if her father's gatekeeper was at her desk, then strode confidently toward the door. She glanced back at Sara, who had slowed to a steady crawl and hovered near the elevator. Kaylee motioned for Sara to hurry as she knocked on her father's door.

A woman said, "Come in."

Kaylee pushed open the door. A long-legged brunette sat on her father's desk. Her skirt pulled high on her thigh, and her blouse plunged between ample breasts. Kaylee cleared her throat.

"Father, I know you're busy, but I want you to meet my best friend, Sara. We roomed together at ASU."

As Kaylee spoke, the brunette slid off the desk and straightened her skirt. She picked up the steno pad, glared down at Sara, wiggled her hips, and closed the door.

"OMG! What's going on here?" Kaylee asked.

Her father shrugged.

"Are you kidding me? Is that the type of woman you hire at Chambers Towers, sluts?"

"Careful—"

"Is she going to sue me for defamation? The truth *is* the best defense. What professional, self-respecting woman does that? And what jury is going to side with a woman who sits on her boss's desk, wearing a neckline plunged to her navel, parading her breasts in front of him? Not to mention, who flirts with his daughter in the room? It's disgusting."

"When did the law become your forte," Michael asked?

"I took law classes at ASU with Sara; it doesn't make me an expert, but I'm sure most people aren't going to side with your sultry, gold-digging employee."

"Is that why you came here, to insult my employees and me?"

Kaylee blew out an exaggerated breath. "If I had known you were entertaining, I wouldn't have wasted my time. What about mom? Have you just forgotten her, swept her under the carpet, as you did me?"

"I have never sought the attention of, or engaged in any activity, with any woman of ill repute. And what my secretary does or does not wear is not your concern."

She reached for the chair and sank onto it. Sara gently squeezed Kaylee's shoulder.

Why had she brought Sara? It had been a bad idea. Sara had been right to be nervous. Michael was a formidable opponent, and Kaylee was always on the losing end. What should she do now? Tell him to go to hell or finish what she started?

She fidgeted in her chair.

"Well?" Michael asked.

"I know I haven't given you much time, but have you been able to locate Jeff's partner?"

Michael sneered. "You think I should help you after that immature tantrum?"

"Just because you disagree with my opinion doesn't mean it's childish." Kaylee paused a moment to make sure she had his attention. "And I do think you should help me."

He leaned back in his chair. "I made a couple of inquiries but have not heard anything yet."

"Are you going to help me or not?" Kaylee snapped.

Michael ignored her latest outburst. "Jeff could have been working with a dozen or more firms, been associated with hundreds of people. I need some time."

"All I need is one name."

"I will make some more calls, but—"

"The police have procedures to follow, which takes time, so the investigation is going nowhere. I'm not burdened by those restraints, and the Chambers name will open doors that the police will never have access to."

"You have always been determined to do everything on your own; why haven't you found a way to resolve this?"

"Time's a luxury I don't have; besides, I'm not experienced in solving crime."

"Then you should let the police handle this; I am trying to run a business."

She jumped up. "Just once, I would like to come first."

Sara cleared her throat.

"Forget it." Kaylee turned to Sara. "Let's go."

Kaylee hurried out of the office, and Sara followed close behind.

"Can you believe him? I'm starting to believe he never cared about Mom, which infuriates me. All those years she spent alone, and all he cared about was making money."

"His love of money and success gave you a good life," Sara interjected.

"All I ever wanted was to be a family. I would give it all back to have a little time with him, to have him love me and tell me he's proud of me. But that's never going to happen."

"Don't get upset; you know how he is."

"Why are you taking his side?"

"I'm not. I'm just stating the facts. Michael's never going to change."

Her father cared more about his employees than he did his own daughter. It would've taken him one call and could have saved Kaylee valuable time, but he couldn't be bothered. Kyle was the only other person who could help her, and there wasn't a snowball's chance in hell she would ever ask him for anything. Kaylee had endured her father's presence and insults for nothing.

Kaylee longed to open up about her relationship with Jeff and her fears about the investigation with Sara. Still, Sara had been acting strangely, leaving without telling her and not listening to her when she spoke. If she divulged her most painful secrets, would Sara be receptive or judgmental? Back in college, they were closer than best friends, and she wouldn't have doubted Sara's loyalty, but now she wasn't so sure.

Kaylee drove home and dropped Sara off; Sara seemed eager to be alone. Kaylee sensed she had been right to hold back. She would wait to see if they could recapture the trust they once shared in college.

After dropping Sara off, she dialed 411, gave the operator the city and state, and waited to be connected. The receptionist said Mr. Goldman wasn't in but was expected soon, and sometimes he could be reached at Jobot Coffee & Bar, a coffee shop directly across from the office. Kaylee asked for the crossroads and backed out of her driveway.

She decided to approach her search from a different perspective. Instead of trying to track down a multitude of Jeff's potential business connections, she would explore

70

Jeff's personal relationships. This would allow her to see Jeff as the rest of the world did. She would start by visiting Greg.

At Jobot Coffee & Bar, Kaylee ordered a large Angel's Kiss, a heavy blend of chocolate, coconut, and almonds, and sat in a small booth in the back. She sipped the hot liquid and instantly understood why it was named as such; it tasted heavenly. The chocolate and the coconut were smooth and sweet. Kaylee wasn't sure if Greg would show up here or at his office, and for a moment, she didn't care.

When the door swung open, a curvy brunette walked in, ordered, and took the booth directly west of her. She sat facing Kaylee, but Kaylee could only see the top of her mocha-colored hair. The barista delivered Kaylee's coffee to her table, and the brunette called someone, asking them to meet her at the coffee shop. The brunette looked vaguely familiar. Kaylee shrugged, continued to enjoy her coffee, and glanced up at the clock on the wall. She came here to get answers and had to wait in a room filled with a bouquet of espresso. What a great way to start the day.

Moments later, the door opened again. This time, a tall, thin man in an expensive three-piece suit scanned the room. He nodded in the direction of the brunette and headed to her booth. As he approached, Kaylee could see him clearly. She hadn't seen him in years, but the lanky build and distinctive red hair were unmistakable: Greg Goldman.

Greg sat facing the door and waved to the barista. She brought over a tall cup.

Kaylee leaned closer, averted her face, and listened to their conversation. They exchanged pleasantries, and Greg called her Stephanie. Could this be the woman who had had dinner with Kyle on the night Jeff died? As the brunette spoke, Kaylee realized it was her former high school classmate, Stephanie Ortiz. Stephanie told Greg the police had come by her fitness salon and questioned her about Jeff's death. Stephanie expressed concern about being a suspect and said that the detective trounced all over her. Greg urged her not to worry. Kaylee waited patiently for Stephanie to tell Greg if she knew anything about Jeff's murder. Still, it was a huge letdown when she denied any involvement. When Stephanie told Greg that the detective had asked about her relationship with him and the note left in Jeff's locker, Greg assured her no one would be convicted for participating in a prank.

By eavesdropping, Kaylee risked hearing unflattering things about herself, Jeff, and their relationship. However, what Stephanie said next knocked the wind out of her. She reminded Greg that the one person from high school everyone hated was dead, and they both had reasons for wanting him that way. Kaylee swallowed too much coffee and instantly regretted it. She put her napkin to her lips to muffle the sound as the hot liquid burned her throat. She had no idea people felt that way about Jeff.

Her burnt tongue hurt and started to tingle; she needed to focus on what they were saying, or she might miss something important.

"I have a secret; do you want to hear it? But if I tell you, mum's the word. You can't repeat it, or I'll have to kill you." Stephanie laughed.

"Poor choice of words, but yes, do tell."

"In our senior year, the day Jeff and Kaylee fought in front of the entire school, Jeff and I bumped into each other at the mall. We talked for a while, and I invited him to my house for a small get-together."

"Why would you do that?"

"Don't be silly. My parents were out of town for the night, so when he came over, we were all alone."

Greg smirked. "You didn't?"

"Yes, I did. That poor sap had a hard-on all night, and we had sex in every room. I really stuck to his bitchy girlfriend."

Kaylee knocked over her drink and frantically wiped it up.

"That was cruel, even for you, and you must be careful what you say out loud. The police are everywhere, and if you keep saying things like that, they might make you their prime suspect."

Stephanie laughed. "Don't worry about me. I have the perfect alibi, and no one, not even the prima donna Kaylee Chambers, can question it."

Stephanie told Greg that she had called Kyle out of the blue because she needed his expert advice on some property she wanted to buy. Stephanie laughed again and said that it must have been fate that the same night she tried to seduce Kyle, a man who still loved Kaylee, Jeff, the man Kaylee planned to marry, died.

Stephanie asked Greg what he was doing the night Jeff died; he didn't answer but told her he felt sorry for Kaylee, when Stephanie asked him why, Greg said that a few months before he died, Jeff had cheated on Kaylee.

Kaylee had heard enough. She wanted to tell them to shut up and to stop lying, but she would never get another chance like this, so she continued to listen, and no matter how much it hurt, Kaylee knew in her heart that some of it was true.

Greg described in graphic detail how Jeff and a voluptuous redhead had danced suggestively at a Scottsdale club, and that he had seen the two having sex in Jeff's car. And when they re-entered the club, the redhead wore an expensive diamond pendant and matching earrings. It surprised Kaylee that Greg seemed to enjoy reciting the story of her fiancé's tryst. Maybe everything Kyle had told her was true–Greg had a crush on her in high school, and his feelings never subsided. Greg had skillfully avoided

73

answering Stephanie's question about his alibi on June first. Perhaps he did have a motive to kill Jeff?

A cell phone rang, and Greg answered it. He informed Stephanie that he had to get back to the office.

Kaylee stood, hurried to their table, and blocked Greg's exit.

"Greg. I couldn't help but hear that you didn't answer Stephanie's question." Kaylee put her hands on the table, leaned close, and asked, "Where were you when Jeff died?"

Greg's face paled. "I—"

"Did you kill Jeff?

"Why would I do that?"

Kaylee straightened up. "Maybe you were jealous of him or wanted to put him in his place for good."

"He was with me."

Kaylee turned and faced Stephanie. "Really?"

Stephanie brushed her hair from her face and fidgeted with her coffee mug. "We've been dating for a while—"

"You're lying. Kyle already told the police you two were together."

Greg's phone buzzed. "I have to go."

"This isn't over, Greg. I'm not going to let this go."

He squeezed by Kaylee and headed out the door.

She turned to Stephanie. "If he killed Jeff, you'd be foolish to protect him. Covering for a murderer is a crime.

Stephanie grabbed her purse and brushed past her.

Kaylee shook; she had never confronted anyone so brazenly before. What if one of them had killed Jeff, and she just let on that she was coming after them? She took a deep breath. The things they said about Jeff made Kaylee's stomach turn. He had been cheating on her since high school and throughout their engagement. How many women had Jeff slept with? Did he sleep with any of her friends? Kaylee committed to finding Jeff's killer, and her

74

parting words to Greg reaffirmed that she was going to see this until the end. Had Kaylee unwittingly put a target on her back; had she tipped off the killer?

She wondered if the woman at the club had been the one who had marked Jeff's collar with her lipstick. And if so, did Greg know her? Kaylee didn't know many women with red hair and curvy figures. Still, Kaylee had met someone with similar features at a party last year hosted by her client, Eric Carter. Jeff hadn't known the Carters, but thousands of women in Arizona likely fit the description. With so little to go on, Kaylee wouldn't be able to identify the woman at the party as Jeff's lover, though finding Jeff's lover could be the key to finding his killer.

Chapter 8

Jensen had been waiting in Steinberg and Goldman's lobby for twenty minutes, but Goldman hadn't arrived yet. Conducting interviews outside of the precinct gave the interviewees a slight advantage. They could control the surroundings and the number of distractions to an extent. Jensen had been forced to meet Goldman at his office today or wait three weeks while Goldman finished a high-profile case.

The door swung open; Greg Goldman walked in and motioned for Jensen to follow. They entered a large corner office decorated with walnut furniture.

Jensen glanced behind the L-shaped desk; framed degrees and certificates covered the wall. A floor-to-ceiling hutch, overflowing with Law books, covered the north wall, but he noticed an absence of pictures. Jensen had imagined Goldman's office filled with higher-end, more ostentatious furniture–something flashy to overcompensate for his personal inadequacies and pictures of his hobbies or conquests. Goldman appeared to be more interested in giving the perception that his intellect and career were more important than money or status.

"You said it was urgent; how can I help you?"

Greg appeared to be flustered and slightly flushed. Jensen wondered what had caused him to be late. "Our meeting yesterday was cut short; I need answers to some important questions. First of all, where were you the night of June first from six to ten?"

Goldman flipped open his calendar. "I had a date; I picked her up at six, and we arrived at Franco's Italian Caffe in Scottsdale at seven. Dinner lasted until about nine-thirty, then we went to see a movie at Scottsdale and the 101. I think the movie ended about midnight."

"I'll need to verify your whereabouts; who did you go out with, and where can I reach her?"

"I'd rather not say; I don't want to get her in trouble."

"The woman you're seeing, is she married; does she know the deceased?"

Greg leaned back in his chair.

"Mr. Goldman, as an officer of the court, you know the procedures, so please tell me who you went out with."

"Her name is Manara Thompson."

"Miss Chambers' friend?"

"Yes."

Jensen glared at Goldman. He was tired of playing games. "Tread lightly, Mr. Goldman; lying to a police officer is a serious offense."

"I told you I hadn't thought about Jeff or Kaylee in years. I didn't say I didn't know where she worked or hadn't seen her occasionally."

"I'm conducting an investigation into the death of Miss Chambers' fiancé, and you didn't think to tell me you've been dating her friend?"

"I didn't want to get her into trouble."

"I don't see how dating you would affect Ms. Thompson, but you made a poor decision when you decided to date Miss Chambers' friend."

"It shouldn't matter who I date."

"But it does. You're dating Miss Chambers' friend, and you might have killed her fiancé."

"This is ludicrous."

"Is it? When did you start dating Miss Thompson?"

"About two months ago," Greg stated.

"Miss Chambers' boss, James Canon, died two months ago, and just about six weeks later, Miss Chambers' fiancé was murdered. You had access to both of the deceased through your new girlfriend. Please explain that to me?"

77

"I have no knowledge about either of those deaths."

"I think you stalked Miss Chambers at her work and deliberately started dating her friend to keep tabs on her. And by dating her friend, you had access to her boss, co-workers, and her private office."

"I never went into Kaylee's private office."

"Why should I believe you?"

"It doesn't matter if you believe me; it's what you can prove," Greg smirked.

"If you have nothing to hide, why are you so uncooperative?"

"I know my rights, and I will answer accordingly."

"With all the women in Arizona, you chose to date Miss Thompson. Why?"

"Have you seen her? She's hot."

"As a model, she could date anyone; why do you think she picked you," Jensen asked?

"I'm smart and rich."

"So, it's not your good looks or dedication to justice that attracted her?"

Greg leaned forward, "Is that supposed to be funny?"

"No, but you are attracted to women out of your league. You figured if you couldn't have Miss Chambers, why not go after her hot friend, the model?"

"I'm done with this. Move on."

"How did you feel when you found out Miss Chambers had agreed to marry the deceased?"

"I didn't care."

"Mr. Swanson proposed over a year ago. Is that when you decided to stalk Miss Chambers and watch her every move? Did you decide then to date anyone at her office just to be close to her?"

Greg drummed his fingers on the desk. "It's interesting, don't you think, that only after Jeff proposed to

Kaylee, he died. I knew Kyle would finally man up and take care of business."

"You think Mr. Masters killed Mr. Swanson?"

"It's just speculation, but he had it bad for Kaylee."

"Funny, he said exactly the same thing about you."

Greg shrugged. "Maybe Kyle found out that Jeff was screwing around on Kaylee and got angry and killed him to save her from the humiliation of living with a cad."

"Do you have proof that Mr. Swanson cheated on Miss Chambers?"

"I saw him with a busty redhead about three months before he died. They had sex in his car in the parking lot of Scampy's in north Scottsdale."

"Did Miss Chambers know?"

"I didn't tell her."

"Did you tell Mr. Masters instead?"

"No, but I saw a black Lincoln, like Kyle's, in the parking lot with the engine running."

"How do you know Mr. Masters drives a Lincoln?"

"Kyle and I have mutual friends and clients; we sometimes attend the same event."

"You're positive it was Mr. Masters' car; what year is it? Did you see him?"

"It's two years old, I believe it's a 2007. If you're asking if I would swear to it under oath, I would, but I didn't see the driver."

"So, you think Mr. Masters suspected his best friend of having an affair, and he followed him to the nightclub to confirm his suspicions. And when Mr. Masters verified that his friend was cheating on the woman he loved, he killed him to save her from public humiliation," Jensen asked.

"It seems more likely that Kyle killed Jeff to eliminate his rival."

"You've wanted to be with Miss Chambers since high school. It seems reasonable you would kill him for the same reason."

"There's only one woman in my life, and her name is Manara, not Kaylee."

"You didn't start dating her until two months ago; the nightclub incident, according to you, happened three months ago. Was it the catalyst that motivated you to date Ms. Thompson so you could worm your way back into Miss Chambers' life?"

"Your obsession with this line of questioning is tiresome. Kaylee is a beautiful and intelligent woman, but I'm no longer interested in or have feelings for her. She made her choice long ago, and it doesn't include me."

"You may no longer be interested in her, but what about her money?"

"I'm wealthy in my own right. I don't have as much money as the Chambers; no one does."

"You've told me your relationship with the deceased had been a tumultuous one. Maybe Mr. Swanson did something to set you off. You stated he was a philanderer; did he try to seduce your girlfriend, Ms. Thompson?"

Greg bolted forward. "He wouldn't dare."

"Did he know you were dating her?"

"No, we kept it from everyone."

"What makes you think they weren't lovers?"

"Manara would never sleep with a scumbag like Jeff, and she would never do anything to hurt Kaylee."

Jensen's cell phone rang. "Jensen."

"You asked me to call you when Larry Lawson arrived. He just walked in." Detective Lopez said.

Jensen had urgent business at Kaylee's work. Blanchard wanted him to investigate a lead that ties Kaylee's boss' death to that of her fiancé's.

"Get the team down to 32nd Street & Camelback on the northeast side. I'll meet you in the parking lot in thirty." Jensen jumped up.

"I have to leave and might need to speak with you again."

Jensen didn't like the guy, but Goldman had given him some new leads. He wondered how many people knew the victim had been screwing around and how Kyle would explain his presence at the nightclub the same night the victim had had hot and steamy car sex.

*****

Jensen, followed by a forensic team, walked through the doors of Lawson and Canon's Consulting Firm, introduced himself to the receptionist, showed his badge, and requested to see Mr. Lawson. Manara rang Lawson's office and requested that he come down to the lobby.

A few minutes later, he strolled across the lobby and extended his hand. "I'm Larry Lawson. How can I help you?"

"I'm Detective Randy Jensen." Jensen shook Larry's hand and handed him some papers. "I have a warrant to search the office and private stairwell of the late Mr. James Canon."

"I don't want anyone in his office, and I've sealed off the stairwell." Lawson stared down at the papers. "This isn't even your jurisdiction. Who's your superior?"

"The person in charge is Commander Blanchard. He's out of the Violent Crimes Bureau at the Central City Precinct. This is related to one of our cases, so we are working with the Squaw Peak Precinct. A judge signed off on the search warrant—it's legal. I'm sorry, but you don't have a choice."

"This is ridiculous. James's death was an accident."

"Unfortunately, the medical examiner could not determine the cause of death."

"It's been months since James died. Why are you coming out here now? Does this have anything to do with Kaylee Chambers," Larry asked?

"This is an ongoing investigation, and I'm unable to discuss it with you or anyone else. Rest assured, Mr. Lawson, we have enough proof to merit a search. You can call the judge or Commander Blanchard, but the search will proceed." Jensen looked toward the elevators. "Now, if you will have someone show us to the stairwell."

Larry crumpled the warrant and said, "This way." He then went straight to the elevator with Jensen and the forensic team close behind. They went up to the third floor, where Larry ushered them to the office on the north side. While Larry dug into his front pant pocket for the keys, Jensen and his team put on their gloves.

Lawson turned the key and pushed open the door. The room was devoid of light. The drapes, made of a dark, lavish, sun-resistant material, were drawn. Lawson stepped in, felt along the wall, and switched on the lights. Plastic sheets covered the furniture. The walls were decorated with high school and college team photos, college degrees, and business awards. A lone portrait, painted by a local artist who attended college with Lawson and Cannon, hung on the wall near the light switch.

The local artist's depiction of Salvador Dali's *The Persistence of Memory* featured reddish-orange hues, evoking the feeling of abundant sunlight. The clocks had large, exaggerated faces. The second hand of each clock remained straight and unyielding, reminding us that time waits for no one. Cannon had purchased the painting at a charity auction to support his friend, and because Carpe Diem, seize the day, was his mantra.

Jensen glanced around the room; it appeared to be a shrine to James Cannon. Kaylee had told him that Cannon's death had crushed Lawson. Jensen had dug into some basic information about their childhood and how Cannon and

82

Lawson had grown up together in Scottsdale, attended the same schools, and even dated the same girl. Jensen wondered if Lawson struggled daily to deal with losing his best friend. Jensen knew he would. Kaylee also confided that Lawson had refused to talk about the accident and had refused access to Cannon's office and stairwell *until now*.

Jensen moved toward the west wall and pulled back the drapes. A faint cigar odor hung in the air; its pungent stench overwhelmed the senses.

"Mr. Lawson, has anyone been in this room recently?"

"No, I'm the only one who has access."

Jensen motioned for the forensic team to split up, directing some to Cannon's desk and others to the filing cabinets.

"Don't move or destroy anything," Lawson pleaded.

"Don't worry, Mr. Lawson, we're wearing the appropriate gear and will take care not to disrupt your memorial."

Lawson glared at the detective. "We all have our own way of grieving. This *is* mine."

"You're right. I'm sorry." Jensen sniffed the air. "Do you smoke?"

"No, but I light one of James' cigars when I'm here."

"Mr. Lawson, please show me the entrance to the stairwell."

"It's right through here." Lawson pointed and headed to the northwest corner of the office. He unlocked the door, pushed it open, and entered.

Jensen and three of the five forensic technicians hurried behind him.

"I thought this was a file room," Jensen mused.

"James stored his football awards and cigars here, but its main purpose is a passage to the stairs."

83

Jensen reached the front of the door leading to the stairwell. "Did you alter this door?"

"After James died, I had our locksmith seal the door."

Jensen shook his head. "They put a blank, a flat piece of metal, on the inside of the door to prevent it from being used. This doesn't meet the city code. You can't block an exit—it's a fire hazard."

Larry shrugged. "They didn't tell me, and I didn't ask."

"My team will have to remove this door to give us access to the stairwell."

"Can't you find another way?" Larry implored.

"No, we must process the stairs and the door leading outside. I'll need the locksmith's name and number."

"You can't possibly think James was murdered."

"I'm sorry, but I can't discuss the case with you. It's covered in the warrant. Please go back to your office. My team has work to do."

"Don't break anything, or your commander will hear from my attorney." Larry stormed out.

The forensic technicians finished the doors and the stairwell, then started on the main office and the storage room. Jensen needed the door company's number and wanted to speak to Miss Manara Thompson, so he took the elevator to the lobby.

While Jensen waited for Manara to give him the door company's information, he asked about her relationship with Kaylee. Manara seemed to like and respect Kaylee genuinely. When Jensen asked about the deceased, Manara stressed that she didn't like him, and Mr. Swanson had, on several occasions, hit on her.

Jensen asked if she had a boyfriend and, if she did, whether she had told him. Manara confirmed what Jensen already knew. She had told Goldman. He asked her where she was on June first, and Manara said she went out with her boyfriend, but the timeline didn't match Goldman's version. He noted to speak to Goldman again.

Chapter 9

Greg and Stephanie's revelations about Jeff had shocked Kaylee, and she needed someone to talk to. She had doubts about Sara, and Manara was at work. No one else knew her history well enough or understood her situation, so the only person who could empathize with her was Kyle. Kaylee had squashed the uneasy feeling building in her gut and called him. She had agreed to meet at his office for lunch. Kaylee was still mad at him, but he had been Jeff's best friend; maybe he could help sort out this ugly mess. She ordered another Angel's Kiss to go and went to her car.

She pulled into the parking structure, went to the third level, and parked next to Kyle's Lincoln.

They pulled out onto Central Avenue and headed north. "Where are we going," Kaylee asked?

"We're going to a sandwich shop on Camelback. They have the best sandwiches around. They also have salads."

Kaylee frowned.

"I saw that."

"What?"

"You grimaced when I mentioned salad. You need to start eating food that doesn't contain a truckload of sugar."

Kaylee shrugged; she did need to eat better, but Kaylee would never tell him that.

They pulled into the lot, parked in front of the sandwich shop, and walked past two planters filled with white and yellow flowers. The soft, sweet fragrance hung in the air near the entrance.

"I could have met you here; it would have saved you some time," Kaylee said.

"Actually, I'm surprised you called. I thought you weren't speaking to me. So, it's a win-win."

Kyle held the door, and Kaylee stepped in. The aroma of fresh-baked bread and spices flooded her senses. She inhaled deeply, and her mouth watered. After they ordered and got their drinks, they sat down at a table for two in the back. Full-color photos of the menu covered one wall. If the incredible aromas didn't entice you to order, the pictures on the wall definitely would. The table arrangement maximized space while giving customers enough room to move freely through the dining area without tripping over anyone. Kaylee would wait to see if it cleared out before telling Kyle what happened this morning. She didn't want strangers or anyone to overhear how her fiancé had betrayed her.

When their food arrived, Kaylee bit into hers hungrily. The turkey had a great smoky flavor, the bread was still warm, the apples were crisp, and the tart cranberries offset the apples' sweetness. The mustard sauce was spicy–a good spicy with a little kick and full of flavor. The deviled egg potato salad's creamy texture complemented the heat of the mustard sauce. Kaylee's taste buds danced as she chewed. She inhaled her sandwich and wished she had more.

"Are you still hungry?" Kyle asked.

"No, I'm good."

He waved the second half of his sandwich in front of her face. "I'll trade this for your potato salad."

"Really?"

She bit into the sandwich and smiled. The lean ham, avocados, and tomatoes were refreshing. And when you least expected it, the Chipotle sauce kicked it up a notch.

Kyle shook his head. "If you start eating better, you'd find a whole world of food just waiting to be gobbled up."

She wiped her lips with her napkin. "Funny."

87

"I'm glad you called, but when you did, you sounded rattled. What happened?"

"I heard some distressing news today and didn't know who I could count on."

He leaned forward. "Why are you whispering?"

"I went to talk to Greg Goldman but stopped for coffee first."

"Why would you do that? You know the police want to speak to him. You should stay out of it."

She shrugged, "Too late."

"Let the police do their job; they will catch Jeff's killer and keep you safe."

"I appreciate your concern, but don't want this investigation hanging over my head."

"You appreciate my concern? We're friends."

She stood, "This was a bad idea."

He motioned for her to sit. "I don't want to fight with you."

She took a drink and wished she had gone home. At least there, she could have mulled over what Greg and Stephanie had said without fear of judgment.

Kyle knew everyone involved; she had no choice but to confide in him.

"Jeff and Stephanie Ortiz had sex."

"What?"

At Kyle's startled response, the people at the next table glanced their way.

"Keep it down," She moved closer to him. "I went to a coffeehouse across from Greg's office, hoping to run into him. A woman came in and sat in the booth right in front of me, and when Greg came in, he sat with her. It was Stephanie Ortiz, and I overheard their conversation."

"You eavesdropped on them?"

"If Greg hadn't sat with her, I would have approached and asked to speak with him. I wanted to ask him about Jeff and why they fought and to get some insight from his perspective."

"Greg's viewpoint is tainted; you shouldn't listen to anything they said. And leave the investigating to the police. How many times do I have to remind you? What if one or both of them were involved in Jeff's death? You could have been in real danger."

"It seemed harmless enough; besides, the coffee house had people coming and going. I was never alone with them."

"That's not what I mean, and you know it."

She leaned toward him. "Do you want to hear what they said or not?"

"Is it relevant to the investigation?"

"Decide for yourself." Kaylee glanced to the right, then left–the other diners were busy enjoying their food. "Stephanie said she had sex with Jeff to get back at me, and then Greg mentioned he saw Jeff having sex with a curvy redhead at a Scottsdale club."

Kyle's eyes narrowed. "What else did they say?"

"They talked about Detective Jensen questioning Stephanie and what they were doing the night Jeff died. Greg sidestepped the question, but Stephanie said she had dinner with you to try to seduce you and get back at me. It sounds like she really hates me; it could be a motive for murder."

"Did you know Stephanie in high school," Kyle asked?

"I would say hi to her, and I think she dated Greg, but I can't be sure."

"Do you remember doing anything that would evoke such hatred?"

"No. Stephanie wasn't part of my circle of friends, so I barely remember her."

"I find it hard to believe she could overpower and kill Jeff. Did Greg hint at what he was doing on June first?"

"No, he sounded confident that he had a solid alibi; he just didn't want to tell her."

"Did they mention anything else about the case or Jeff dying?

She thought for a moment; it was hard to relive the conversation. They both seemed to despise Jeff, and she hadn't fared well either.

"Once I heard Jeff and Stephanie had sex, I spilled my drink, and it took me a few minutes to recover, so I missed some of what they said."

"Did Greg say if he'd talk to Detective Jensen?"

"No, but he got a call and tried to leave; that's when I confronted him."

"You did what?" Kyle shook his head.

"I asked Greg where he was when Jeff died. He didn't answer me either. I had more questions, but he got another call and rushed out. I warned him to be careful because I'm not giving up. I'm going to find out what happened to Jeff. I think he got the message–I'm not letting it go."

"Damn it, Kaylee." Kyle hit the table.

The couple at the next table was looking their way and whispering.

"Let's go back to my office. We'll have more privacy."

"I'd rather not be cooped up in an office."

"Sorry, I'm due at a meeting in an hour, and I can't be late. Besides, I want to give you the tour. It's different from your dad's office."

Kyle pulled Kaylee's chair out, and they hurried to the car. They headed south on Thomas Rd.

Kaylee fidgeted with her seatbelt. "You should've heard them. They were vicious. They attacked Jeff and our relationship, and Greg laughed as he retold the story about the redhead. He sounded happy someone was hurting me. I don't remember mistreating them. Is that why they were inflicting so much pain on me?"

"If you were discreet—"

"I was."

"Then, they didn't know you were listening until you confronted them. You did nothing wrong. Haven't you heard that saying: people will love you, and people will hate you, and it has nothing to do with you?"

She looked out the side window. "Yeah, but it doesn't make me feel any better."

The Chambers' name was a blessing and a curse. Back in high school, Kaylee had let it dictate her circle of friends. Kaylee loved Coronado High, but she now knew not everyone had. Her family's wealth had sheltered her from a lot of ugliness, which had robbed her of learning skills needed to deal with everyday situations, including those with men.

After she met Kyle and Jeff during freshman year, the three became good friends, and when Kyle asked Kaylee out, she accepted. Kyle was bright, confident, and focused; he had a plan for his future and worked toward it. After months of dating, it appeared they would finally be a couple, but Jeff had also asked Kaylee out. Since Kyle never discussed going steady, she accepted Jeff's offer to go out. Jeff worked hard to make her happy. She found his attempts to please her, surprising her with flowers in homeroom and showing up in P.E. with a cold water bottle, refreshingly different from her relationship with Kyle.

Kyle knew what he wanted and went after it. He reminded her of her father, and, looking back, that may have been why Kaylee had agreed to be Jeff's girlfriend. Kyle never mentioned her choice to her, and all three remained devoted friends. Kyle had hidden his feelings well, and she never knew how much she had hurt him then, but Kaylee's decision to be with Jeff had been the beginning of a fierce rivalry between the two.

Kaylee realized Kyle was right. Stephanie and Greg might have a reason, real or imagined, for hating her, and it might have nothing to do with what she may have done.

They parked and went to the private entrance.

Compared to Chambers Towers, the atmosphere in Kyle's office seemed relaxed and friendly, and the décor had functional yet stylish pieces. Kaylee could see herself working here. The culture was professional yet welcoming. Based on what she saw, Kyle's employees seemed to respect one another and work well together. It didn't have the suffocating, competitive environment her father had established at his office.

Kyle introduced her to his secretary and guided her to his corner office down the hall. He motioned for Kaylee to sit, and she did. He walked around his desk, angled the blinds to keep the sun out of Kaylee's eyes, and sat across from her.

"What a great chair; you should call me before you buy anything else. I can get custom, handmade furniture at cost."

"I didn't ask you here to talk furniture. You need to finish telling me what happened at the coffee shop."

Kaylee wondered whether she should tell him everything they'd said or stick only to what was relevant to the case. Kyle's feelings for her could shed light on what happened to Jeff. Kaylee decided to tell him all of it.

"Stephanie said you loved me," Kaylee chewed her bottom lip. "Do you love me?"

She waited for Kyle to answer, but his strained facial expression spoke volumes. Maybe he had loved her once, but didn't anymore. Why should he? She chose Jeff, not him. She couldn't expect him to wait for her. Her question, the elephant in the room, wouldn't be answered.

He stood, asked if she wanted some water, and hurried out of the office.

Kyle's silence disappointed Kaylee. If he didn't love her, he should say so, and if he did love her, now would be the perfect time to let her know.

When he returned, Kaylee stood solemnly by the window. "I didn't know you were just down the street from my father; how often do you see him?"

"Not often, we're both busy."

She turned to face him. "Yet, you were able to visit him on the anniversary of my mother's death."

"I dropped by to see if he needed anything."

She eased herself onto the chair and stared out the window. "She was my mother, but you didn't drop by to see if I needed anything. What about when Jeff died? Where were you then?" Kaylee asked.

It had been a humid, cloudy June evening, and Kaylee had been working late when her cell phone rang. She had thought it might be Jeff calling to try to get back together, so she had hesitated before answering. Instead, it had been the police telling her that Jeff had had a fatal fall. Kaylee had gripped the phone tightly. Had the worst happened? Did Jeff take his own life?

She had barely heard the policeman offer his condolences and instruct her to meet so she could identify the body. To Kaylee's surprise, her father had been waiting for her when she arrived at the M.E.'s office. He had nodded when she walked past, but hadn't said a word. The picture of Jeff on the cold steel table had been horrific: his face caved in on one side and covered in blood. She had turned away; she couldn't believe that mangled flesh had once been her fiancé.

Her father hadn't offered support, and she remembered wishing Kyle had been there.

Kyle, who had been standing by the window, went to her. "What's wrong?"

"I needed you. Why didn't you call or come over?"

Kyle ran his fingers through his hair. "I was grieving, too."

She exhaled. What good would it do to discuss it now? Kyle had his reasons for staying away, but she couldn't shake the feeling he had forgotten her. Was that how Kyle felt when she chose Jeff?

"Did you know," she asked?

"Know what?"

"About Jeff having sex with Stephanie and the redhead."

"This is the first I've heard of it."

"You didn't keep quiet because of some football code of honor or something?"

"No, I never knew he slept with Stephanie."

"I want to believe you, but I'm having trouble. You've kept secrets from me before."

"If I'd known, I would have said something."

Kaylee wanted to believe him. If he had known about Jeff's affairs and had told her, all of this ugliness could have been avoided.

"I planned everything, college, and my career, around his happiness. And he had the audacity to cheat on me. You were his best friend; why didn't you know what he was doing?"

"After Jeff announced your engagement, we didn't stay in touch. I tried to stay out of his way and let you two plan your future."

"Did you want me to marry Jeff?"

Kyle blew out a heavy breath. "What choice did I have?"

"If you cared, you would've fought for me. Jeff worked hard to let me know he cared."

"And I didn't?"

"Not as much as Jeff."

"We had backstage passes to No Doubt, and—"

"Jeff couldn't afford expensive gifts–he gave me things from his heart."

"So, you dumped me because my parents had money? That's rich."

"I didn't dump you—"

Kyle went back to the window. "Why are we rehashing this?"

She didn't want to argue with him, but Kyle's refusal to tell her he loved her had hurt, and Kaylee was still shaken by the confirmation that Jeff had been cheating. She would deal with her feelings for Kyle later; she needed his help.

Kyle stood and stared out the window. Kaylee knew her repeated attempts to force him to reveal his feelings were wearing on him, so she decided to lighten the mood.

"Thanks for lunch; you hit a home run with the sandwich, but the tea, well, better luck next time."

He turned to her. "It tasted fine; you just can't imagine a world without sugar."

"Sugar is what makes me so sweet."

Kyle laughed. "Oh, please…"

Kaylee licked her lips, and Kyle stopped laughing. A strange look crossed his face.

"What? Did you remember something?"

"Yeah."

She went to his side. "What is it?"

Kaylee looked up at him and waited. Kyle gazed into her eyes and caressed her cheek. Kaylee's whole face tingled; she saw something in his eyes, but he turned away again, and the moment was gone.

She stood beside him, breathing in his clean, earthy scent. Kaylee missed him and all the fun they used to have. When she was with Kyle, she had felt alive, but after their kiss, he seemed to turn his back on her. She couldn't understand why. The kiss wasn't planned; it just happened. Kaylee felt guilty about their kiss; maybe Kyle did too. As

95

her relationship with Jeff fizzled and he became more unstable, she longed to resume her previous friendship with Kyle.

Kyle had been her rock for so long that she thought he would always be around, and when he wasn't, he forced her to find her own way. It had made Kaylee stronger, and she would always be thankful for that, but his friendship meant the world to her. Despite all the recent ugliness in their lives, Kaylee wanted to reach out to Kyle. Did he want more, or was he done with her?

In high school, they studied, socialized, and trained together. Kyle and Jeff had competed in the 440-yard dash and the high jump, and she had run cross country. Kyle gave her tips for improving stride frequency and length and pointed out that Kaylee needed to work on timing and foot contact. His advice paid off and helped her take a national title. Kaylee never wanted to be an athlete, but while dating Kyle, he convinced her it would be fun, and it had been.

Running also helped Kaylee to get in shape; she had a trim figure, but being thin didn't mean she was fit. When she joined the team, she could barely run a quarter mile. In fact, after her first lap around the track, Kaylee had collapsed on the ground. Kyle stood above her, the sun at his back; his tanned skin glistened, and a luminous cloud danced above his shoulders and head–she imagined him as the Greek Sun God, Helios. She had stared up; he reached down and yanked her to her feet–forcing her to try again. With Kyle's continued encouragement, Kaylee gained strength, speed, and confidence.

When Jeff attended class, Kaylee and Kyle studied, watched movies, or hung out with friends. When she went to class, the guys would hang out together. She wondered if it had been awkward and if they had talked about her. Kaylee treasured her time with Kyle; their friendship made her feel at ease. She never had to worry that he wanted her money or used her to get to her father. It almost felt like

96

Kaylee had two boyfriends, as their three lives were so closely intertwined, but she didn't. Kaylee had chosen Jeff.

While dating Jeff, he confided in Kaylee that his stepfather had left because of him, and his mother struggled financially since he left. What could a thirteen-year-old boy do that would warrant a grown man abandoning his family, Kaylee had wondered? The fact that his biological father had never been in the picture only added to the guilt Jeff had felt. No one, not his birth father or his stepdad, had stayed. Jeff grew up believing he wasn't good enough, and Kaylee's heart had connected with him.

Both Jeff's father figures had left and never returned; her father was present, yet inaccessible. Kaylee had wanted to prove to Jeff that he deserved to be loved and that she wanted to make his life better, but it hadn't turned out that way. During their senior year of college, Jeff had become irritable and withdrawn, giving Kaylee more time to spend with Kyle. Did Jeff's refusal to look her in the eye signal the end of their relationship?

Chapter 10

The door opened.

Kyle's secretary appeared in the doorway. "Tim Barnes is on line one for Miss Chambers."

Kyle handed Kaylee the phone.

"Mr. Barnes, is there any news on my house?"

"Call me Tim. Your father would insist."

"Okay, Tim. Am I going to lose my house?"

"The title company is under investigation, and all its assets are frozen. If you continue to make payments, you should be able to keep your house. I will do everything I can to assist in the investigation."

Her shoulders sagged. She loved her home. Kaylee had worked hard for it, and Jeff stole it from her. If he weren't dead, she would...

"What's going to happen to the families Jeff evicted?"

"If it's proven they were evicted illegally, they will have legal recourse to get their homes back. This process may take months or years."

"Can you speed it up?"

"Unfortunately, this isn't an isolated incident, and my office is inundated with these cases. We're doing our best."

Kaylee thanked him and hung up.

"What did he say," Kyle asked?

"Tim said I should be able to keep my house, but he didn't make any promises, and the families Jeff threw out can only get their homes back if it's proven Jeff did something illegal." Kaylee sighed. "I'm sorry he called here; I thought he'd call my cell."

"Why are you sorry? You weren't looking into the investigation, were you," Kyle asked sarcastically?

Kaylee cleared her throat. "When I first called Tim, I asked specific questions about how the mortgage fraud may have been the motive for Jeff's death, but Tim told me he couldn't discuss it. Do you think Jeff was killed because of his title scam?"

Kyle rubbed his neck. "It's hard to say, but I'm sure Detective Jensen will be angry if he finds out you're interviewing prominent figures about Jeff."

"Are you going to tell him?"

"No, but I should. First, you question the Attorney General, and then you confront Greg. You are putting yourself in danger. I know you want answers, and so do I. I feel like I didn't know Jeff at all. Can you think of anything that might explain his behavior?"

"Why are you asking me?"

"You were his fiancée. You knew him better than anyone else."

"The man I agreed to marry was not the same man who scammed innocent families out of their homes or slept with other women."

"I'm not accusing you of anything. My best friend is dead, and I want answers."

"I do too, but I don't know what drove him over the edge," Kaylee stated.

"You would tell me if you knew anything, right?"

"Are you serious? You're the one who lied to me."

Kyle looked her directly in her eyes. "I don't want to keep rehashing this."

"Neither do I. Apparently, this all started in high school, or Jeff wouldn't have cheated on me. Do you remember anything at all about when his behavior changed?"

Kyle didn't respond; he appeared to be thinking, and just when she thought he would say something, he slammed his fist on the desk.

Kaylee moved closer. "Are you all right?"

"I have a meeting I need to get ready for. We'll talk soon. Okay?"

Something had made Kyle angry. Did he say or do something to Jeff that changed him forever?

"Sure." She grabbed her purse and headed home.

*****

What had made Kyle so mad? Had he remembered a vital piece of the past, one that would finally answer the question as to why Jeff had gone from a fun-loving, faithful friend to a murder victim? Kaylee tried to expunge the horrible things she had heard about Jeff. If what Greg and Stephanie said were true, why hadn't Kaylee seen it then, too? She went to her bedroom closet, pulled out her high school yearbooks, and read messages from friends and classmates. She couldn't find one nasty comment or any hint that she or Jeff hadn't been liked. Kaylee should've realized no one would write anything negative; her father's reputation had significantly impacted her social life. If someone had felt slighted, they wouldn't have risked the wrath of Michael Chambers by making it public.

She speculated on whether attending private schools for the first twelve years of her life had cultivated her naivety or whether it stemmed from her mother's trusting nature. Kaylee had often wondered if her classmates had known her father had no interest in her life, would they still have been friends?

Kaylee's cell phone rang. It was Michael. After their earlier discussion, she felt sure her father would ignore her request for help.

"Michael, do you have information for me?"

"I would like to discuss my findings with you at lunch. How does Ruth's Chris Steak House sound?"

"No, thank you."

100

"I know the thought of having lunch with me makes you uncomfortable, but the food is first-rate. The stuffed chicken breast, mozzarella, and heirloom tomato salad are excellent. Chicken is what you order when you eat there, right?"

"I've already eaten, but who—"

"Your mother informed me of your activities, including your eating habits."

Just because her mother had kept him abreast of what she had been doing didn't mean he knew her.

"Mom reported my comings and goings to you, and you think that makes up for all the times you weren't around?"

"No, I merely stated that she kept me up-to-date."

Kaylee could spend an entire afternoon rehashing his failures as a father, but why waste her time? "What did you learn about Jeff?"

"I checked with my financial partners, advisors, and friends, and the consensus is the same. No one lent Jeff any money, and he did not have a partner."

"He must have. Where else would he get money if he didn't borrow it?" Kaylee asked.

"My associates and I could not find the origins of the large deposits in Jeff's bank accounts. We checked out a lead that he might be gambling, but were unable to find proof that he frequented casinos or visited the tracks. If his transactions were legal, we would have found a paper trail. Our sources indicated no one would lend him money. His credibility was shot."

Everyone seemed to have the same opinion of Jeff– he wasn't trustworthy. Why hadn't she seen it?

"I spoke to Tim Barnes earlier, but I don't believe he gave me all the information. Did you speak to him," Kaylee asked?

101

"I did; all of the properties, except yours, are in a centralized location, and it appears a large developer wants the land."

"Innocent, hard-working families were forced out of their homes so Jeff could sell the land?"

"If money were the reason, that would be a logical conclusion."

"What other reason could there be, and why buy my mortgage?"

"Speculation makes for inferior business—"

"Can't you just once tell me something without switching into corporate exactitude mode? Why do you think he would do this?"

"I did not know Jeff well."

"You know people. You know what motivates them. Your business has flourished because of these skills."

Kaylee had better be careful; she didn't want to inflate his massive ego.

"It seems you are convinced I have superhuman powers, but I have no idea why Jeff did what he did."

It made sense to Kaylee why Jeff would try to capitalize on a land deal. He had wanted to prove he could compete with her savvy businessman father, but why involve her in his mortgage scheme? Had Jeff figured out that Kaylee wanted to leave him?

"I guess I needed a plausible answer as to why the man I agreed to marry would rip people off and think he could get away with it."

"No one will ever know."

"Was Jeff involved in any other plots to defraud honest people?"

"Tim is still looking into his financial activities. If he finds anything else, I will call."

"Thank you."

Her father had been uncharacteristically polite. Maybe he felt sorry for her. After all, Kaylee did get taken in by a con artist–something that would never happen to him. The more she learned about Jeff's criminal activity, the more she despised him. Kaylee had endured unspeakable things at his hands, but to involve innocent families was a new low even for him.

Kaylee went upstairs to check on Sara. Her clothes and suitcase were thrown about on the bed, but no sign of her. Kaylee checked the guest bath and living areas. She went downstairs to the front window and pulled back the drapes; Sara and her car were gone. Sara had been acting distant and nervous. Maybe her breakup with Ben had upset her more than Kaylee realized. The next time Kaylee saw her, she would ask Sara if she wanted to discuss it. Sara probably didn't want to burden Kaylee with her issues when Kaylee was in the middle of an investigation. That seemed more consistent with the Sara she knew and loved. She headed downstairs to make a drink.

The custom-built Cortina Bar, made of Rosewood, complemented the coffee table. The intricate lines, deep carvings, and beveled-edge granite top reminded her of one of her mom's favorite pieces. Kaylee looked for furniture that evoked positive emotions. If she couldn't find them, she would pay extra to have them made to her exact specifications. Kaylee didn't mind waiting or spending more; she was creating a home where she could be happy and safe. She ran her fingers across the smooth countertop and prayed she wouldn't lose it.

Two months before Jeff had proposed, Kaylee had signed the contract for her house but hadn't told him. Construction had taken twelve months, and she had been ecstatic when she moved in. Three weeks passed, and Kaylee still hadn't shared the good news with Jeff. It had been challenging to keep it from him, and before he died, Kaylee had convinced herself she had kept it secret to surprise him. But now, she knew their life together had been over.

The vodka and cold cranberry juice slid down her throat, and Kaylee let out a deep breath. As she lifted the glass for another sip, she heard her phone ringing. She hurried upstairs to her office and searched her purse for her phone. Kyle wanted to meet her at The Capital Grille on Camelback to discuss an important issue regarding Jeff. Kaylee didn't expect to hear back from Kyle so soon. What could be so important that he would need to see her twice in one day?

*****

At the bar, she ordered a Cape Cod. Kaylee sipped slowly and waited for Kyle to arrive. She played with the rim of her glass as she took in her surroundings. She liked the dark wood and the high-back barstools. She had selected a booth right across from the bar to give her access to food and drinks, just in case the wait staff was busy, and she guessed they would be. Her booth glowed under the recessed lighting. The bartenders moved quickly from patron to patron to keep the booze flowing and hype up the fun.

After the lights dimmed, Kaylee checked the time. It had been over ninety minutes since Kyle called. She wondered if she should have another drink or switch to water. While she mulled over what to do, Kyle approached and sat across from her.

"You look like hell," Kaylee stated.

"Thanks."

"Do you want me to get you a drink?" Kaylee asked.

"I ordered one."

"Do you come here often?" She smiled suggestively.

"Occasionally, I meet clients here; I don't normally come alone."

104

Kyle missed an opportunity to tease her about the pick-up line she used. Or did he intentionally ignore it? Either way, Kaylee wondered what they'd be discussing. It couldn't be good if he glossed over her attempt at humor.

"I wasn't implying you were a barfly; I just wondered why you picked this place."

"It's a great place to unwind from a hard day."

"How did your meeting go?"

"It was short and gave me time to prepare for my meeting tomorrow morning."

"You seem to spend a lot of time in the office. How do you actively promote your real estate ventures?"

Kyle nodded to the woman wearing a white ruffled blouse and black slacks and slipped her a ten. He downed one-third of his drink and set the glass down.

Kaylee waited for his answer, but apparently, she wouldn't get one.

"I need to tell you something, and it's going to be upsetting, but in light of what we discussed this afternoon and your repeated jabs about me being secretive, I'm going to tell you so you don't find out some other way."

"You're only telling me so I don't hear it from someone else."

Kaylee's curiosity piqued. Kyle had denied knowing about Jeff's affairs. What could he possibly have to tell her?

"No. You need to know, and I have to be the one to tell you." He took another drink. "Your father asked me to take you to the Senior Prom. I said no."

"Why would he ask you to take me when he knew I was going with Jeff?"

"I'm guessing he thought you two were too young to be exclusive."

"We weren't engaged; we were just dating."

"Maybe Michael wanted to give you other options. If you want answers, you'll have to ask him."

Kyle knew Kaylee would never ask her father why. Michael didn't like anyone second-guessing his decisions. He would never tell and probably yell at her again. She played with the rim of her glass and considered the timing of Jeff's car accident. It happened two weeks before prom, and now that Kaylee knew her father had tried to sabotage her date, she wondered if it was an accident or something more sinister.

"Did Michael hurt Jeff so you could take me to the prom?"

"Michael had nothing to do with the accident."

"You don't know that."

"Yes, I do."

"How could—"

"I did it," Kyle confessed.

"You're responsible for his scar?"

"It just happened. We were racing, and Jeff swerved into my lane. I hit the brakes, and Jeff slammed into the wall."

"You shouldn't have raced Jeff. He had a Mercedes, and you had a sports car. He had no chance of winning. You should've said no."

"Jeff wanted to prove he could beat me. He was relentless."

"Seriously?"

"It's a guy thing."

"You were the mature one. You should've stopped him—"

"Damn it. I'm only human."

She had no idea when Kyle called that he would reveal a secret, so distressing that Kaylee almost doubled over. Her current pain didn't compare to what Jeff had gone through. He had lost all feeling on his left side and had been hospitalized for a month. The scar on Jeff's forehead had been a constant reminder of the accident and his pain. It had been agonizing for her to watch as he had

106

struggled to regain his strength and coordination, and her guilt had made it worse.

"If I could take it back, I would. Jeff never fully recovered from the crash, and everything–sports, grades, cars, money–became a competition. My best friend's spirit died that day, and it's my fault."

Kaylee reached for Kyle's face, but she let her hand drop. She wanted to stroke his cheek and tell him to forget about the tragic accident. But this heartbreaking event could have been prevented if Kyle had said no. Could he have, or was it wishful thinking on her part?

"So, in the end, you took me to prom."

Michael had won. He always did.

"Jeff knew you'd be disappointed if you didn't go, and he didn't want anyone else to ask you, so I agreed, only to make him happy."

She swirled the ice in her glass. "*I see.*"

"*I* owed him. He could've been killed–I'm to blame."

Kyle felt guilty about Jeff's accident. Who wouldn't? But his soulful confession tainted the memories of one of the best nights of her life. Kaylee didn't want to miss prom; it was a rite of passage, and since Jeff couldn't go, she assumed Kyle would take her. It seemed natural that Kaylee would go with him, but now the truth had come out. He had only escorted her out of obligation to Jeff.

For Kaylee, prom had been magical. Kyle had arrived at her door in a Giorgio Armani tuxedo, and she had worn a midnight-blue strapless dress and matching heels. Her mom had taken dozens of pictures and made a big fuss, as moms do. They danced, laughed, and mingled like a real couple, but Kyle insisted they leave an hour after their only slow dance. She thought it odd; he seemed to be having a great time.

They'd taken off in his 1957 Corvette and sped down the road. Kyle glanced her way and then accelerated.

As the convertible raced through the desert night, Kaylee's hair whipped around her shoulders, and the wind kissed her cheeks. She had never felt anything so exhilarating. She looked at Kyle; he seemed focused, maybe even mad or annoyed. She asked him why they had to leave, but he didn't answer. They drove in silence for a while longer, and she couldn't stand it; the silence drove her crazy.

Kaylee remembered asking, "Why are you driving so fast?"

He slowed down and pulled onto the shoulder. His hands gripped the steering wheel tightly.

"What is it?" She asked.

He turned toward her. "While you're with Jeff, it's not a good idea for us to be alone."

"Why not?"

He exhaled. "It's hard to explain, and now is not the time."

"Why are you mad at me? What did I do?"

He groaned. "I can't be with you, so I need to get away from you."

"What are you talking about?"

He looked down at his lap and closed his eyes. "Forget it... I need to get you home."

"It's too early to go home; it's prom night."

Kyle didn't take her home. He had spent the rest of the night teaching Kaylee to drive his Corvette. He had been patient and supportive when she tried to change gears without holding down the clutch or killing the engine. Kyle had grimaced, and Kaylee wondered if he regretted trying to teach her how to drive a stick. After she had mastered it, he had let her drive home, and a car enthusiast was born.

She should've known Kyle cared for her, but Kaylee had been young and had no real experience with guys. If she had, she wouldn't have realistically expected Jeff to wait until they were married to have sex. Did Jeff figure out that Kaylee's repeated requests to wait were her fumbled hints about her true feelings for him? Kaylee couldn't be sure, but his repeated affairs made it clear that what he felt for her was not love.

Chapter 11

Detective Jensen arrived at Kyle's office at nine and waited in a large conference room. The long oval table seated sixteen, and the chairs had thick, leather seats with tall, flexible backs. Color photos of commercial buildings covered the south wall, and a sixty-inch flat-screen was mounted on the east wall. Fifty percent of the north wall contained glass. It let in additional light into the room, but Jensen wondered whether the window would be a distraction during meetings.

Kyle arrived and took a seat at the east end of the table.

"Good morning, Detective. Do you want coffee or water?"

"No, but thank you. I asked you here to discuss your relationship with the deceased."

Kyle leaned forward. "If you don't mind, I have some new information that I would like to discuss first."

Jensen nodded.

"I know everyone, including myself, is a potential suspect. However, I think you will agree that keeping Michael Chambers happy and his daughter safe is a primary objective."

"Go on."

"I spoke with Kaylee yesterday, and she told me she confronted Greg and asked him if he had an alibi for Jeff's murder and would have continued interrogating him until she got what she wanted, but he had to leave. I've known her a long time, and Kaylee won't stop. Can you do something legally to prevent her from endangering herself?"

"If Kaylee directly interferes with the investigation, I can, but I'm sure Mr. Chambers won't like me arresting

110

or putting his daughter in jail. When Commander Blanchard assigned me this case, he assured me you would assist in keeping Kaylee, let's say, out of the way and out of my hair."

"It's going to be tougher than I thought. Kaylee's angry and more determined than ever."

"Did Mr. Goldman say anything to her?"

The intercom buzzed.

"Jessica, please, no interruptions."

"I'm sorry, Kyle, but your friend is on her way to your office; she insisted."

"I'll take care of it. Thank you."

The door opened, and Kaylee walked in. "I'm sorry to interrupt." When she noticed Detective Jensen, she said, "I thought your meeting was later. I'll come back."

"Did something happen? Are you all right?" Kyle asked.

"I'd hoped to speak with you, but I should've realized you'd be busy."

"Miss Chambers, I'd wanted to interview Mr. Masters alone, but your arrival seems perfectly timed. Please sit and tell me why you are interviewing persons of interest in my investigation."

She glared at Kyle.

"I went to see Greg Goldman; I wanted to ask him why he didn't like Jeff. Stephanie Ortiz was with him, and they were discussing Jeff and their alibis—"

"Miss Chambers, I'd appreciate it if you leave the detective work to me."

"Are you saying I can't talk to old classmates?"

"Not if your purpose is to discuss your fiancé's murder. Stay away from anyone who might be involved in this case."

"Do you want to hear what they said?"

"Possibly, but first, I would like more information on Mr. David Swanson. Do you know why his company went under or where he went when he left town?"

"David didn't have a good relationship with Jeff, but even if he did, I don't think he would have talked to him about it. Jeff was only thirteen. David probably told Jeff's mother, but she's gone too. Are you trying to find him now, after all this time?"

"I want to speak to anyone connected to the deceased. Please let me know if you hear anything about David's whereabouts." Jensen waited for Kaylee to meet his gaze. "Miss Chambers, did Mr. Goldman or Ms. Ortiz say anything relevant to the case?"

"They had a lot of hateful things to say about Jeff and me, but they did talk about their alibis. Stephanie bragged about having an air-tight one, but Greg refused to tell her where he'd been."

"Mr. Goldman said he was on a date the night Mr. Swanson died, and I corroborated it with the woman he went out with. An aspect of his story concerns me, and it affects you, Miss Chambers," Jensen paused, "The woman he went out with is someone you know; her name is Manara Thompson."

"He's dating Manara," Kaylee asked?

Jensen watched Kaylee closely. He wondered if this was the first time she had heard about it, or did she already know?"

"He's pretending to date Manara to be close to Kaylee. It's obvious he's fixated on her—she's in danger."

"Mr. Goldman may have ulterior motives, but I won't know until I finish the investigation."

"What are you going to do about it? He can't be trusted," Kyle insisted.

"Mr. Masters, my team, and I will closely monitor his movements to ensure Miss Chambers is not harmed."

"Should I be worried?"

"I would, as always, be aware of your surroundings and don't go to questionable locations at night. It's my job to find Jeff's murderer, but it is also my job to keep you safe. And although I appreciate your willingness to help, this is a police matter. Understood?"

Kaylee nodded.

"Miss Chambers, I will be exploring a new line of questioning. I know this has been difficult for you, and I apologize if my questions are painful. Your honesty is crucial to the success of this investigation."

"I will help anyway I can."

"Did you know Mr. Swanson was having relationships with other women while you were engaged?" Jensen watched as her smile fell, and her fair skin seemed to pale. "Please answer the question."

"Yesterday, I overheard Stephanie tell Greg she had slept with Jeff in high school."

"Your fiancé slept with Ms. Ortiz? She doesn't have red hair."

"How did you hear about the redhead?" Kaylee asked.

"I didn't tell him."

"Mr. Masters, how'd you find out?"

"Kaylee told me yesterday."

"Is that the first time you heard about it, or maybe you saw it yourself at a Scottsdale nightclub?" Jensen asked.

"Kyle, what's he talking about?"

"A witness places him and his black Lincoln at the same club where the deceased engaged in sexual activity in his Mercedes."

"Is it true?"

"It was my car, but I wasn't there. I'd loaned it to a couple of friends."

"Mr. Masters, I'm going to need their names."

He nodded.

"Did they see Jeff having sex? Did they tell you?"

Kyle rubbed his temple. "Sam told me he'd seen Jeff having sex, but because he'd been drinking, I didn't believe him, so I asked Brad, the designated driver, and he said he didn't see Jeff, so I believed Brad."

"Why didn't you tell me," Kaylee asked?

"Tell you what? My drunk friend saw someone having sex in a car? I had no proof it was Jeff."

"Miss Chambers, let's move this along." Jensen waited until he had her undivided attention.

"Why didn't you sue Mr. Swanson when you found out about your mortgage?"

Kaylee stared at him with her mouth slightly open. "Why would I sue him?"

"The other victims of the scam filed a suit against your fiancé's company."

"I just found out a couple of days ago, and those families were evicted from their homes."

"So, you're telling me the first time you heard about it was Saturday when Mr. Masters notified you?"

"Yes, I am."

"Why didn't he evict you?"

"I don't know? He never mentioned anything like this to me."

"Did you receive any notice that your mortgage company had changed?"

"The new company notified me, but I had no idea Jeff owned it."

"A newer, less established company purchased your mortgage; weren't you concerned?"

"Why should I be? Mortgages are bought and sold all the time."

"Your potential net worth is extensively more than the cost of the house; why didn't you pay it off and not worry about a mortgage?"

"I don't have access to my father's wealth; if I did, I wouldn't use it. Besides, I didn't know Jeff purchased my mortgage."

"Can you prove that?"

"The burden of proof is on you, and I'm tired of your insinuations."

"Did you receive any useful information from Greg," Kyle asked?

Jensen paid close attention to how Kyle changed the subject when Kaylee seemed to be on edge.

"He gave me a new potential suspect.

Kyle asked, "Who?"

"You."

"Me? Jeff and I were friends, and Greg and I barely spoke in high school. How would he know what I wanted?"

"According to Mr. Goldman, the entire school knew you had feelings for Miss Chambers."

Kyle shook his head in denial. "What does that have to do with this case?"

"Jealousy, love, and greed are all strong motives for murder. Most people don't find them worth killing for, but some people get so enraged and consumed that all rational thought leaves them in the heat of the moment. At least, that's what the lawyers want you to believe; it eliminates the element of premeditation."

"Kyle wouldn't kill anyone."

Jensen had a hard time believing she was that naïve. She appeared to be an intelligent woman, and Kyle's feelings for her were blatantly obvious.

"Mr. Masters, other than the pool party where Mr. Swanson flirted with some girls, have you and the deceased ever fought over Miss Chambers?"

"No!"

"What did he do to make you hit him? What did he do that made you so mad?"

Kyle glanced over to Kaylee, "He made Kaylee cry. An honorable man wouldn't do that."

"Does a respectable man kiss his best friend's fiancée?"

Kaylee whipped around to face Kyle. "Don't blame him. It was my fault."

"Kaylee, don't."

"I won't let him attack your integrity. Kyle came to my aid, and I got caught up in the moment. I kissed him."

"Why did you need assistance?"

Kaylee's lips quivered, and she turned toward Jensen.

"In the pool house, Jeff and I were arguing. He frightened me, and I fell onto the ottoman and then to the floor. When the door opened, Jeff left. Kyle came in and helped me up. He held me while I recovered. Then I kissed him."

"Did Mr. Swanson see you kissing?"

"I thought he left; maybe he came back."

"Did he know?" Jensen asked.

"Know what?"

"I don't think so," Kyle replied.

"Know what?"

Jensen rolled his eyes.

"Mr. Masters, don't you think it's about time you come clean?"

"It's none of your business."

"Under normal circumstances, it wouldn't be. But your feelings for Miss Chambers give you a reason to want Mr. Swanson out of the picture, which *is* my business. Don't you think she deserves to know?"

Kyle drummed his fingers on the table.

"Kyle…" Kaylee pleaded.

Kyle turned to Kaylee. "I didn't want to tell you until Jeff's killer had been caught, and this isn't how I'd planned to tell you." Kyle glared at Jensen. "But I can see I have no choice." Kyle took a deep breath. "I love you. I always have."

"Why didn't you tell me?" Kaylee asked breathlessly.

"You were with Jeff and seemed happy. If I had known what a creep he was, I would have—"

"Mr. Masters, your motive is as strong as, or stronger than, Mr. Goldman's. Is there anything you'd like to tell me?"

"I *did not* kill Jeff."

"You have quite the temper; are you sure you didn't get angry and push the deceased to his death accidentally?"

"I thought Kaylee loved him; hurting him would've destroyed her. And my so-called anger is frustration. I was nowhere near him or his building the night he died."

"No, you were out with Ms. Ortiz."

"You've already checked my alibi. Move on."

Jensen's phone rang; dispatch informed him about a disturbance and possible robbery at the victim's grave, and he needed to get to the cemetery ASAP. Dispatch gave him the address and told him she had contacted the officer in charge to let him know Jensen would be responding to the call. She informed Jensen that Detective Stone had arrived at the scene.

"I'm sorry, but duty calls."

*****

It had been a cloudy August morning, and Jensen had been on his way back to the precinct. A call had come in over the radio about a kidnapping; an escaped felon had stolen a Honda with a young girl in the back. He had responded to the call and followed the Honda down a deserted alley; the perp rammed the Honda into the Crown Vic and had been ejected from the vehicle. Jensen restrained him and waited for backup to arrive. The girl sustained no injuries, and the look of appreciation her frantic mother gave him reminded him why he, his father, and his father before him had joined the force: to protect and serve those who couldn't defend themselves. He had been put on desk duty for ninety days. It had been the longest three months of his life, but if he had to, he would do it again.

His perceived mistake in taking a vacation at a crucial time made Jensen acutely aware of the additional commitment he needed to make to his profession. He couldn't have foreseen that a major case would have occurred while he had been away. Still, he felt immeasurably responsible for the outcome. At the precinct, Jensen tried to ignore it, but sometimes, he would hear rumors about how he conveniently left when his team needed him most. He had vowed never to let that happen again.

As a child, he had worshiped his father, but his father's belief that justice was always served lulled Jensen into thinking that criminals would always be punished for their crimes. One day, while walking home from high school, Jensen came upon an elderly man being jumped by a group of teenagers. When Jensen saw the old man being attacked, he remembered how his grandfather had been victimized and had rushed to the old man's aid, ending up with a broken arm and bruised ribs in the process.

The victim had still been robbed, but because of Jensen's intervention, he had only sustained minor injuries. Unfortunately, the older man took a hit to the head. He couldn't help with the investigation, and when Jensen had been interviewed, he could not describe or identify any of the perpetrators. At sixteen, he had gotten caught up in the moment, trying his best to be heroic.

Jensen had forgotten everything his father had taught him: be aware of your surroundings and remember the unique details specific to the perpetrator. Since the law was on his side, Jensen naively believed everything would be all right, but the criminals had gone free.

He had hoped his father would be proud, but instead, his father told Jensen that his efforts were merely what was expected and that he had let the public down. His father and grandfather were decorated officers, yet he had failed in his first opportunity to prove he was worthy of following in their footsteps. The physical pain of his injuries masked his self-loathing, and immediately after the mugging, he used it as an excuse to sulk, but that only displeased his father further.

A horn blared as Jensen swerved into the right lane to exit at Shea. He took the access road to the cemetery and parked near the office, where the security guard waited. He advised Jensen that he had subdued a man who had been digging up a grave, and the suspect was being detained in the security office. Officer Stevenson, from the Desert Horizon Precinct, stayed with the perpetrator. When Jensen entered the office, a man in his forties, covered head to toe in dirt, sat on a plastic chair. Jensen extended his hand to Stevenson and thanked him for waiting. After arriving on the scene, Stevenson had cuffed the man and read him his rights, and so far, he hadn't uttered a word.

"I'm Detective Jensen. Are you injured?"

The man turned to the side and spit, but didn't answer.

"Officer Stevenson read you your rights; is that correct?"

The man stared at the ground.

Jensen turned to Stevenson. "Does he have a disability, or do you think he has mental issues?"

The man coughed and spat dirty mucus on the floor. "I'm not disabled, and I'm as sane as the next guy."

"Then why were you digging up Mr. Swanson's grave? Trying to rob him?"

"Anything that pansy had is mine, so I guess it wouldn't be stealing, now would it?"

"Why do you think you're entitled to his stuff?"

"Because I'm his only living relative."

Jensen paused. "What's your name?"

The man smiled. "Don't you know? I'm his step-daddy."

"You're David Swanson?"

"Yup."

Jensen turned to Stevenson. "Where's his ID?"

Jensen searched the man's wallet and pulled out an Arkansas driver's license. He examined the photo and compared it to the man before him. "Mr. Swanson, I've been trying to reach you."

"Well, here I am."

"So, it would seem, but why were you desecrating your stepson's grave if, as you say, anything he owned is rightfully yours?"

Swanson grinned. "I wasn't looking for possessions. I had to see if the little weasel had really died."

"What makes you think he's not dead?

"I have my reasons; besides, you didn't know him as I did."

"Well, unfortunately for you, vandalizing a grave is a serious crime. I'll be taking you downtown."

Stevenson headed out and nodded to Jensen as he left. Jensen grabbed Swanson's right arm and pulled him up. Stone waited outside and told Jensen that Lopez would stay behind until the scene was processed.

The ride back to the precinct had been quiet; Jensen had hoped Swanson would elaborate on his theory that the victim was still alive. It would've made the drive back more entertaining. But instead, Swanson had stared into the rearview mirror with a lopsided grin as if he didn't have a care in the world. He probably didn't realize his actions had severe consequences. Swanson's stepson had been buried for months; Jensen wondered why he chose now to return.

Stone booked David Swanson and took him to Interview Room 1. Jensen waited with a bottle of water and a dozen questions.

Swanson pulled on the chain, tightening his cuffs.

"Don't move around too much; you might hurt yourself," Jensen stated.

"Where's my lawyer?"

"Do you want a lawyer?"

Swanson nodded toward the bottle. "Is that for me?"

Jensen handed him the bottle and watched as he quickly removed the lid and downed all the contents.

"Do you need more?"

Swanson shook his head no. "Had to wash down the rest of the dirt. The other guy roughed me up pretty good; he shoved my face into the ground."

"You were in the commission of a crime, and you had a weapon."

"A shovel."

"A weapon. The officer had every right to take you down by any means necessary. Do you want me to call you a lawyer, or are you giving up your right to remain silent?"

"I guess it wouldn't hurt to chat a while."

"Good. You said you thought your stepson might still be alive. Why do you think that?"

"While he was alive, he was a thorn in my side, and when I heard he died, I had to come see for myself."

"He died; we conducted an investigation, and the family buried him. Why wouldn't he be dead?"

"Things aren't always what they seem?"

"What things?"

"For a cop, you're not very smart," Swanson quipped.

"Enlighten me."

"Some people get what they want because they are who they are. You get my drift?"

"Are you implying someone covered something up?"

"Now, you're getting it."

"Why would anyone fake your stepson's death?"

"Why don't you ask him?"

Jensen started to believe a straitjacket was in order, or maybe a trip to the hospital to see if he had hit his head. "I can't ask your stepson, so why don't you tell me who you think it is?"

"A man with money and secret power."

"Mr. Chambers?"

Swanson shook his head. "It's not the devil, not this time."

Jensen decided to play along. "Then who?"

"A man who can bring the dead back to life."

Jensen stared at the man sitting across from him and wondered why he had been listening to the ramblings of someone who'd probably escaped from a mental institution to rob a grave.

The man stared back, a weird look on his face as if he was waiting for Jensen to have an epiphany. When his words sank in, Jensen realized the dirty, disheveled man hadn't completely lost his mind.

"The funeral director."

Swanson nodded.

"What can you tell me about him?"

"I'm done. Where's my mouthpiece?"

Jensen didn't leave the precinct until eleven. After David Swanson lawyered up, Jensen returned to his office and researched Heavenly Stars mortuary. The owner, James Fuller, was also the Director of Services. He searched the Better Business Bureau and only found two complaints filed by the same family.

The deceased's family had requested an open casket, but the director had sealed it shut, and after the family sued, their money had been refunded. Jensen couldn't find anything else that seemed suspicious. Tomorrow, he would speak with the director; he needed sleep.

Chapter 12

Jensen dropped down onto his bed, and just as his eyes were closing, the damn phone rang. He glanced over at the clock. Midnight. This had better be important. Stone called, urging him to return to the precinct; a suspect in holding requested to speak to him. Jensen said he would see the perpetrator in the morning, but when Stone revealed it was Kaylee's best friend, he dressed and headed back in.

Stone greeted Jensen with a large coffee and informed him that the silent alarm at Lawson and Canon's consulting firm had been triggered. The officers of the Squaw Peak precinct had arrived just as Miss Hill had tried to flee the scene. Since the suspect was involved in the Swanson case, she had been arrested and taken to Central City Precinct booking.

Jensen downed the coffee and rubbed the back of his neck. The woman sitting across from him, dressed in a black jogging suit and ski cap, had been crying when he entered the room. He made sure Miss Hill's rights were explained to her and asked whether she wanted to confer with an attorney; she informed him that she was an attorney. Sara seemed remorseful, guilt-ridden, and embarrassed, but refused to tell him why she had broken into her best friend's office. He told her he had seen the pictures she had on her at the time of her arrest and that he had a pretty good idea why she had broken into the office.

Sara broke down and admitted to being blackmailed for having an affair. The blackmailer had threatened to expose her to her lover's family. And since he had seen the pictures, he knew why she couldn't let that happen. She identified the blackmailer as Jeff Swanson and confessed to paying him several large sums, but he had kept asking for more. So she told her lover about the blackmail, and he said he would take care of it.

While at Kaylee's home, Miss Hill had received a special delivery. The envelope contained three keys and a note explaining how she could retrieve the incriminating pictures. She had followed the directions and used the first key to get into the building, the second to access Miss Chamber's office, and the third to open the filing cabinet. Miss Hill had found the negatives and pictures inside and had tried to leave when the officers detained her.

Jensen planned to visit the funeral director first thing in the morning, but this development required his immediate attention. He downed the last of the coffee and instructed Stone to call it a day and get some rest. Jensen intended to do the same, but when he got home, he jumped on the computer. He researched Miss Hill's law firm and gathered as much information on her as he could. She seemed credible, and Jensen believed she was being blackmailed. The pictures confirmed her story, but everyone he had spoken to had lied about something.

He fell asleep and dreamt of David Swanson digging up his stepson's grave, only to uncover Miss Hill's lover buried inside.

*****

Chambers Towers showcased one-of-a-kind paintings and intricately designed stone and woodwork. Jensen wore his best suit, yet he felt grossly underdressed. The highly competitive atmosphere felt stifling, and Jensen fought to squash the uncomfortable feeling that seemed to engulf him. He wondered why anyone would want to work in a place like this. Jensen knew it was for money and power. He would stick to murder: at least then you knew you were going to get stabbed in the back.

Jensen knocked and pushed open the door. He took a seat opposite the sophisticated and impeccably dressed magnate.

125

"Thank you for meeting with me today, Mr. Chambers. I know you have an important schedule, so this won't take long."

"Good. I'm meeting the governor at the golf course in an hour, and I don't want to be late."

"I'd like to start with where you were the night of June first, from six to ten?"

"I met Kirk Underwood, the Arizona Department of Real Estate Commissioner, at the Biltmore for dinner and drinks."

"You didn't consult your appointment book; how can you be sure?"

"I received a call about my daughter's fiancé. I am not likely to forget what I was doing when I found out he had died."

"It's procedure, you understand, but I must verify that with him."

Chambers nodded.

"Did you know the late Mrs. Swanson, Jeff's mother?"

"No, but she did try to get money from me."

"Did you ever give her any?"

"Never."

"After her husband left, she sustained a comfortable lifestyle, and based on her meager income, we believe she was getting money from someone."

"She did not get it from me."

"Why did she ask you for money?"

Chambers leaned back in his chair. "She thought I deliberately ruined her husband's business, and after he left, she felt it was my responsibility to take care of her and her son."

"Did you purposely destroy Mr. Swanson's stepfather's construction company?"

"The construction industry has always been volatile, and some people are not equipped to run a thriving

126

business. What I did or did not do did not affect the outcome of his success or failure."

"So why did she blame you?"

Chambers brows pinched together. "Detective Jensen, I have answered your question. Move on."

Jensen leaned in. "When Mr. Swanson died, you asked the Attorney General to oversee the investigation, guaranteeing it would be handled swiftly and privately."

"Yes, and…"

"I'm wondering why you made that particular request."

Jensen watched as Chambers gazed up at the life-sized portrait of his loving wife and replied, "I was trying to save my daughter from the pain and embarrassment of a protracted investigation. She had suffered enough at the hands of Jeff; I wanted to give her some well-deserved peace."

"What did Mr. Swanson do to your daughter that she would need relief?"

"You will need to speak with her about it."

"If he was hurting her, wouldn't you have tried to stop it?"

"My daughter is capable of taking care of herself."

"But she's your daughter—"

"Next question."

Jensen paused; Chambers' lack of concern for his daughter was troubling. "If he'd been prone to violence, he probably had more than one victim, and it's possible that one of his victims fought back and killed him."

"Move it along, Detective."

Throughout his career, Jensen interviewed several important people who all seemed to share one quality: entitlement. "If we get the person or persons responsible for Mr. Swanson's death off the street, your daughter will be safer, and anything you can tell us regarding his behavior might help."

Chambers checked the time on his Rolex.

Jensen waited for a response and, when he didn't get one, handed Chambers a bank statement. "Have you seen this before?"

"Yes." He returned it.

"A friend of yours is in trouble, and she said you were helping her. Is that correct?"

Chambers nodded.

"Due to your friend's vulnerable situation, you might have been forced to take extraordinary measures to help her."

"Are you insinuating I killed my daughter's fiancé to help a friend?"

Jensen straightened in his seat. He needed to choose his words carefully. "Your friend said that due to the private nature of the situation, you became overly concerned about your friend and your daughter's safety. It's not unreasonable to presume a man, any man, would do whatever was necessary to protect his family."

Chambers' lips curled up. "Is that your diplomatic way of saying I flew into a rage and pushed Jeff to his death, all in the name of family?"

"No, what I'm saying is, under the most precarious of situations, no one, including yourself, is exempt from doing what they can to keep their loved ones from harm."

Chambers leaned forward. "I am tired of mincing words. I did not kill Jeff Swanson. Not for the reason you politely suggested or any other reason. If I wanted him gone, I could have done it any number of ways, none of which would have violated his rights or taken his life. If you want to question someone with a motive, you should speak with David, Jeff's stepfather. He has called and threatened my secretary and has left several accusatory messages on my voicemail."

"Why do you think he's threatening you?"

"I believe he said it was my fault his business went under, and I killed Jeff because my daughter was too good for him, yet she would never leave him. He had been kind enough to offer to keep quiet if I paid him a substantial sum."

"Why would Mr. Swanson kill his stepson?"

"Jeff had a life insurance policy for two hundred thousand dollars. His mother and stepfather were the beneficiaries. Jeff's mother passed away, so the entire amount went to David."

"Why would he kill his stepson for two hundred thousand dollars when he could demand much more money from you?"

"I have not done anything illegal or immoral; why would I pay for something I did not do. Besides, I do not pay blackmailers or any other kind of con artists. If you want to know why he would kill his own stepson, you need to ask him."

"Did you save the messages?"

"No."

"Did he call you from in town or suggest a place to drop off money?"

"I did not give him a chance."

"When did he start leaving messages?"

"The first time he called occurred right after Jeff's funeral; the last time I spoke to him was yesterday."

"Based on that call, did he sound like he would stop threatening you?"

"I warned him to stop harassing me, or I would have him served with a restraining order. I am sure I made my point."

Jensen wondered if Chambers used his political connections to ward off Swanson's repeated requests for money. He could've easily turned the tables on Swanson and threatened him with jail time. Jensen didn't think Chambers cared what Swanson felt about his involvement,

129

if any, regarding the demise of his business. He just wanted Swanson out of his life.

"Do you think your daughter, if forced to, could've killed Mr. Swanson?"

"She is smart and resourceful, and I am sure, under the right circumstances, she would do whatever it takes to survive."

"What would you have done if she came to you for help?"

"The issue is resolved; I avoid speculation at all costs."

"What if I told you someone believes Mr. Swanson is alive?"

"I would say someone needs some quality mental health care."

"As a law enforcement officer, it is my duty to investigate all viable leads; sometimes those leads may seem intrusive and offensive."

"Is that your prelude to another question?" Chambers jeered.

"I'm trying to respect your relationships while asking tough questions. I know you and Mr. Masters are close, but new evidence has come to light that he probably had the ultimate motive to kill Mr. Swanson."

"Kyle is an honorable man; he loves my daughter and would not jeopardize her or his life with her. Find Jeff's killer, and stop wasting your time trying to convict my friends." Chambers stood to leave.

Jensen strode quickly to the parking garage and thought, all things considered, that went rather well. He would prepare a perfunctory apology, just in case. Jensen called Stone and instructed her to meet him at the Heavenly Stars mortuary in thirty minutes. As he approached his car, he heard heavy footsteps and quick, shallow breaths. He glanced over his shoulder; a stout man in his late forties, with a determined look, was heading straight toward him.

Jensen stopped at the back of the Crown Vic and waited as the man approached. After the man took a couple of deep breaths, Jensen asked, "May I help you?"

"Yes, I have some information about a murder."

"What murder?"

"The one Michael Chambers' daughter is involved with."

Jensen pulled out a pen and a pad.

"I'm Robert Deakin; I own Deakin's Securities. I'm in the building next to the deserted construction site–the one the dead man owned. It's across the street from Chambers Tower."

"Did you know Mr. Swanson?"

"I'd recognize him when we passed on the street, but I didn't know him. I'm out of town most of the year, but I did see him in a heated fight right before he died."

"Do you remember the date?"

"It was May 31st, and he was with a young woman."

"How can you be sure of the date?"

"I had a plane to catch at Sky Harbor."

"Where did you see them?"

"They were on the fourth floor of the dead man's structure."

"Could you hear what they said?"

The man took another deep breath, "No, but their voices were loud enough to disrupt my thoughts–that's why I looked up."

"Can you describe the woman," Jensen asked?

"She had light brown hair with blonde highlights, was thin, and well-dressed. She had on stiletto high heels. She had been swinging her arms while she had been yelling, and I remember thinking, if she weren't careful, she would fall to her death."

"Did the fight get physical?"

"Not that I saw. I woke up late that morning and didn't want to miss my plane. The woman I saw in May was on the news this morning."

"Miss Hill," Jensen asked?

"I don't remember her name–she got caught trespassing."

"Are you sure about the woman fighting with Mr. Swanson?"

"Positive. I'd seen her in this area before."

"Was she with anyone?'

"No."

"Why didn't you come forward when you heard Mr. Swanson had died?"

"I'm only in Phoenix for a few weeks at a time, and I've only been back a couple of days, so I haven't had a chance to catch up on the local news. In fact, if I don't leave now, I'll miss my plane."

"Where can I reach you?"

He pulled out his wallet, thumbed through it, and handed Jensen a business card.

"If you have any more questions, let me know." The stout man turned back toward Central Avenue. The back of his jacket swung back and forth, and his head bobbed up and down as he shuffled across the sidewalk. He wiped his forehead with the back of his hand as he hurried to his car.

Jensen took a moment to consider what he had just learned. Not only had Miss Hill been a victim of blackmail and confronted Mr. Swanson, but she was in town the day before he died and had been fighting with him at the crime scene. Funny, she hadn't mentioned that.

Based on the blackmail pictures, Jensen knew that if her secret got out, her relationship with her lover would probably end, and her other relationships would be in jeopardy. Since Sara couldn't seem to convince Mr. Swanson to stop threatening her, she had a strong motive to kill him. But why give her access to the negatives? Did he

132

try to trick her, pretending to stop, then hit her up later with another demand? Jensen would talk to Miss Hill again, but he was running late and had to meet Stone.

He took the 101 to Shea Boulevard, drove past the cemetery, and pulled into the parking lot. Jensen walked past the large black hearse and greeted Stone, asking if Miss Hill had seen the judge yet. Stone said no, but Mr. Chambers had been notified and said he would bail her out this afternoon. Jensen entered the office and asked to see the funeral director. While he waited in the lobby, Stone came in a few minutes later and pretended to be a customer looking for a casket. The receptionist escorted her into a large, well-lit display room, and Stone faded out of sight.

Jensen sat on the pale green flower-embellished sofa and glanced around the room. It was regal with its crystal chandelier and solid mahogany coffee table. The design looked so intricate that it had to be hand-carved. Just those two pieces alone had to cost more than his monthly salary. The lush carpet looked inviting, and he wondered what it would feel like to have the soft fibers between his toes. The drapes on the floor-to-ceiling windows had been pulled back, letting the sun brighten what would typically be a sad, depressing place.

He thumbed through brochures on funeral services, casket options, and grief counseling. It was, on the surface, a legitimate business. Jensen hoped David Swanson was right about his stepson faking his death. He couldn't afford to waste time chasing after useless leads. And if Jeff had faked his death, where was he?

Thirty minutes had passed, and no sign of Stone, and the funeral director hadn't come out of his office. Jensen went into the display room and spoke to the receptionist. She strolled down the hall; Jensen followed close behind, and she knocked on the main office door. She knocked again and called out for her boss. When he didn't answer, she turned the handle; it was locked. She went to the front desk, found the spare key, and opened the door. The office appeared in perfect condition. The receptionist apologized to Jensen and said the director must have had another appointment or had received an emergency call.

Why did the funeral director leave, and if he had been called away, why hadn't he notified his staff? Jensen went to his car and called Judge Bromin's office. He knew it was a long shot, but it was a lead, and he had to try. If he could get a search warrant, he might unearth a substantial cover-up or something more nefarious. He trusted his gut, but would it merit a warrant?

He leaned against his car and waited on the phone. He didn't want to leave in case the director returned. Jensen watched as Stone and the receptionist came from the back of the building. The receptionist headed in; Stone walked past the hearse, peeked in, and approached Jensen.

Jensen covered the mouthpiece. "Did he bolt?"

"Looks like it. Sandra gave me a tour of the grounds. In the back, there's a private parking lot for the staff, and the director's car is gone. She indicated he had been acting nervous lately, but she didn't know why, and when he took off without telling her, she thought it was strange."

"Not strange, suspicious."

"You holding for Judge Bromin?"

"Yeah." He motioned for Stone to stay. Jensen listened as the judge's clerk informed him that the judge had denied his warrant request due to lack of probable cause.

"Where to now?" Stone asked.

"Back to the cemetery."

The cemetery, located only a few blocks south of the funeral home, had a steady stream of visitors and mourners. When they arrived, Jensen pulled up next to Jeff Swanson's alleged grave. He got out and walked the perimeter, careful not to disturb the crime scene tape.

Before his arrest, David Swanson had dug down one foot. Jensen wondered what he hoped to find in his stepson's grave. Did David hate his stepson so much that he had to make sure he was out of his life for good? Mr. Chambers had been convinced Mr. Swanson had killed his stepson for money, but if that were true, he would've known for sure he was dead and wouldn't need to disturb his grave.

The small, unassuming office differed from the funeral home. It had crème-colored walls and white lacey curtains that were no match for the Arizona sun. The three desks were constructed of faux oak and didn't appear sturdy. The pictures on the walls seemed to be copies of copies, like ones you'd find at a swap meet or garage sale. The staff was professionally but modestly dressed. Jensen realized that the funeral director and his staff were in a more lucrative business than the cemetery workers.

Jensen and Stone questioned the staff about their long-standing relationship with Heavenly Stars Mortuary, which had benefited both parties. The cemetery staff had never received any complaints regarding Charles Pierce's burial. Jensen asked about the location of Mr. Pierce's plot. The staff confirmed he was on row D13, the same as Jeff Swanson.

He pointed out that the Pierce family had been unhappy with the funeral director for sealing the casket before the services and had filed a complaint with the BBB. They told Jensen they were unaware of the complaint, but it must have been an oversight. James Fuller, the funeral director, was a good friend of the cemetery owner, Roger Goldman.

The receptionist refused to give Jensen the Pierce family's contact information. She offered to have one of the family members call him. Jensen gave her his card, and he and Stone left.

"Do you think the cemetery's owner is related to the Goldmans in our case?"

"I'd bet my salary he is," Jensen replied. "When we get back to the precinct, do a background check and find out if Roger has any ties to our lawyer friend, Greg. I'll call the judge again; maybe I can get a warrant for the cemetery's records. I need Pierce's phone number."

"Do you believe the vic's stepdad? He seems a little off."

"He does come across kind of nutty, but if he's right, and the vic isn't in his grave, I'd like to know who is."

Chapter 13

On her way through the lobby, Kaylee waved to Manara, who spoke on the phone. She should feel happy; Kyle had finally confessed his love for her, but they were in limbo until Jeff's murder was solved. And now that Kaylee learned Kyle had been responsible for Jeff's accident and scar, she felt his death hanging over them both.

A deep despair surrounded her, and Kaylee had a hunch something terrible would happen; she couldn't shake it no matter what she did. She used to get a rush from working and had always felt safe in her office, but lately, she had been inundated with fear and dark thoughts. If she were going to be productive, she would have to focus.

Kaylee flipped on the lights in her office, and as she took in the rich décor, she remembered her first victory at the firm. Larry and James had appealed to her competitive nature. They said that if she could land the Carter account, she could decorate her office any way she wanted, on their dime. Kaylee loved a challenge, and one with such a great reward had been irresistible. She dove in, working twelve-hour days until she finally brought Carter's Culinary Services to the firm. After she completed the work, the fun began.

She scoured the internet for the perfect furniture pairing. Finding each piece took her months, but it paid off. Her hard work resulted in a symphony of style and technology: the rich espresso finish and the clean lines blended seamlessly. The L-shaped desk, credenza, and hutch were the centerpieces. When Kaylee entered her office, they reminded her of her professional achievements.

The mound of folders on her desk was shoulder-high, and the stack of messages looked to be at least two inches deep. She sighed and sat on her leather chair; she had her work cut out for her. If she concentrated, it would take her all day to get through it, but she let her mind wander instead.

Kaylee had an epiphany when she had kissed Kyle at her client's pool party. She had realized she no longer wanted to marry Jeff. By the time she had discovered her mistake, Kyle had faded into the background, and Jeff had turned violent. Her guilt had consumed her waking hours and had tormented her in her dreams. Kaylee had second thoughts about telling Detective Jensen about Jeff's sudden and vicious outbursts; she didn't want to give him another motive as to why she might have killed Jeff. Who was she trying to protect, Kyle or herself? Maybe she should bear her soul and deal with the consequences.

She pulled out her cell phone and, instead of calling the detective, called Kyle, but it went straight to voicemail. She tried his office number, but his secretary didn't expect him back until after five. Kaylee felt disappointed; she wanted to discuss Kyle's declaration of love. She had so many questions.

Was he willing to date her after what had happened to Jeff? When did he realize he loved her? Why didn't he tell her in high school or at prom? It would have been the perfect time to discuss his feelings. If he had told her then, she might have understood that her feelings for Jeff weren't love, and she would have set him free. And the horrible ordeal she had experienced wouldn't have happened.

She heard a faint tap at her door.

"Come in."

"It's me. I come bearing gifts," Manara said, handing Kaylee a large Mocha Java from Hava Java.

"Thanks." Kaylee motioned with her hand. "Sit."

"If I'm not careful, I'll eat my way to a new career. My agent advised me to lay off the bagels and biscotti. And she's the boss, so I'll have to stick to coffee with no extras."

"Has your agent found you anything yet?"

"Nothing big, just local shoots. It's a hard industry to break into."

Kaylee took a drink, savoring the soft citrus flavor and full body. It hit the spot, and she took another sip. She was lost in a coffee daze. When Manara scooted her chair across the floor, it startled her. She put the cup down. Manara sat across from her, her lips slightly turned down.

"I'm okay. It's just going to take a while."

Manara leaned forward; her tone softened. "I know you're hurting, but maybe this was for the best. No one should die like that, but sometimes he was mean and aggressive."

Kaylee froze. "Did Jeff hurt you?"

"He would sulk around the lobby. He'd get mad, yell, and storm out when he couldn't see you. When you told me not to let him back in the office, I figured things had gone south."

"It's a shame. We were once such good friends. It just didn't work out."

Manara fidgeted with her cup. "I want to tell you something…don't be mad."

"Okay?"

Manara twisted her hands. "I wasn't going to tell you because I didn't want to hurt you, but then the detective came by and asked the entire office questions."

"Whatever it is, I know it wasn't your fault."

"Several times, while you were out and Jeff waited in the lobby, he'd asked me out. I said no, but he kept asking. I warned him that if he didn't stop, I'd tell you. That seemed to have worked; he didn't bother me again."

Jeff had hit on her friends right under her nose. Kaylee wondered what else he had done behind her back, but she was too ashamed to think about it.

"I should've said something sooner," Manara apologized.

"I'm sorry he put you through that."

139

"You didn't force him to be a jerk."

"I wish I could do something to make it up to you."

"Stop trying to cover for him. He's dead, and you don't owe him anything. But you could do me a favor and stop refusing my invitation to my pool party next weekend. Once I get a few photo shoots under my belt, I might be jetting off to Paris or somewhere, so this may be our last summer together. Think about it, okay?"

Kaylee paled and became rigid. "I will."

Manara left her deep in thought.

Kaylee took a drink, but the coffee had lost its appeal. She would have to attend Manara's party or risk hurting her friend's feelings. If she didn't get a handle on her Achilles heel, it would forever drag her down. She would address the issue after the police caught Jeff's murderer. She didn't have the strength to do it now.

She thought about what Manara had said about Jeff. Did he prey on all her friends? How could she have been so blind? Perhaps someone she knew killed him because he abused them, too.

She tackled the customer files, writing a three-page summary of her recommendations for each client. She was almost done and needed to make room on her desk; she would need to put the completed files away. Kaylee unzipped the tiny compartment in her purse to retrieve the key to her private filing cabinet, but the key and the Mustang keychain were gone.

She dug deep, searching the bottom of her purse, then dumped its contents onto her desk. Kaylee picked through each item to verify that the key hadn't fallen out or hadn't gotten tangled in her brush. Her annoyance turned to frustration, and she remembered her clothes had been put away on the wrong racks. Kaylee had assumed she did it and chalked it up to grief. But now she wasn't so sure. The order of her clothing was personal and a quirk, and Kaylee learned to live with it. She guarded her work key with her life. Her files contained the private phone numbers and home addresses of some of the state's wealthiest executives, and neither Larry nor James had a copy.

She changed purses daily, sometimes more if she changed for dinner or special meetings, so perhaps she had left it in another purse. Kaylee took a moment to breathe and thought back to this morning when she switched purses. She couldn't remember whether she put the key in it. Kaylee rubbed her temple, and then it came to her. The key wasn't in yesterday's purse; come to think of it, she hadn't seen it in a while, and due to Jeff's death, she had been out of the office and hadn't needed it.

Kaylee flipped through her Rolodex and called Sonoran Locksmiths. They promised her a tech would be out within the hour. She stared at her door and bit her lower lip, considering the implications of the missing key. Was her personal life spilling over onto her professional one? Should she be worried about her clients' secrets or safety?

She tried to finish her reports, but her stomach had twisted into a large knot. Kaylee went to the window and watched as cars sped down Camelback Road. Jeff had invaded every aspect of her personal life; had he tried to control her professional one, too?

The crushing weight that had settled on Kaylee's chest after Jeff had died hadn't gone away. She wondered if her inability to cope with guilt might be the cause of her turmoil. She had to regain her peace of mind, which meant admitting she had made mistakes and that they had determined the course of Jeff's downfall.

She paced across the room and wondered why it was taking so long. Kaylee had to know if anything was missing or misplaced. Her future and her livelihood depended on it. A quick, loud rap disrupted Kaylee's thoughts.

The locksmith, a middle-aged man in faded jeans with a three-day shadow, finally arrived. He wasn't

Kaylee's regular contact at the company and didn't dress like a tech who serviced high-end professional buildings. Still, if he could get her into her files, she didn't care.

The tech worked fast and efficiently. Kaylee's first impression didn't do him justice. He finished and gave her two keys; she gave him a twenty.

She reviewed the files, and everything seemed to be in order. She blew out a long, relieved breath. Kaylee locked the cabinet, put one key in her purse, and looked for a secure spot in her office for the other. No matter how scrambled her personal life was, her clients' privacy was her priority.

Kaylee headed to the lobby to speak with Manara and asked if anyone had been in her office. She was told no one had entered her office, not even Larry. Kaylee checked the guest sign-in sheet for the past couple of weeks, but didn't see anyone on the list who shouldn't have been in the office. She asked Manara to show her the footage from the camera outside her office.

Kaylee reviewed the tape and watched a tall, slender, and agile person in black entering her office. She had heard from Manara that the police were there last night because someone had set off the alarm, but she didn't know they had entered the building or her office. Why hadn't anyone contacted her regarding the break-in?

How did someone get into the building, and how did they get into her locked office? Were her clients compromised? Kaylee felt sick. Her clients relied on her to safeguard their information. How would she explain this breach? She knocked on Larry's door and went in. He leaned back in his chair and stared out the window.

Kaylee asked, "Larry, what did the police say about the break-in?"

Larry turned to face her, "A person was caught leaving the building; no items were missing from the office.

I'm not sure how they got in, but the silent alarm on your office door had been activated."

"Did the person photograph my files? Is my clients' financial information safe?"

"The police will have more information later today. I asked Manara to rekey the entire building, and the security company will be out to check the alarm system."

"I can't believe this is happening," Kaylee mused.

Larry came around the desk and gave Kaylee's shoulder a comforting squeeze. "It's not your fault. Nothing's missing; they caught who did it, and we've taken measures to prevent it from happening again."

She headed back to her office. Larry's comment haunted her–it's not your fault. Did he think this was about Kaylee or Jeff's murder? She dove back into work. She needed the distraction and had to focus on what she could control.

At twelve-thirty, her cell phone rang. Bridget Carter, a good friend and the daughter of her most prominent client, called to see if she wanted to meet at Scottsdale Fashion Square. Kaylee agreed to meet her at Macy's.

She hadn't seen Bridget since Jeff passed away. And the last time Kaylee went shopping was when she tried on engagement rings with Jeff. At first, she had been dreading it, but when she slipped on a platinum four-carat ring and rotated her fingers, the diamond shimmered. It was mesmerizing.

For a brief moment, Kaylee wondered what it would be like to be Kyle's wife. Would she have to learn to cook? Maybe it wouldn't matter to him whether or not she cooked as long as she loved him.

The moment hadn't lasted; her fantasy ended when Jeff insisted she choose the most expensive option. Kaylee wondered if Jeff would still be alive if she had had the courage to refuse the ring and break up with him.

Chapter 14

While browsing through the newest Michael Kors purses, one caught Kaylee's eye. She breathed deeply, enjoying the scent of the Italian leather. The snake-trimmed straps popped with color and texture. A familiar rush enveloped Kaylee. She remembered watching her mother glide through this store a few years ago, looking for the perfect gift for her friend's birthday. Her mother had had exquisite taste. She could glimpse an intended gift, a diamond tennis bracelet or a champagne flute, and know whether the recipient would like it.

Kaylee missed her mother terribly. Her mother would never have found herself in Kaylee's current predicament. She would have been strong and decisive, telling Jeff she valued his friendship but didn't love him. Why wasn't Kaylee able to be strong? Had she really been trying to be nice, or had she been trying to save face? Admitting she had chosen the wrong man could have been a devastating blow to her ego and to the Chambers' pride.

She met Bridget at the makeup counter, and Bridget confessed she had made an appointment for them to get massages. Kaylee had never had a massage before and wasn't sure how she felt about a stranger touching her, but she didn't want to let her friend down, and she needed to relax, so she agreed.

They discussed the pros and cons of lipsticks versus lip stains. Kaylee picked up a tube, pulled off the top, and twisted it until the pink-and-orange shade was visible. It looked familiar, but she couldn't recall where she had seen it. Bridget reminded Kaylee that her brother's ex-girlfriend, who had red hair, large breasts, and a fake laugh, used to wear that shade.

Kaylee remembered the party at the Carter house where she had been introduced to Cory's girlfriend. The redhead had been brazen, flashing her perfectly rounded and fake breasts to anyone who would dare to look. Kaylee had stayed away from her and had wondered why Cory had gotten mixed up with her. She had seen the silly grin on Cory's face and knew his hormones were dictating his every move.

Kaylee put back the lipstick. "What's her name?"

"I don't remember," Bridget laughed, "I called her the devil."

"Did you know her well?"

"Well enough to know she only dated my brother for money. Once she realized my dad had him on a tight leash, she tried to go after my dad—"

Kaylee gasped.

"It didn't work, and she moved on to some other rich sap."

A week before Kaylee broke up with Jeff, she had called him and asked to meet after work. He had been running late, so she had let herself into his apartment. She had been waiting for over two hours, and when Jeff finally showed up, his face was flushed and his hair disheveled; he had fresh marks on his neck and refused to look her in the eye or to tell her where he had been. Kaylee immediately noticed the makeup smeared on his shirt. His appearance and actions had left her confused, but never in a million years did she ever imagine Jeff would cheat on her. They weren't lovers; how long did she expect him to wait?

Jeff's continued insistence that they consummate their relationship annoyed and frustrated her, and then it angered her. Kaylee didn't know when she would be ready, but she needed time to work through her feelings. Deep down, she had known something was wrong and had been right. Jeff must've grown tired of waiting because he had tried to initiate sex with her every time they were together. His pawing made her feel dirty, as if he were trying to win a prize, taking the virginity of Michael Chambers' daughter, as opposed to making love to his fiancée.

Bridget called her name, and they headed toward the salon. Kaylee was grateful for the interruption; the trip down memory lane was painful and best forgotten.

The tranquil floral scent in the salon helped to reduce Kaylee's tension. She looked forward to a soothing, full-body massage. They were seated in the relaxation room, where the lights were dimmed, flameless candles flickered, and a video of soft, rippling water played in the background. While they waited, the receptionist brought a glass of cucumber water and instructed them to drink it. The cold water was refreshing, and when they finished, their masseuse took them to their rooms.

Kaylee followed the instructions and stripped to her underwear, slid under the sheets, and positioned her face into the headrest. It felt odd to be half-naked in a darkened room with a stranger, but she promised Bridget she would try to relax. She hoped she could; her mind drifted back to the lipstick and Jeff's shirt. Had he slept with someone while they were engaged? If he did, why did Jeff pressure Kaylee to have sex with him?

As the bed warmed, Kaylee felt the stress melting away. Her masseuse found and worked out a huge knot centered between her shoulder blades. The vanilla- scented lotion reminded her of her mother's kitchen during the holidays. The lights were low, and as the masseuse kneaded her body into a pliable mound of flesh, she closed her eyes. She dozed off despite her reservations. She wanted it to go on forever, to stay in this peaceful, relaxed state with no worries or responsibilities, but all good things must come to an end. She dressed, left a twenty on the table, and met Bridget in the lobby, where they both scheduled another appointment.

Kaylee and Bridget went to the Caketini Coffee Lounge. They each ordered a salted caramel cupcake and a

Frappitini with homemade whipped cream. Kaylee took a big bite and slowly chewed the sweet treat. Bridget sipped her Frappitini; she slightly frowned and lowered her eyes.

"I'm sorry to hear about Jeff. Do you need anything?" Bridgett asked.

"No, but thank you," Kaylee put down her fork, "I really need to know who killed Jeff." Seeing the surprised look on Bridget's face, she added hastily. "I wish the police would find his killer so I could move on with my life. The investigation is eating away at my energy. I feel like my soul is being devoured."

"I dated a detective once," she paused, "For a moment, I thought he was the one."

"You dated a law enforcement officer? What happened," Kaylee asked?

Bridget played with her napkin. "It takes a special breed of man to do what he does; his heart belongs to the job. If you can't accept that, it's over before it starts."

"Are you sure you couldn't work it out?"

"I'm sure. Randy made it crystal clear about where our relationship was heading."

Randy? "What's his last name?"

"Jensen. He works homicide."

"Detective Jensen is the lead on my case, and he's tough." Kaylee couldn't believe it. She never imagined he had time to date anyone, much less one of her friends.

"Randy's a good guy and the best at what he does. He'll figure it out and give you your life back."

Kaylee chewed her lip. "I can't be sure, but I think he has Kyle or me pegged for the killer."

"You'd never kill anyone, even if they deserved it."

She was keeping a secret, a painful, frightening secret. Guilt consumed her. With the investigation in full swing, Kaylee needed unbiased advice, but would she be able to share her traumatic experiences with Bridget or anyone else?

Although she knew Bridget would be supportive, Kaylee wasn't ready to reveal her innermost pain. She had survived the physical abuse, but it was over. It had been terrifying, and she would need time to heal, but the effects of the emotional torture would take longer. Kaylee thought the reason she couldn't sleep was that Jeff had died, but maybe the pain he had inflicted upon her and the subsequent nightmares caused her not to sleep. She would wake up shaking, covered in sweat, and frightened. Perhaps Kaylee should talk to a professional.

She hugged her friend, thanked her for a great afternoon, and promised to call soon. Kaylee walked Bridget to her car, waved goodbye, and headed to the parking garage.

As the sun set, the horizon burst with orange and yellow hues; the temperature dropped a few degrees, but it still hovered around the one-hundred mark. Kaylee took the elevator to the third level and headed east to her car. The lights in the garage flickered off and on, and she looked over her shoulder. A tingling sensation crept down her spine. She kept walking but couldn't find her car. In her haste not to be late, she hadn't paid attention to the row number, and now she couldn't find her car. Kaylee glanced down each of the rows. Her Mustang, typically easy to spot, was hidden from view by the multitude of luxury cars or large, expensive SUVs.

She couldn't shake the nagging feeling someone was watching her. Kaylee spotted her car and hurried down the row, but as she approached, she realized it wasn't hers. She looked behind her but didn't see anyone. Kaylee hit the button on the car remote and searched for the flashing headlights. She turned and headed down the next aisle, pressing the button repeatedly. At the sound of heavy-labored breathing, she whipped around.

A man in black jeans and a grey t-shirt leaned against a black Escalade. As she walked past, he tipped his baseball cap, exposing piercing blue eyes. She took a closer look. She knew those eyes and that chin; she stepped closer, and the man backed up.

"Who are you?" Kaylee demanded.

When he didn't respond, she moved closer.

"What's your name? Why are you following me?"

The man turned and ran.

"I know you; what's your name?"

He looked to be in his mid-forties but was quick and spry; he dodged in and out between the cars. Kaylee chased after him, shouting as she ran. She yelled for him to stop and pulled out her phone. He jumped into a primer gray station wagon, knocking off his cap. She snapped pictures of his car and hoped she got the license plate. His tires squealed as he sped off. Kaylee stood in the middle of the row, breathing hard and wondering what had happened.

Armed only with her cell phone, Kaylee had chased down a man who had been following her. Not smart. Her heart pounded in her chest, and as her breathing slowed, she took a picture of the fallen, sweat-stained cap but didn't recognize the logo. She dug into her purse, found a tissue, and picked up the cap by its brim. Kaylee held it out in front of her as if it had been exposed to a contagious disease. She hit the button on her remote and located her car. She emptied the makeup from Macy's onto the front passenger seat, stuffed the smelly cap, and wadded up tissue into the bag.

She hurried back to her office and searched for the baseball team online. The red cap with a red A on a white-and-black patch must be an out-of-state team. One of Jeff's passions had been baseball, and he knew the stats for all the teams; Kaylee had attended a few Diamondbacks games with him, but she preferred football.

It turned out the cap belonged to an Arkansas minor league team, which she had never heard of. Kaylee had the license plate number of the station wagon, but it wouldn't do her any good unless she could get a name and address.

She called Bridget and asked her to call Detective Jensen and ask if he would research the plate for her. Bridget pointed out that if she called him about a license plate, he would know she was up to something. Bridget said he had an uncanny ability to drag the truth out of people, but if Kaylee insisted, she would call.

The man with the intense blue eyes seemed so familiar, but why would he follow her? What did he want? On the surface, he appeared harmless. If he hadn't done anything wrong, why did he run?

Back at her office, Kaylee had finally stopped shaking. Her encounter with the stranger had left her frightened but motivated. She finished the paperwork, filed it, and locked it up. She rechecked her watch; forty minutes had gone by. The police ran plates all the time. Did Detective Jensen see through Bridget's request and figure out Kaylee asked for the information? But how could he? Kaylee only found out today that the two had dated. Perhaps he refused to take her call, or he did, and they were still talking.

Bridget didn't answer, so Kaylee decided to leave. She pulled on the filing cabinet door, turned out the light, and locked her office. Kaylee rode the elevator to the first floor; everyone, including Manara, had gone home. A car's horn blared, and she looked across the street and noticed movement near the front entrance. A tall, well-dressed woman in a navy-colored skirt and jacket, and a shorter, huskier man in a dark suit, were in the front parking lot, standing by what Kaylee presumed was their car.

She hovered near the unlocked door. "May I help you?"

They turned and headed toward her.

"Miss Chambers?"

"Yes."

150

"I'm Detective Olivia Stone, and this is Detective Jose Lopez. Detective Jensen wants to speak with you."

"About what?"

"You need to come with us," Stone insisted.

"I'll call him from home."

"Detective Jensen has requested you come down to headquarters."

"Am I under arrest?" Kaylee asked.

"No."

"I'm not going anywhere with you." She closed and locked the door. The two detectives returned to their car, and Detective Stone made a phone call.

How did Kaylee know they were really police? They drove a plain car and didn't bother to show ID. After a few minutes, they were still hovering by the car, so she called the precinct and left a message for Detective Jensen. The dispatcher promised she would contact him immediately.

Chapter 15

The last thing Jensen expected, tonight or any night, was to receive a call from Bridget, and he didn't want personal entanglements getting in the way. He had broken it off with her to make their lives easier. Jensen knew his chosen career didn't fit her lifestyle and regretted hurting and disappointing her. Jensen had his hands full with grave robbing, the B&E, and the funeral director, and from the look of things, this case was about to become even more convoluted than it already was.

Jensen had been unable to follow up with Greg Goldman to ask about the discrepancies in his alibi, so he had sent Stone. Jensen instructed her to tell Goldman his girlfriend didn't back up his story and see what happened. Jensen had played a hunch, and it paid off. Goldman remembered they'd missed the movie; Greg had returned to the office to finish some work, and they saw the film the following day. Stone verified the movie time, but as of now, Goldman didn't have an alibi for the time of the murder. Jensen had difficulty swallowing Goldman's reason for dating Kaylee's friend, Manara. She was exotic, beautiful, and articulate. Did Greg believe he could actually fool anyone?

Jensen had checked the license plate Bridget had given him. When he found out it belonged to David Swanson, Jensen checked to see if he had posted bond, which he had, and had been released on his own recognizance. Jensen delegated the responsibility of finding David Swanson to Stone.

After receiving the call from Stone telling him Kaylee had refused to come to the station and had locked herself in her office, Jensen advised Stone to make sure she didn't leave. He had a few questions for her, and when he got to her office, he would reiterate that this was his investigation and that she would need to stay out of it *or else*. Jensen didn't want Commander Blanchard, Michael Chambers, or the governor reprimanding him or worse because Kaylee got hurt or killed.

Jensen pulled into the parking lot and parked next to Stone's car. He instructed her and Lopez to return to the precinct, and he headed to the entrance.

Kaylee yanked open the door. "Why didn't you just call?"

"I left four messages, but you refused to respond."

She pulled out her phone and frowned. "I turned off my phone during an appointment and forgot to check my messages when I was done. I'm sorry; I shouldn't have yelled at your detectives. Do you have a new lead?"

Jensen ushered her to the couch. "Sit." He took the seat opposite her and checked his watch.

Jensen watched her take stock of the lobby. Her brows pinched together a few times.

"Are you expecting someone?" Kaylee asked.

Several minutes later, the door swung open, and Kyle came in. He sat down next to Kaylee.

"Sorry, I'm late."

"What are you doing here?"

Jensen met Kaylee's questioning gaze. "I asked him to meet me. I have a problem and would like to resolve it now." He waited until he had her complete and undivided attention. "How do you know Bridget Carter, and why did you ask her to call me?"

Kaylee leaned back on the cushion, "We're good friends, and her father is an important client of mine. What makes you think I asked her to call?"

"This is my interview; I'll ask the questions."

Kaylee brushed her hair from her eyes and sat up taller. "I asked her to call you because I needed some information; it seemed like a good idea at the time."

153

"I want to be clear," Jensen leaned closer and looked her in the eyes, "You are not to participate in my investigation in any way, and you are not to have any contact with Miss Carter until I resolve this case. Is that clear?"

"Why?"

"To prevent a potential conflict of interest situation, you cannot have contact with her."

"But—"

"I will not have you, your father, or anyone else undermine my efforts to solve this case. If there is the perception that I am giving my ex-girlfriend's friend, who has not been eliminated as a suspect, special treatment, important evidence may be thrown out."

"I am not interfering with your work," Kaylee tightened her hold on the bag.

"What's in the bag?" Jensen asked?

She tucked the bag under her arm.

Jensen exhaled; two hours of sleep wasn't enough. He had to stay on top of his game. He relied heavily on Stone; she was driven and didn't take crap from anyone, but she was exhausted, too. He needed to delegate more to Lopez.

If Jensen chose the direct method and demanded an answer, Kaylee might clam up and go to her father. He didn't need more complications or distractions. "Please, tell me what happened."

"Bridget and I did some shopping in Scottsdale, and after she left, a stranger approached me in the parking garage. He didn't seem dangerous, but he ran when I asked why he was following me."

"Did he hurt you or say anything?"

"No. I've never seen him before, but he seemed familiar."

"What did he look like?"

"He wore a grey t-shirt, black jeans, and a baseball cap. Early to mid-forties, clean-shaven, and he looked like me."

"You?" Kyle asked.

"It sounds bizarre, but he had similar eyes and my chin. Looking into his face freaked me out. If I didn't know better, I'd say he could be my dad. I asked him his name, and that's when he drove off in his car."

"Did he drive a gray station wagon?"

"Yes."

"You had Miss Carter call me to run the plate for you." Jensen knew she had, but wanted to see if she would be honest and forthcoming.

"I didn't mean to get her into trouble, but were you able to find out who owned the car?"

This could get interesting. Jensen knew the case had taken a new direction. Still, after Kaylee had described her assailant as a possible relative, he was preparing for the shit to hit the fan.

"Did you?" Kaylee asked again.

"The car's owner is a North Little Rock, Arkansas resident."

"I don't know anyone from there. What's his name?"

"David Swanson."

Kaylee fell back on the sofa cushion. "What? You're wrong."

"Miss Chambers, he may have similar facial features—"

"I have his eyes and chin. Is David my real dad? Is that why Michael never loved me? He's not my father?"

"Michael is your dad, and you know it," Kyle stated adamantly.

"No, I don't. Michael and I never fit. There has been this awkward disconnection between us; maybe that's why he hates me. I'm not his biological daughter."

"Miss Chambers, I know you're upset, but a DNA test will prove your parentage."

Kaylee waved the bag at Jensen. "I have his DNA."

"What's in the bag?" Kyle asked.

"It's the man's cap from the parking garage. His sweat and hair are in it; maybe you can get his fingerprints, too."

"How did you get it," Jensen asked?

"He ran; I chased him. When he jumped into the car, it fell off."

"You chased him? Are you crazy?" Kyle asked.

"I didn't think. It happened so fast."

"Pursuing a stranger is a dangerous thing to do."

She handed Jensen the bag. "I took pictures of the hat before I put it in the bag."

Jensen jotted down his number. "Here's my cell; send me the pictures."

Kyle glared at Kaylee.

She glanced over at Kyle and shrugged, "What?"

Jensen examined the photos on his phone.

"It's a hat from a team in Arkansas," Kaylee stated.

"The Travs play in the minor league. You like baseball," Jensen asked?

"No, I researched the team while waiting for Bridget to call back."

"I thought you weren't helping me?"

"I didn't know it was related to Jeff's case until you told me David owned the car."

Jensen nodded and pulled out a pair of gloves from his coat pocket. He put them on and carefully removed the hat. "Did you touch it?"

"No, I used a tissue to pick up the cap."

Jensen put the hat in one evidence bag and the Macy's bag and tissue in another.

"Are you going to do a DNA test?" Kaylee asked.

"The man didn't commit a crime, but if it was David Swanson, it could be related to his stepson's death. I'll have the CSU team process it. I'll get you a number if you want a private DNA test run, but you must provide your own samples."

"Is that really necessary," Kyle asked?

"I'm the spitting image of David, and if he's related to me, I want to know. Detective, are we done? I want to go home."

"I have more questions, but if you answer honestly, it won't take long." He put the bags on the table. "Your fiancé's prints were found all over Mr. Canon's office. When would he have been in there and why?"

"What does Jeff have to do with my boss?"

"Please answer the question."

"No one but James and Larry were allowed in James' office; I have no idea how he gained access."

"You never gave him the key?"

"I don't have a key. And I would never betray James. It was his sanctuary."

"The deceased's fingerprints were found on both interior doors and stairwell walls. Did Jeff have any reason to dislike your boss or want to hurt him?"

"You think Jeff killed James?"

"Only two sets of prints were found in the stairwell. It's possible your fiancé fought with your boss, and when your boss was in the throes of a heart attack, your fiancé pushed him down the stairs to finish him off."

"But why?"

"Robbery, or if Mr. Swanson surprised your boss, it could have led to a struggle."

"Why would Jeff be in the office?"

Jensen took copies of the pictures found on Miss Hill at her arrest and put them on the table between them. He wondered how Kaylee would react to them. Viewing

157

the images would be a shock, and he felt terrible about the timing, but time was of the essence.

"Early this morning, the Squaw Peak Precinct arrested an intruder who had used keys to enter your office building and then your private office. Since the intruder is your friend, she was transported to the Central City Precinct. It's possible she killed Jeff Swanson to retrieve the items from your office."

"My key...I knew I didn't lose it."

"Who broke into Kaylee's office," Kyle asked?

Jensen pushed the pictures closer to Kaylee. "Sara Hill."

Kyle's lips pressed into a thin, hard line, "What the hell?"

"Why would Sara break into my office?"

"She was being blackmailed for having an affair and had gone to your office to retrieve the incriminating pictures."

Kaylee shook her head no. "It's not true."

Jensen wasn't sure Kaylee would cooperate once she found out that her best friend and father had been shacking up, so he decided to drop the bomb later and ask her about the new lead regarding Miss Hill.

"Miss Chambers, did you know that your friend, Miss Hill, was in Phoenix the day Mr. Swanson died and that she had argued with him?"

"What?" Kaylee paused. "That's ridiculous."

"We have a witness who puts her and Mr. Swanson fighting at the same place where he died."

"Why wouldn't she tell me?"

Jensen didn't have any reassuring way to tell Kaylee why her best friend would betray her. Kaylee's reaction seemed genuine; he had to keep pushing. "We also have evidence, including Miss Hill's sworn statement that she has been seeing someone and, due to the sensitive

158

nature of their relationship, kept it secret, but somehow Mr. Swanson found out."

"Who's she dating?"

Jensen braced himself. "Your father."

She jumped up. "No, it's not true!"

"I'm sorry, Miss Chambers—"

"She's my best friend. She knows I hate him—"

"Don't—" Kyle interjected.

"Sara would never do this to me. She knows what a horrible person he is–how he tore my family apart. He's a sorry excuse for a father, a husband, a human being." Kaylee's entire body shook.

Jensen watched as Kaylee struggled with the news. Her face reflected the emotional turmoil ravaging her.

"Miss Chambers, do you need a break?"

"I don't believe any of this."

"I know it's a shock, but we have proof."

"Proof?" Kaylee sank back onto the couch.

"Miss Hill's bank withdrawals matched some of the deposits in Mr. Swanson's account, and we have the pictures in evidence. Do you want to see them?"

"NO."

"It's possible Miss Hill killed your fiancé. She admitted Mr. Swanson confronted her about the affair and demanded more money. They fought. Now, he's dead."

"She would never kill anyone. I know her too well." Kaylee massaged her temple.

"Miss Hill was sleeping with your father, and you didn't know."

Kaylee glared at Jensen. "He took my mother from me, and now he took my best friend. I hate him!"

Kyle wrapped his arm around Kaylee and whispered something to her. Whatever it was, it calmed her down. Jensen needed her to focus. The next few questions were going to be painful.

159

"Miss Chambers, did your fiancé ever hit you, or was he abusive in any other way?"

Kaylee slouched and averted her eyes.

"I know this is difficult, but I need the truth. Did Jeff hit you?"

Kyle looked over and waited for her to answer.

"I didn't love him. He was a monster, and I'm glad he's gone."

"Did you kill him?"

"NO." Kaylee and Kyle spoke in unison.

"Mr. Masters, let her answer," Jensen warned. "Did you have anything to do with the death of Mr. Swanson?"

"I said I was glad he's gone. I didn't kill him."

"Why'd you lie?"

"I told him I wished him dead, and then he was. I panicked."

"What did he do?"

Kaylee crossed and uncrossed her legs, and she smoothed out her slacks. "About six months before he died, he started acting distant."

"How so?"

"One minute he'd be happy, the next angry. Sometimes, he'd looked afraid."

"What changed?'

"About three weeks before he died, I found evidence he was sleeping with someone."

"The redhead," Jensen asked?

"After everything I've learned these past few days, it could be anyone. Jeff hit on my friend, Manara."

"Why do you think he started sleeping around?"

Kaylee spoke softly and looked out the mirrored doors. "We'd agreed not to have sex until we were married. I guess he changed his mind."

Jensen found it hard to believe that anyone in a long-term, caring relationship would not be sexually active. "You two weren't in a sexual relationship?"

"No."

"Were you waiting to get married or secretly waiting for Mr. Masters?"

"No!"

Jensen felt Kaylee's intense answer appeared to be an attempt to convince herself rather than persuade him. Extracting the truth in the correct context was crucial to his job, and Kaylee made it challenging. Jensen believed she wanted to tell the truth, but struggled to defend her emotions and actions. Living under a microscope could be uncomfortable.

"Other than Ms. Ortiz, are you sure you don't know who he had sex with?"

"No, but the redhead might be someone I've met. I attended a party at the Carters' last year, and Bridget's brother brought his girlfriend. She fits the description of the woman who had sex with Jeff at the nightclub."

"Do you know where I can reach her?"

"You'll have to ask Bridget or her brother."

"Are you sure you don't remember her name or where she works?"

"I'm positive."

"Why are you refusing to tell me pertinent information? Don't you want me to find the person who killed Jeff?"

"If you're mad at Bridget, don't yell at me. I know you don't want to, but you might have to involve her."

This whole damn case was infuriating, and he didn't want to believe Bridget might be involved. Bridget knew Ms. Ortiz and Kaylee; maybe she also knew the victim's mistress. He had sent Stone or Lopez to talk with her–he had been ordered to stay away.

"I need you to tell me everything," Jensen pressed.

"I only remembered because I saw a lipstick today that reminded me of a shade I'd seen on Jeff's collar.

Bridget pointed out it was the same color Cory's former girlfriend used to wear."

"Previously, you called Mr. Swanson a monster. Why didn't you tell me earlier that he had abused you?"

She twisted her hands together and lowered her eyes.

Chapter 16

Before joining Homicide, Jensen had interviewed hundreds of abuse victims, and they all had one thing in common: shame. It wasn't their fault, yet they made the perpetrator sound like the good guy. The victims were usually scared and would lie or recant their stories, allowing the accused to continue the abuse. Sometimes, it turned deadly. It made him sick, but at least now, Arizona's domestic violence laws require charges to be filed by the state.

The anguished look on Kaylee's face spoke volumes. Jensen knew she needed a break. He rearranged the bags on the table, trying to give Kaylee time to compose herself, and then he asked, "Can I get some tea or coffee?"

Kaylee pointed to a granite counter next to the water cooler, which contained all the makings for various beverages. Jensen filled a mug with hot water from the cooler. He placed a tea bag in the mug and let it steep. He hoped the chamomile would calm her nerves. He returned to his seat and handed her the tea.

Kaylee grasped the mug with both hands and sipped slowly. Her eyes had glossed over. Jensen knew the key to getting to the truth was patience. Retelling her life's most vulnerable and terrifying moments could be the most challenging thing she would ever do. Kaylee seemed content to drink, as if stalling might make it easier. In his opinion, delaying the inevitable only made it worse. It gave victims time to try to convince themselves it didn't happen or wouldn't happen again.

"Are you ready?"

Kaylee nodded and gripped the mug tightly.

"One week after the Peterson's pool party, I went to Jeff's apartment after work. I was late, and when I came in,

I found him staring at his clenched fists. I told him I'd been delayed at work, but he didn't believe me. I went to the kitchen, and he snuck up behind me and started kissing my neck."

Kaylee's hands trembled. Kyle took the empty mug from her.

"I tried to get away—"

Kyle tapped his foot angrily.

"He whirled me around and tore the buttons off my blouse. He slammed me against the wall." She jumped up. "He unbuckled his pants—"

The mug hit the wall and crashed to the floor. Dozens of tea-stained pieces covered the immaculate stone flooring.

Jensen turned toward Kyle. "Go on."

Kaylee glanced over to Kyle and eased back onto the sofa.

"Where was I?"

Kyle responded through gritted teeth. "Jeff was ripping your clothes off."

She chewed her bottom lip a moment. "Jeff's pupils were dilated, and his lips were twisted into an unnatural grin. It creeped me out. I begged him to stop, and he did. He started mumbling and left."

"Where did he go?"

"I don't know. I stayed the night at Manara's, and I didn't see him for a few days, but then he started calling and wouldn't stop, so I met him at a coffee house near ASU. I gave back his ring and told him it was over. When I suggested he get help, he laughed at me. I waited for him to leave and went back to work. I honestly thought he would stop tormenting me."

Kaylee paused and took several cleansing breaths.

"The next day, he showed up at my office. Jeff apologized and said he didn't mean to scare me. He wanted to get back together, but I refused. He said he'd love me forever, and we belonged together. I demanded that he leave me alone and go away. After he left, I notified Manara Jeff wouldn't be coming back, but if he did, to call the police."

"Did you see or hear from him again?"

Kaylee glanced over at Kyle.

"A couple of days after Jeff came to my office, I called Kyle and asked him to dinner. I was upset about Jeff's behavior and didn't want to be alone. At dinner, I'd sidestepped Kyle's questions about my missing engagement ring. He didn't seem to buy my answers but dropped the subject. After dinner, I drove straight home. I went in, locked my door, and started to change for bed. My door crashed in, and Jeff came straight at me—"

"That bastard!" Kyle boomed.

"I screamed. Jeff pushed me against the wall, and I dropped my nightgown. He wrapped his hands around my neck and squeezed. I tried to loosen his grip—"

Kyle jumped up, his fists curling and uncurling at his side.

"Easy, Kyle. I think you should wait outside."

Kyle glared at Jensen as he thrusted through the lobby doors.

Jensen watched as Kaylee struggled to regain her composure. He saw her glancing toward the door. Outside, Kyle ran his fingers through his hair and paced in front of his car.

"It's best to give him a few minutes. Please continue."

Kaylee closed her eyes. "I was in my underwear. Jeff held my throat with one hand and started to touch me. I tried to scream, but his fingers tightened around my throat. I called him evil and told him I wished he was dead. He laughed and said I might get my wish. His grip tightened. I couldn't breathe; I started swinging at him. His fingers dug into my skin, and blood dripped down my throat. I swung

165

again and hit him on the head. He loosened his grip. I kicked him in the groin and punched him in the nose, and then I ran to my neighbor's house."

"Did you file a report or call the police?"

"We grew up together. I hoped it would blow over and he would leave me alone; when I didn't hear from Jeff again, I thought it was over. About two weeks later, I received the call about his fall."

"Is there anything else?"

"No, but now I know how he found out about my new house. He followed me there. He bought my mortgage to get back at me. Why didn't I remember that?"

"The brain copes with pain by blocking out certain events; it gives the body time to heal and process trauma."

Kaylee glanced over at the stained floor and broken coffee cup.

"Have you seen Mr. Masters hit anyone or portray aggressive behavior?"

She shook her head. "No way."

"A moment ago, Mr. Masters demonstrated how angry he can get when it comes to you."

"He wouldn't hurt or kill anyone."

"He shattered the mug, and he hit Mr. Swanson at a party."

"But—"

"Were you aware your father knew how Mr. Swanson treated you?"

"Who told you that?"

"He did."

Kaylee leaned toward Jensen. "When?"

"Earlier this morning."

"How would he know?"

"Do you think he would kill Mr. Swanson to save you?"

"What did he tell you," Kaylee asked?

166

"He said you were a strong, capable woman, and he did not kill Mr. Swanson."

"My father's concern is touching, but I doubt he'd lift a finger to help me, so you can take him off your suspect list."

Jensen watched as a flood of emotions crossed her face. Humiliation appeared to be the overwhelming reaction to her father's confession. He could only imagine the pain it caused, knowing her father would let her fend for herself against a brute like Jeff Swanson. He was beginning to hate Michael Chambers.

"I wanted to know if you were aware of your father's possible participation in this investigation, but I can see you had no idea, and for that, I'm truly sorry."

"You didn't tell me anything I didn't already know. It was a shock to hear someone say it out loud. Perhaps Michael is not my father. That would explain his contempt for me. Seriously, what kind of a louse would do that to his daughter?"

Her rhetorical question was valid, and Jensen wished he had an answer, but there was no excuse for a father to turn his back on his only child.

"Miss Chambers, did you seek assistance after Mr. Swanson attacked you?"

Kaylee shook her head, "No."

"Violence committed by someone you know or love is still violence. It's traumatic and painful and can have lasting mental and physical effects. The Arizona Department of Economic Security's website lists agencies that can assist you with various services. I can get you the information. Regardless of where you go, I urge you to call someone. It will take time and support for the healing process to begin."

Kaylee nodded.

Since Kaylee could afford top-of-the-line health care, Jensen doubted she would use the state-offered assistance. Jensen hoped she would get help somewhere. He had seen this all too often. The victim believed the pain, mental anguish, feelings of guilt, and regret would go away on their own. They typically didn't. They just festered and exploded.

"Tell me about Mr. Swanson's funeral."

Kaylee shrugged. "It was a closed casket. Some of Jeff's coworkers and a few of his clients showed up. Based on the negative comments I've heard about Jeff, I'm surprised anyone came. If he cheated them, why would they come to his funeral?"

"I don't know, but it's something to consider. Do you remember anyone who looked out of place?"

"The whole thing was a blur; I just wanted it to end. Kyle attended; he might know."

Jensen was curious whether Kyle had any insight and went outside to check on him. Jensen made it clear he would not tolerate any more outbursts. Kyle nodded and followed Jensen back into the office. He sat at the end of the couch, one cushion away from Kaylee. Jensen carefully examined his demeanor.

"I asked Miss Chambers if anyone looked out of place at Jeff's funeral; do you remember anyone who stood out?"

"I didn't know the majority of the people. Besides, Kaylee didn't look well, and I wanted to speak with her."

"Miss Chambers, who decided to have a closed casket?"

"The funeral home director did. He said he couldn't make his face presentable due to the extent of Jeff's injuries."

The funeral director had arranged for the closed casket. What better way to hide a missing body or the wrong body? "Who picked the mortuary?"

"Jeff paid for and took care of the entire process," Kaylee stated.

168

"Do you know when these arrangements were made?"

"I'm not sure. The director would know."

Jensen turned his attention to Kyle. "Did you know Mr. Swanson was terrorizing Miss Chambers?"

Kyle gripped the arm of the sofa. "No, I would have stopped it."

"How?"

"I would have done whatever it took to keep her safe."

Jensen leaned closer. "Does that include murder?"

"No!"

"Are you sure? Mr. Swanson terrorized the woman you love, and you never considered killing him or taking matters into your own hands. I find that hard to believe."

"Believe what you like. I would have found a way to keep her safe if I had known. Besides, some fates are worse than death."

"Is that a threat, Mr. Masters?"

"I don't make threats. I could ruin Jeff's financial and business reputation. I wouldn't have to lay a finger on him, but professionally speaking, his life would be over."

"Interesting… Mr. Chambers said the same thing. Do you consider yourself to be Mr. Chambers' equal?"

"We are colleagues, business partners, and friends. But if you're asking if I have delusions of grandeur, the answer is no. Michael is a self-made man, well-respected and heavily connected. I dare say there aren't many people who can top that."

"Has Mr. Chambers ever asked you to do anything to help his daughter?"

Kaylee looked toward Kyle.

"Kaylee and I are friends; if she were in trouble, I would do whatever I could to help her."

"I know you understand my question," Jensen stated flatly.

Kyle glanced in Kaylee's direction. "Like I said. If she needed help, I would be there for her."

"Do you want to consult a lawyer or Mr. Chambers?"

"Kyle, just answer the question."

"Miss Chambers is right; I would love an answer if you have nothing to hide."

"Michael asked me to take her to Senior Prom."

"Is that all," Kaylee asked?

Kyle drummed his fingers on the sofa. "Due to my feelings for Kaylee, my friendship with Jeff became strained toward the end of high school. A couple of weeks before prom, Jeff challenged me to a race. I knew I'd win, so I refused. One day after football practice, he challenged me in front of the entire team. I was forced to accept."

"What happened?" Jensen asked.

"Jeff crashed and ended up in the hospital. He missed prom."

"Did Mr. Chambers pay you for taking his daughter to prom or getting rid of Mr. Swanson?"

Kyle turned toward Jensen and said, "What the hell is wrong with you? It was an accident."

Kyle didn't take the bait; it seemed he could control his temper. Now, if only he could be sure Kaylee was telling him everything. She had a habit of forgetting key details. She neglected to let him know that Mr. Swanson had been abusive and that she had broken off the engagement; she also forgot to tell him she had kissed Kyle.

"Miss Chambers, is there anything else you 'just remembered' that might be relevant to the case?"

"Are you accusing me of sabotaging your investigation?"

"To be fair, you have, at least twice, waited to reveal important details—"

170

"No matter how Jeff treated me, I would never have killed him."

"I have to follow every lead."

"Stop harping on things I forgot to tell you; they're leading you away from the real killer?"

"Kaylee—" Kyle interrupted.

"It's true; the more he focuses on me, the less time he spends finding the murderer."

"I have to balance professional courtesy with hard-hitting questions and innuendos, but I aim to find Jeff's killer and get him or her off the street."

Jensen empathized with her. Losing a loved one and being considered a person of interest must be emotionally draining.

The loss of his father had hit him hard. He had been consumed by grief. It had taken months to return to his routine, but it was never the same. His father's partner had retold stories of their glory days; it should have helped, but it had only reminded him of what a great man he had lost. The loss he endured would be with him forever. He could only imagine the added strain of trying to prove oneself innocent of a murder.

Kaylee grabbed her purse and waited at the door. "I've had enough for one day. If you have any more questions, call me tomorrow."

Chapter 17

Kaylee put the folder away and locked the cabinet. She might as well go home; she couldn't concentrate. Yesterday's events had reopened old wounds and a plethora of reasons why her father might not love her, all starting with the fact that she might not be his daughter. Was that why he never made time for her? All those years wasted trying to please him, and he never bothered to reciprocate. Now she knew why. Had her mother conceived her before she met Michael, and he gave her his last name to appease his new wife, or had she been the product of an affair? Imagining her kind, loving mother as an adulterer seemed impossible. Despite how her father had mistreated her mom, Kaylee knew she would never cheat on him.

Or would she?

Everyone had a limit. Maybe Kaylee's mother had reached hers. She had spent long, isolated days and nights alone while Michael worked. Had she reached out for the comfort of a stranger, someone to give her what he couldn't?

A year ago, Kaylee had been naïve enough to think Jeff would wait until they were married to have sex. After all the lies and pain, had she become jaded and believed everyone, including her dear, sweet mother, might be a cheater?

She rubbed her temple.

The ringing was a welcome distraction.

"Hello."

"Miss Chambers, it's Detective Jensen. Are you able to stop by headquarters?"

She exhaled; she didn't want to hear more bad news or any news. Was one day without drama asking for too much? "How about tomorrow?"

"We're finally making progress with the case, and I don't want to stop the momentum. I can drop by your office. It shouldn't take long."

Kaylee didn't want to disrupt the office staff. Earlier, she had had difficulty explaining the broken mug and stained floor–best to keep the investigation out of her office. "I'm swamped and can't get away until later. How about four?"

Jensen agreed. Kaylee had four hours to finish her paperwork and get to his office. She grabbed a blueberry bagel and coffee from Hava Java. Upon returning, she tackled the stack of folders on her desk when she received a call from Kyle, who offered to take her to the precinct. He, too, had been invited to speak with Detective Jensen.

Due to the investigation and her stress level, Kaylee's productivity suffered. She worked fast and completed her tasks in record time. She would come back later and double-check her work. She didn't want to make mistakes to appease Detective Jensen.

On their way to the precinct, Kaylee asked, "Did Detective Jensen tell you why he wanted to see us?"

Kyle shook his head. "He said he had questions regarding some new information."

"What information?"

"He didn't say."

Kaylee looked out the passenger window and wondered if Jensen had a lead on David Swanson or knew why he had followed her to the parking garage. She prayed he wouldn't mention Jeff's attack. She couldn't relive that event again, at least not so soon. Retelling it yesterday almost broke her, and Kyle didn't fare too well either.

Walking down the hall at police headquarters, Kaylee heard a commanding voice, one she knew all too well. What was her father doing here? She reached the center of the room, stopped, and searched for him. He stood with his back to her, appearing to speak to the sergeant in

173

charge. Kaylee bolted over to the information desk. The thought of the two of them together incensed her.

"Father!"

He turned.

She slapped him.

The whack echoed through the station.

All eyes turned toward them.

Michael rubbed his face.

"She's too young for you. She's my best friend!"

"Sara is old enough to make her own decisions," Michael stated blandly.

"She's practically my sister."

"Kaylee, grow up. Sara is an adult."

"What about mom? Don't you care about her?"

"What's going on here?!" Jensen boomed.

The squad room fell silent. The clock's second hand ticked away; its low rhythmic beat resonated throughout the room.

"My daughter and I are disagreeing over my choice of companions."

"Mr. Chambers, Detective Stone will take your statement; it should only take a few minutes."

"Go ahead. Have me locked up—" Kaylee fumed.

Michael, unfazed, headed down the hall.

"You shouldn't have hit him," Jensen grabbed her arm, "I'm going to have to charge you with domestic violence."

Michael turned back; his eyes bored into Jensen's. "Do not arrest my daughter! If you do, the governor will speak to your commander. He might even suggest a transfer to a less-than-desirable location."

Jensen dropped her arm.

Jensen entered his office. Kaylee stared at the floor, and Kyle's brows were pulled tightly together. Jensen felt like a principal getting ready to dole out punishment to misbehaving kids. He knew the relationship between Mr. Chambers and his daughter had been strained to begin with, and these circumstances only added to the stress. Still, he never imagined it would escalate to a physical assault.

One of the advantages of being wealthy was the ability to evade due process. Anyone else who had physically assaulted someone in front of a squad room full of cops would have been arrested on the spot. Jensen understood the pressure an investigation of this type caused, but he had to let her know that this kind of behavior would not be tolerated, and he had to do so in a manner that would allow him to keep his job. He wasn't keen on getting transferred.

"Miss Chambers, it is my duty as a law enforcement officer to uphold the law, and when I see the law being violated, I —"

"I shouldn't have hit him. I'm sorry—"

"It's okay," Kyle whispered.

"No. It's not," Jensen cautioned.

"Kyle, he's right. If Michael didn't have money, I'd be in jail. I'm a hypocrite–I'm no better than Jeff."

"You lost it for one minute, one time in your life. It was wrong, and you're remorseful, but you're nothing like Jeff."

"Jeff had been put in a situation where he had no control and went crazy. How is that any different?" Kaylee asked.

"You regret what you did and won't do it again. That's how it's different," Kyle answered.

"Violence is never the answer, Miss Chambers. I strongly suggest you see someone about the items we discussed earlier."

Kaylee nodded.

Jensen watched Kaylee slump down in her chair. The investigation had just begun, and he had no idea when it would end. She would need all the energy and perseverance she could muster to get through it. It seemed she was truly repentant for what she did and needed a minute to gather herself. He shuffled some folders before asking his first question.

"I asked you here to discuss the results of the toxicology tests run on Jeff before he was buried."

"What tests?" Kaylee inquired.

"Due to the circumstances surrounding Jeff's death, an autopsy was not performed, but a Forensic toxicology screening had been, and these are the results from the blood and urine tests—"

"At the time of Jeff's death, everyone believed he fell. Why did he need testing?" Kaylee demanded.

"When the cause of death is found not to be by natural causes, and falling from a building is not considered natural, these tests are run. They can determine whether levels of toxic substances, drugs, or poisons contributed to a death. The samples are tested for things like opiates, alcohol, marijuana, and barbiturates, and if those drugs were in the system, were they at a lethal level? It can take up to three months to receive results. The results came in yesterday, and I have some questions for you."

"When he died, were there drugs in Jeff's system," Kaylee asked?

"There were trace amounts of marijuana—"

"Marijuana?"

"Don't act so surprised. Jeff cheated on you, attacked you–what's a little recreational drug use?" Kyle quipped. "He never did drugs when we were together. Maybe he did them with…." Kaylee's voice trailed off.

"The amount of marijuana in his system was negligible. It's the drug Etomidate I'm interested in. Did Mr. Swanson have a surgical procedure right before he died?"

"I don't think so."

Kyle shrugged. "I don't know; I hadn't spoken to him for months before he died."

"Maybe he was trying to minimize the scar on his forehead," Kaylee suggested.

Jensen shook his head. "The drug found in his system is a fast-acting anesthetic used for short procedures such as tracheal intubation or reduction of dislocated joints."

"I saw him two weeks before he died, and he looked fine," Kaylee said.

Jensen tapped the folders on his desk. Should he reveal David Swanson's theory and suggest to Kaylee that Jeff, her sociopathic ex-fiancé, might be alive? Jensen believed David was missing a few screws. He wanted concrete proof and needed time to find it. Telling Kaylee Jeff might be alive, even to elicit an honest response, could be detrimental to her situation, and Jensen wasn't willing to risk that. He would find another way to get the information he needed.

"I'll look into the discrepancies," Jensen said.

"Are there any new leads on David Swanson," Kaylee asked?

"You know I'm not able to divulge information regarding the case, and just a reminder, this is my investigation. That means you, Miss Chambers."

Chapter 18

Kyle owned a two-year-old 2007 Lincoln Town Car, but the smell of new leather still permeated the interior. Kaylee loved leather–its look, feel, and smell–it reminded her of when she had purchased her Shelby. Several people had advised her against getting leather seats. The Arizona sun can be brutal, and if not properly cared for, the leather can dry out and be ruined. Not to mention, sitting on hot leather seats could be painful.

Kaylee put the seat back and appreciated the spaciousness of his Lincoln. It was a luxurious sedan with plenty of leg and headroom. Kyle stood over six feet tall; she guessed that was one of the reasons he bought it, but she would never buy a four-door. Kyle had two cars, a sedan and a sports car. She only had one, a muscle car—her Shelby, and wouldn't trade it in for the world. No matter what life dished out, driving her Shelby seemed to put everything back into perspective. It gave her time to think and enjoy the important things in life. It also made her feel invincible, and that feeling alone was worth every dollar she had spent.

After only a few questions, the interrogation ended. Detective Jensen had said he would be in touch. Kaylee wondered when her life would return to normal and if Kyle would be a part of it. The past few days had been exhausting; she closed her eyes and listened to the soft cooing of Sarah McLachlan.

"Have you eaten?" Kyle asked.

"I'm not hungry."

"How about some coffee?"

At the Java Shack, Kaylee drank coffee and ate a cookie; Kyle demolished a ham sandwich and side salad and downed a raspberry tea.

After finishing his meal, he asked, "Do you want to talk about it?"

She shook her head no and sipped her coffee. Just when Kaylee had convinced herself that Michael was not her biological father, he finally defended and protected her. He even threatened a police officer. Maybe she dreamt the whole thing. Why would he choose now to make a stand? Did he love her, or was this just another way to exert his power and keep his good name out of the paper?

While Kyle drove back to her office, she rubbed her temple and wished she had stayed in bed.

As he turned into Lawson and Canon's parking lot, he muttered.

Kaylee opened her eyes and sat forward in the chair. The seatbelt tightened, cutting into her throat as she craned her neck to the right. Several patrol cars and a fire truck were blocking the entrance to the parking garage.

Kyle shut off the engine, "Lock the doors, and don't move until I say it's safe."

She gazed into the darkness. A ghostly hue hovered over the manicured lawn, and Kaylee heard faint sounds drifting through the night. Police officers huddled at the entrance. A vein in her neck pulsed, and she twisted her hands together. She moved the seat back to see better, but the men at the main entrance blocked her view.

She released the seatbelt and got out. Kaylee hurried to the entrance, squeezed by the group of men, and headed toward her car. The smell of burnt rubber hung in the air. Kyle, Detective Jensen, and several officers were clustered together.

She moved closer, and the caustic odor stung Kaylee's nose and throat—a piercing pain shot through her chest.

"My car! Where is it?"

"Miss Chambers, I'm sorry, but this is your car," Jensen stated flatly.

Kaylee shook her head in denial. That mound of incinerated metal could not be her car.

"Miss Chambers, I'm Officer Housner. My department received a call about an arson in progress, and when we arrived, this vehicle was engulfed in flames. Is it yours?"

"Who are you?" Kaylee stroked her temple.

"Officer Housner, I'm from the Squaw Peak precinct. This is my jurisdiction, but due to the location and possible murder connection, I called Detective Jensen."

"What?"

"Miss Chambers, my men have identified the frame as a Shelby Cobra. Do you drive a Cobra?" Housner asked.

She searched the far corners of the garage for her cherished Mustang.

"How can you be sure it's a Cobra or if it's mine?" She asked.

"The back portion of the car burned at a lower-intensity flame, which made it easier to identify."

"Did the license plate burn?"

"We found no plate."

"I have a personalized plate. Mustang Lover spelled MSTGLVR. If you didn't find it, maybe this isn't my car?"

"We identified two colors of paint, blue and white. What color is your car," Jensen asked?

"It's Vista Blue with white Lemans stripes." As soon as she confirmed the color, she assumed Jensen had made up his mind that the burnt heap was hers. She had only been gone for two hours. How could this happen?

"Miss Chambers, did you keep anything of value in your car," Officer Housner asked?

"No, I keep all my important items locked up or with me. Why?"

"The car had been partially dismantled and badly damaged before it was set on fire. Robbery doesn't appear to be the motive; it looks like a crime of passion."

180

Crimes of passion usually involve domestic violence or stalking.

Stalker.

Goose bumps formed on her arms and legs. "Crime of passion?" The only person who had stalked her was dead, and he wasn't coming back.

"We don't have any answers yet, Miss Chambers. Officer Housner and his men are coming back tomorrow to speak to your coworkers," Jensen asserted.

She stared at the rubble.

"Miss Chambers, did you see or hear anything unusual before meeting with Detective Jensen," Housner asked?

"I didn't see anything out of place when Kyle picked me up, and when we returned, the police were the only ones I saw in the lot."

Kaylee stepped closer to the scorched debris. The seats had melted into the frame, and everything inside had melted down; only ashes remained. She turned away from the blackened pile of metal. It sickened her.

Nausea welled up inside her. Kaylee touched her forehead; she felt warm and dizzy.

"Miss Chambers, go home. You're looking a little peaked." Jensen turned away from them and spoke with Officer Housner.

Kaylee and Kyle walked back to the Lincoln and drove off.

She wasn't paranoid, but something about the arson felt wrong. Why wasn't her license plate found in the charred wreckage? Kaylee had been parking in the garage for three years and never had a problem. No crimes had ever been reported in the twenty years the firm had been in the building. Why her and why her car? Kaylee wasn't convinced the foul-smelling pile of rubble was her Mustang.

Detective Housner's crime of passion theory lingered in Kaylee's mind, but she refused to consider it. If she did, she would have to admit someone wanted to harm her. It was all happening too fast: Jeff's death and the murder investigation, Sara and her father, and now the fire. She didn't want to accept Detective Housner's assessment. It sent chills down her spine.

The shoulder strap cut across her neck. She yanked it down, rubbed her arms with short, quick strokes, and adjusted the dual climate control. Kaylee leaned back in the seat and pressed down on her stomach to calm the storm that raged within.

Kyle glanced over at her. "How are you holding up?"

"My brain is overloaded, and if I don't get home soon, I will hurl."

"Try to relax. It should only be a few more minutes."

Kaylee closed her eyes, but it didn't help. Question after question formed in her mind. Was it really her car that went up in flames? Would Larry be able to handle another tragedy? Was Jeff's killer stalking her and trying to kill her?

She blew out a deep breath. The finality of the situation was sinking in. Her Mustang could be replaced, but it had been the embodiment of all her hard work, the hundreds of hours Kaylee spent in college, and the two years straight she had worked twelve-hour days to make a name for herself. Kaylee had earned her clients' and colleagues' respect and trust, and did it without using the Chambers name.

After acquiring Carter Culinary Services, Kaylee purchased the Shelby Cobra to bond with her father and prove she could make it on her own. But now it was gone, and another pivotal part of her life had vanished, with it, an opportunity to repair her relationship with her father. She

182

hadn't rescheduled another meeting to show him her car—the timing always seemed wrong. Kaylee had started to doubt that using the Mustang to form a rapport would work, which frightened her. If she didn't have the Mustang, would she have any chance of building a relationship with him, or could she use something else to bridge the gap?

She had followed in Michael's footsteps, overachieving at everything, and all her free time had been spent trying something new to impress her father, which never worked. He had continually buried himself in work, and Kaylee's efforts resulted in mental and physical exhaustion. Her friends had complained about being neglected, so she returned to a slower pace and regained her life.

Kyle pulled the Lincoln into the private drive, parked near the main door, and turned off the engine.

She opened her eyes, sat straight, and realized this wasn't her house.

She stared up the driveway. The sky-high rotunda loomed over the thriving landscape. Lush plants and a three-tier fountain filled the Spanish-style courtyard. Two enormous Indigenous boulders adorned the entrance. Kaylee never guessed Kyle would buy something so extravagant and beautiful. He had impeccable taste, and the blend of plant life and stone was aesthetically pleasing.

"When did you buy this place?"

"After Jeff called to tell me you two were engaged, I knew I had to move on."

"You sold your other house because Jeff and I were getting married?"

Kyle went over to the passenger side and opened the door. "I kept it as a rental and built this one."

Kaylee got out, glanced down the driveway, and then back to the house. "It's huge."

He closed the car door and pulled the keys out of his pants pocket.

"Don't you get lonely all by yourself?"

"I'm not always going to be a bachelor."

"I meant it's a lot for one person to care for."

Kyle arched his right brow.

"You know what I mean."

He stared at her and said, "No, I don't."

"I thought you'd buy something more practical."

As soon as she said it, Kaylee regretted it. Kyle turned on his heels and headed to the main entrance. Her compliments turned to insults, and her words became weapons. It had been a horrible night. She was tired and wanted to go home.

"Wait. Where are you going?" She hurried to the front door and hovered in the foyer.

Kyle put the keys in a small silver dish and sorted through a stack of mail.

She shouldn't have run. She had been feeling nauseous, and running only made it worse. "Are you going to take me home?"

"No."

"I'm having stomach pain."

"Come in, and I'll get something for your stomach."

"I know you mean well, but you're being a little bossy."

"I'm trying to be a friend," Kyle replied tersely.

Kaylee followed Kyle to the living area. He pointed to the sofa and left the room. She sat down; sick or not, she couldn't help herself. She took a moment to admire the décor. The split-stone walls and vaulted-beamed ceilings added texture and charm to the room. The furniture was rich and dark. His eye for detail and natural style were evident: every piece fit seamlessly.

He returned with a glass of water in one hand and pain relievers in the other. He handed Kaylee the glass and put the bottles on the table.

Kaylee took two pills for her head pain and popped three antacids into her mouth, chewed them up, and swallowed. "This is quite a stash of medicine."

"I stock up so I don't have to make unnecessary trips to the store."

Kyle hovered near the table. It made her nervous. She sipped the water.

"I didn't mean what I said earlier. Your home is beautiful, and it suits you."

He shrugged. "It's just a house."

"It's perfect for you."

"Yeah, maybe."

"Earlier, when I unintentionally implied it wasn't for you, you seemed angry, and now you don't care?"

"You made a good point, and I've reconsidered how I view this place."

"Don't put any stock into what I said earlier. I suffered a huge shock and was rambling."

He rounded the table and sat next to her. Kyle angled himself so he could see Kaylee's face. "Are you afraid?"

"I'm angry, confused, and a little scared."

Kyle's knee touched her thigh. She could feel the heat from his body. He shifted, and his knee bumped her thigh again. The earthy scent of Kyle's cologne surrounded her. An unfamiliar feeling stirred in her. A wave of warmth washed over her. Kaylee could feel his breath on her shoulder. She never felt so alive and wanted to feel that way again.

Kyle touched her face. "Are you all right?"

His light embrace stirred more memories, "I…" He was too close. Kaylee needed a distraction. She leaned back, trying to put some distance between them, and ran her finger along the curvy, scalloped back of the pub-style sofa. She avoided eye contact and continued to admire the fine craftsmanship.

"You look flushed." Kyle moved closer and put his hand on hers, holding it still. "Look at me."

She tried not to, but she was drawn to him. His eyes were dilated, and his moist lips were tempting her. Kaylee remembered his lips, his hands…

Kaylee groaned.

"What is it?"

She jumped up and grabbed her stomach.

He pointed. "Upstairs to the left."

Kaylee rushed upstairs and rounded the corner. She went down the hall to the first room on the left, closed the door, and leaned against it. It had only been a few months since Jeff had died, and Kaylee wanted to make out with his best friend. Did she have any morals at all?

She splashed cold water on her face. Kyle confessed his love for her because he had to, but was it real? Kaylee had thought she loved Jeff and planned to marry him, but she had been wrong. What if Kyle felt some misguided loyalty to her, and she was stuck in the friend zone with him, as Jeff had been with her? If Kyle had parted his lips, Kaylee would have thrown herself into his arms as fervently as she had done at the pool party. Would he have kissed her back?

Kaylee gripped the edge of the counter. Why did it take her this long to realize she loved Kyle? And she had all along. Did Jeff know this? That might explain why he had turned on her and had flown into rages. Kaylee dashed more cold water on her face. She had misled Jeff and blamed Kyle for kissing her and betraying Jeff, and it wasn't him. She was the liar and traitor, not Kyle.

A quick rap on the door startled her.

"Are you okay?"

Kaylee's reply stuck in her throat.

The door handle shook. "Kaylee?"

"I'll be out in a few minutes."

Kaylee waited until she heard him walking away and exhaled. She would have to face him sooner or later, but needed time to gather her thoughts. Whenever she felt overwhelmed or pressured, she would take deep, cleansing breaths and focus on the décor. It felt like a productive way to escape, at least temporarily, from a hectic situation.

She took her time wiping up the water on the counter, a dark marble infused with gold flecks. Kaylee stood between the double sinks and saw a reflection in the mirror. She turned around to get a better look. A massive vintage soaking tub, in the same dark marble as the vanity, sat in front of the window, allowing bathers to view the pool with its rock-water feature and well-manicured landscape. Kaylee glanced around the spacious room. Like the rest of the house, each fixture complemented the other but stood on its own merit.

The glass shower walls exposed the ceiling-mounted rainfall showerhead. Kaylee could imagine herself taking a shower and basking in the hot water as it cascaded down, in a steady stream, over her aching body. Kaylee didn't know what she would do about Kyle, but she couldn't stay in the bathroom all night.

She headed down the hall to the sweeping grand stairway. The staircase, constructed of the finest dark wood and a wrought-iron railing, was similar to the pub-style sofa in the living room: elegant but unassuming. Kyle's house was a goldmine of distractions. Until Kaylee could devise a plan, she would probably critique his entire house.

She stepped off the bottom stair and scanned the living room, where Kyle paced back and forth with long, determined strides. Kaylee approached cautiously. How would she tell him she loved him? Should she tell him? Until Detective Jensen completed the investigation and arrested the killer, Jeff's murder loomed over them. Should they pretend to be just friends until the investigation ends, or go on living their own separate lives indefinitely?

"How are you feeling?"

Kaylee mustered a weak smile. "I've had better days."

"Maybe you should eat something."

"I can't." She grabbed the antacids and popped two more into her mouth. The fruity flavor couldn't hide the chalky texture or bitter aftertaste.

"You have a beautiful home. Who picked the furnishings?

"I did."

"I didn't know you had a passion for décor."

Kyle sat on the pub-style sofa and ran his fingers along the trim. "I wanted furniture that has character and depth."

"I know exactly how you feel." Kaylee paused. "After Jeff had proposed, he wanted to buy a velvet sofa and chrome ottoman. It was a stunning set, but—"

"I'm guessing you didn't buy it."

Kaylee arched her brow.

"You want to discuss furniture?"

"Your home is amazing; I'm taking the time to appreciate it fully."

"You sound as if you'll never be coming back."

Before she would commit to returning, she needed to know whether they had a future together.

"Tell me what you're feeling about what happened to your car?" Kyle urged.

Kaylee's cherished Mustang had been torched, and she had found out her best friend had been sneaking around with her father. She needed time to process the news.

Sara had deceived her in a way Kaylee had never imagined possible. The time they'd spent in college, sharing dreams, planning their futures, and building a strong, trusting friendship, had been one of the happiest in Kaylee's life, but Sara had thrown it all away. Kaylee wished Sara had stayed in New York to finish her schooling. She would never have met Michael if she hadn't moved to Arizona. Then Kaylee wouldn't be experiencing the pain of Sara's egregious betrayal.

She sat opposite Kyle, "Do you think someone is stalking me?"

"I'm not sure. Why would someone trash your car? Can you think of anyone who might've done this?"

"Destroy a seventy thousand dollar car?"

"This isn't about money."

"My Mustang was my last attempt to connect with my father. I'd wanted to show him we had something in common."

"Michael likes muscle cars?"

"Strange, isn't it? Mom had told me that as a teenager, he'd wanted a Mustang but couldn't afford one, and when he could, his pride had prevented him from getting one. The day my grandfather died was the day my father had sworn he'd never be poor again."

"Maybe he's afraid that if he lets up, even for one minute, he'll lose it all?"

"All my life, I've tried to show him how much he means to me; you'd think he'd realize working himself to death isn't the answer. I'm at a loss; I'm beginning to feel I can't do or say anything to make him proud. It's a good thing I grew to love my Mustang. Otherwise, it would have been a total bust."

"Don't give up on your father; things will work out."

She had doubts, but had more pressing issues to worry about.

She wondered if the fire department had notified Larry. News of the fire would upset him. He was still reeling from James' death, and she wasn't sure how he would react. Larry used to be the epitome of composure, but lately, he has suffered from sudden bouts of depression.

Kaylee didn't want a group of detectives to ambush him regarding the fire and send him spiraling out of control.

Chapter 19

Kyle's phone rang; he answered it and left the room. Kaylee wondered why he didn't take the call in front of her. Was it business or personal? Did he have a girlfriend? Is that why he said he wouldn't always be a bachelor? How could he love her *and* have a girlfriend? When she accepted Jeff's proposal, did he give up on her and move on with someone else? She had been secretly in love with Kyle for years, and now that she realized how much he meant to her, he might not be available.

Why had she said yes to Jeff's proposal? All the clues had been present: a lack of passion and chemistry, dissimilar goals, and clashing styles. She liked hand-crafted luxurious comfort with deep historical meaning. Jeff had wanted trendy items; his style had constantly changed.

Yet, looking back, they'd been together so long she hadn't known how to break it off without hurting him. Kaylee's directness paid off professionally. Her clients appreciated her honesty, and her career reflected that. Her mom had taught her to be kind but straightforward. Kaylee didn't want to intrude on Kyle's call, so she checked out the kitchen.

The open-concept floor plan made it easy for Kaylee to navigate Kyle's house. The French country cabinetry immediately caught her eye. The doors were garnished with metallic gold handles that blended well with the subtle gold theme of the granite and marble countertops. The classic eighteenth to twentieth-century designs included fine woods, crown moldings, and sophisticated details she loved. Tall, cherry-wood side-by-side windows allowed the sun to flood the room in the mornings and early afternoons.

She put her elbows on the granite counter, rested her chin on her hands, and stared out the window. Darkness engulfed the city, and the intermittent twinkling of faraway stars was all she could see. She wondered what treasures the Arizona sky hid and couldn't wait to see them in the sunlight.

Kyle returned, his face strained.

"Work," Kaylee asked?

"Your dad."

"What did he want?"

Kyle pulled the top off a domestic beer and took a long drink.

"Did he ask about me?" The question sounded ludicrous, even to her, and Kyle's hesitation confirmed it.

At the police station, her father had threatened Detective Jensen. He made her doubt her earlier concerns that he wasn't her birth father. He had shielded her, and Kaylee hoped it was a step in the right direction, but Michael had a reputation to maintain. He couldn't have her tainting it by going to jail. They shared the same name, but did genetics link them, or was it something else?

David Swanson's eyes haunted her. Intuitively, she knew the two of them were related. She didn't understand how or why. If she shared DNA with David, he would be family, and she would move heaven and earth to find out.

A burst of vivid colors ricocheting off the pool siding, intensifying the textured finish, caught her attention. The kaleidoscope of lights cut through the water. She watched transfixed as the colors continued their mesmerizing show. She wondered what it would be like to move through the water, having the lights reflect off her skin.

Kyle put down the beer. "I'm going for a swim; you should join me."

"I'm beat. I need to rest."

"It's hot, and it's been a long day. Come on. It's refreshing and will relax you."

"No, I don't feel well. Where do I get to sleep?"

192

"You can have my room. I'll take the sofa."

"I'll take one of the other bedrooms."

"The other rooms aren't guest-ready."

"If I sleep on the couch—"

"You're my guest—"

"I'm just a guest," Kaylee asked?

"You know you're not."

"Do I?"

"There's nothing I can do. At least, not until we finally put Jeff to rest."

"Am I supposed to continue waiting and do nothing?"

"I had to shelve my feelings for a long time. It's frustrating, but you get through it."

Kaylee sighed; hadn't they waited long enough?

As she climbed the stairs, Kaylee peeked into one of the bedrooms. Boxes were stacked high and scattered throughout the room, but it was empty of furniture or a bed. She wondered why the rooms weren't ready; Kaylee guessed he had been busy and, like her, had thrown himself into work.

She rummaged through the main bedroom closet and found a faded football jersey from high school. Kaylee put it on; it hung past her thighs. She had always remembered high school fondly, but the recent ugliness of her situation threatened to spoil those memories.

Kaylee sat on the bed and combed her hair, and when she heard splashing, she went to the window. Kyle was outside swimming laps; his tanned, muscular body cut through the water effortlessly. Arizona's summers were brutal, and Kaylee had often wondered what it would be like to swim surrounded by cool, refreshing water, but her fate had been sealed long ago.

As a child at a friend's pool party, Kaylee had fallen in and inhaled the chlorinated water. Her eyes and nose had stung. Her chest burned. Kaylee had kicked and screamed, causing her to ingest more water. She couldn't breathe, and fear blinded her. She had felt as if the water was swallowing her up. Kaylee had started to tire and sink to the bottom. One of the adults pulled her out. It had taken a few panicked gasps to breathe, and she vowed never to get into the water again. Her mother had scheduled her for swimming lessons, but she had refused to go.

Growing up, Kaylee had always found ways to avoid getting into the water, but she had wondered what it would be like to conquer her demons and control her fear instead of the other way around.

She watched from the window. Kyle's strokes and kicks were perfectly timed; the synergy between his body and the water fascinated her. While driving her car, Kaylee felt as if she was one with it, but it was the only time she had ever felt that way. Kaylee knew most people wouldn't understand, but she felt lost without it, and amidst the chaos, she had realized Kyle was the only constant she could count on. Unlike Jeff, who had drained her emotions and resources when it mattered, Kyle had been there for her.

She went outside and stayed in the shadows; Kaylee didn't want to disrupt his rhythm or get too close to the water. His vigorous strokes slowed, and he appeared to be in the cool-down portion of his swim. Kaylee lingered, delighting in his physical prowess. He swam to the edge and dried his face. He turned and stared in her direction.

"Are you going to stand in the dark all night or come over and talk to me?"

She stepped into the light and walked toward him. She stopped several feet from the edge. "If you exercise before you go to bed, it interferes with your sleep."

"Most nights, I have no problem sleeping. How about you?"

Until recently, Kaylee had no problem, but the past couple of months wreaked havoc on her daily routines. "I haven't slept well, but I guess, all things considered, it's to be expected."

"Come in. Some exercise will do wonders for your mood."

"I'm good."

"Jump in and enjoy the water."

"I can't, not today." She said timidly.

"Oh."

"Not that."

"Then get in."

Her never-fail excuse went out the window. No one wants to pressure a woman on her period. Now, she had no valid reason not to get in.

"What's the problem?"

She didn't want to drown. Kaylee had successfully gone her entire adult life without getting into a pool and wasn't about to start now. Kyle probably wasn't afraid of anything, but fear could be debilitating; it strangled your spirit, forcing you to succumb to its power. In the past, she had used dozens of excuses not to get into the water; why couldn't she remember them?

He swam toward the stairs. "Are you all right?"

"Why wouldn't I be?"

"You turned ghostly white."

She wanted to run, but her feet were planted solidly on the ground. "I was just thinking."

He sat on the second step. Kaylee should've run and quickly escaped, but his words sent chills down her spine.

"When I first realized you didn't swim at any of the parties, I thought you were networking and didn't want to get wet. Then I'd thought maybe you didn't want to get sunburned, but now I'm not so sure."

Kaylee had never felt more vulnerable. If Kyle thought she was hiding something, he would dig until he unearthed her secret. He would try to convince her to get in the water, but she couldn't let him. Her fear would weigh

195

her down like an anchor, and she would drown. Her heart pounded, and acid exploded in her stomach. Her arms and legs trembled. Kaylee had to get away from the pool.

She stepped back, turned toward the house, and fell to her knees. Kaylee groaned, leaned on one knee, and tried to steady herself.

"Are you hurt?"

"I'm fine."

"Really?" He challenged.

As he lifted her, she could feel his breath on her face. "I lost my balance."

"I saw the terrified look in your eyes, and when you crashed to the ground, I knew. Why didn't you tell me?"

"I—"

"You're afraid—"

"I need to eat."

He squeezed her arm. "Talk to me."

In the past few months, Kaylee's trust in people had diminished. How could she make Kyle understand her fear? The day at the party, she hadn't just almost drowned, which would've been a pivotal moment in any child's life when they realized they were no longer invincible. Still, it had been the day her father's indifference toward her could have killed her. Kaylee had never told anyone, not even her mom, but she blamed her father. He had taken her to the party and promised to watch her. He knew she couldn't swim and was frightened of water. He had gone inside to take a business call, and she had fallen into the pool. That was the first of many times he had let her down.

Kaylee eased her arm from Kyle's grip, and he stared at her encouragingly. She couldn't believe she had agreed to share her feelings, but she had no choice. Baring her soul to Kyle would be far less dangerous than getting into the water. Even now, the thought of retelling the events of her near tragedy would ignite paralyzing anxiety. Still, if

Kaylee could trust anyone, it should be Kyle. But how could he empathize with her situation? He probably didn't understand the complexity of terror and how it dominated one's life.

They sat with crossed legs and faced each other. Kyle's chest and stomach glistened; for a moment, Kaylee fantasized about kissing him. She knew it was terrible timing; he wanted to talk about her aquaphobia, but she started to relive their first kiss and how her body had responded to his. His slow smile indicated he knew what she had been thinking, so she focused on the patio furniture, and as she became engrossed in the backyard layout, he touched her arm and pulled her attention back to him.

"Where do I start," Kaylee asked?

"Wherever you're comfortable."

She drew circles on the wet tile.

"Mom suffered so much at the end; I hated seeing her once vital body fragile and inundated with tubes. I felt as if I was dying, too, and the thought of being alone in this world with my father terrified me. If her twin brother had lived, I probably wouldn't have felt so alone after she passed. I used to imagine spending time with him as a family, enjoying dinners and holidays, and getting to know one another. I saw how much it hurt her to speak of her brother. It broke my heart. After my mom's funeral, my father barely left his office. I know he was grieving too, but when I'd needed him most, he completely bailed."

Kyle squeezed her hand. "I wish I'd been there for you."

"Me too, but you know, the only time Jeff showed me he cared was after Mom died. Whatever else he was, he knew about loss and empathized with me. He's been murdered, and I don't know if I can do this on my own."

"You're not alone."

He leaned in and brushed her lips with his. She reached up and touched his face.

"I wonder if my father showed my mother his tender side. I don't see him as the compassionate type."

"I believe he'll do something that will change your mind about him."

"He can't decide whether or not I'm family. At the police station, when he defended me, I was proud of him, but it must have been an act. After the fire, he didn't even ask about me. Maybe he's not my father."

Maybe Michael couldn't stand the thought of having a weak child, and he considered her weak because of her fear of water. Perhaps she should get a DNA test?

"Michael is your father. If he wasn't, I'd imagine one of his competitors would've found a way to use that information against him. Besides, how could David, a man who had been married to Jeff's mom, be your dad?"

"It does sound weird when you say it out loud. Why does Michael act like he hates me?"

Kyle caressed her palm with his thumb. "He just doesn't know how to be the father you need him to be."

Trying to figure Micheal out exhausted Kaylee.

She steered the conversation toward Kyle, "I've met your mom, and she's great, but tell me more about your family."

"Growing up, we were inseparable, but my parents divorced when I was seventeen—"

"Why didn't you tell me?"

"You were Jeff's girl—"

"We were friends.

"There was nothing you could've done."

Kaylee linked her fingers with his. "I had a shoulder you could've leaned on."

"You were busy with Jeff."

Trying to appease Jeff's never-ending demands had consumed most of her time, and it had never been enough.

"I lost time with my mom; of all the things Jeff took from me, that hurt the most."

Kaylee asked Kyle, "Are you still close to them?"

He stared past her.

"After the divorce, I refused to speak to them. I should've supported them. I'm always disappointing the people I love." Kyle leaned in. "I made a huge mistake by not telling you how I felt. Jeff was my friend, and I chose to be the bigger person and sacrificed what I wanted. And because of me, you were hurt. I won't let anyone hurt you again."

She was taken aback by the forcefulness of his admission. He seemed angry he had chosen to be Jeff's friend and not interfere with their relationship.

"If Jeff were alive, what would you say to him," Kaylee asked?

Kyle tapped the empty water bottle on the tile. "I'd tell him I'm sorry about the accident–that stupid race ended our friendship. And if I'd addressed my feelings for you sooner, the accident and everything that followed wouldn't have happened."

"Declaring your feelings wouldn't have changed anything."

"At least we could've talked it out—"

Kaylee leaned forward. "Do you think he'd tell the truth—how he would use me to get to Michael?"

After learning of Jeff's death, Kaylee had been angry she didn't get the chance to confront him about how he had terrorized her. Jeff had hurt her, and she had wanted to tell him what a monster he was.

"We mishandled our feelings, but Jeff committed crimes and tried to trick me. His goal was to gain access to the Chambers' money. Convincing me to love him would've only boosted his ego. He's the guilty one!"

When she stood, her leg buckled.

"You need to eat," Kyle warned.

199

"My foot's asleep."

"Consider yourself lucky. I'm postponing your swimming lessons until tomorrow."

Kaylee's voice squeaked, "Lessons?"

"I'll go over water safety, treading water, and the basic strokes, and before you know it, you'll be swimming like a fish."

Her stomach turned. "What?"

"You must learn to swim. I didn't wait my entire adult life to be with you just to watch you drown."

"I can't do it." She screeched.

She jumped up. Her foot slid on the wet deck. Kaylee plunged into the pool. She hit the bottom and sucked in water. Her nose and throat burned, and salty water stung her eyes. She flailed, trying to reach the surface. Kaylee was sinking; her limbs felt heavy. She thrashed wildly. Her chest contracted; she couldn't breathe. Her heart felt as if it would burst. Darkness surrounded her.

She lashed out and stuck something hard. Strong fingers gripped her arms and lifted her out of the water.

"I've got you."

Kaylee continued swinging her arms. She gasped for air. Kyle pinned her arms at her side and encouraged her to take deep breaths. After several painful heaves, she could breathe and tried to break free from his grip.

He eased her back into the water until her feet touched the bottom. "We're in three feet. Stand up."

After several agonizing minutes, Kaylee realized her feet were planted firmly on the bottom, and she wasn't going to drown. "Okay, you can let go."

She pushed her hair out of her eyes and wiped water from her face. The soaked t-shirt clung to her curves, and Kaylee remembered she wasn't wearing a bra. She tugged at the shirt, pulling it away from wet skin.

"It's a little late, don't you think?" Kyle grinned.

Her cheeks grew hot.

"You play dirty."

"Are you ready to go in?"

Kaylee nodded, turned to face the stairs, and froze. The water sprayed up around her waist, sprinkling her face with salty water. She remembered how it had burnt her nose and throat. She watched it splash over the steps, forming tiny waves as the pebble tec shimmered in the moonlight. Kaylee wondered how something so beautiful could elicit such terror.

"Just start walking. You'll be fine."

She turned and said, "Apparently, you didn't see me face-plant into the pool."

Kyle chuckled, "I was going to wait until later to critique you, but your form could use some work."

Kaylee couldn't help it. She laughed.

Chapter 20

Jensen rolled over, knocking the alarm clock off the nightstand, but the noise wouldn't stop. He reached for his phone.

"Stone?"

"Yeah, there's been a murder, and you're never going to guess who it is."

Jensen wrote down the address, changed his shirt and tie, and headed out. Based on what Stone had said, he would be in for a long day. He stopped at Dunkin Donuts and bought two large black coffees; if he didn't drink them both before arriving at the crime scene, he would give one to Stone. Jensen thought about how Kaylee couldn't catch a break. Her fiancé had been murdered, most likely by an old classmate; her old man was banging her best friend, and now her Cobra was toast.

He headed to a new housing subdivision in Glendale. The victim had been found slumped over in a driveway on the third block. A barking dog had alerted one of the residents, and when he saw a body, he called nine-one-one.

The typically quiet street buzzed with activity. While Stone, Lopez, and the others had kept the frightened and curious residents back, the crime scene unit had started processing the scene. Jensen parked in front of Stone's car and noticed the coroner hadn't arrived, so he approached the body. It appeared from the amount of blood in the driveway that the victim had been killed there. The first officer on the scene had noted the condition of the body and had taken preliminary photographs. Once the paramedics arrived, they pronounced him dead. Jensen knelt by the body, making sure not to step in the blood. Jensen noticed a distinctive scar above the man's left eye. He remembered the description Kaylee had given him.

Jensen leaned closer. Could he be looking into the face of Jeff Swanson?

After years on the force, Jensen had learned to trust his gut, no matter what direction it led him. Although he believed David Swanson had an ulterior motive, he trusted the stepdad's intuition. He waved over Stone and asked her to call Judge Bromin at nine and get an order to exhume the body in Swanson's grave.

Jensen walked around the parked Mustang. "Is this Miss Chambers' car?"

"It matches the description she gave Housner," Stone replied. She jotted down the VIN and called it in. "The M.E.'s here."

Jensen nodded and went to speak with the coroner, who determined the preliminary time of death: between seven and midnight. Due to one fatal laceration to the throat, COD was either exsanguination or asphyxia. The coroner would know more after the autopsy. She told Jensen that a sharp, single-bladed instrument had caused the fatal wound. Again, she would know more after the post-mortem examination. Jensen watched as the victim was lifted onto a stretcher, loaded into the van, and taken away.

He walked around the car again. "Stone, did anyone find the license plate?"

"Mills was the first on the scene, and he recorded it as missing, but I'll check and see if it turned up."

Jensen walked across the street and spoke to the man who'd called nine-one-one. The witness verified that he had arrived home around nine and had dinner. At eleven thirty, his dog had started barking, so he took him for a walk. As the witness approached the end of the street, he saw a man in the driveway in a pool of blood. He took his dog home and called the police.

The witness stated he had seen the dead man hanging around for a few weeks, but hadn't seen the

Mustang before. He told Jensen that the deceased had been driving an older white truck. When asked if the victim had been staying at the house, the witness didn't know. Jensen asked a few more questions, verified the witness's contact information, and suggested he get some sleep. Jensen instructed Stone to meet him at the precinct at five.

Even though Jensen had entertained the notion that Jeff Swanson might have faked his own death, he would have to prove it. He didn't have to now, but he did have to find out who was buried in Swanson's grave. Jensen would bet on Charles Pierce.

At the precinct, Jensen powered on his computer and made a fresh pot of coffee. He inhaled a few times, savoring the richness. Most mornings, the smell got him going until he could down a few cups. Since the next twenty-four hours would be vital to the investigation, he anticipated drinking copious amounts of the hot beverage.

Jealousy and revenge were strong motives. Swanson's recent and final demise opened up a gamut of new ones. Kaylee had the strongest motive to kill Jeff: to keep her ex-fiancé dead. With him gone, she would be safe and free to be with the man she loved, and if she found out he was still alive and had stolen her car, she might have, in an act of revenge, slashed his throat.

Jensen dismissed Greg Goldman; he didn't have the fortitude to do anything. He hid in the shadows, lurking around, and couldn't seal the deal. It would take extraordinary measures to provoke him to commit murder; Jensen refused to waste time on him. If he needed anything from the insipid attorney, he would send Stone.

Kyle's devotion to Kaylee took precedence over everything. And now that he knew Jeff had abused her, maybe he decided to end it once and for all. He had money and a strong constitution. Jensen had witnessed his controlled fury. He had no doubt Kyle could do what needed to be done to protect the woman he loved. The more he thought about it, the longer the list became.

David Swanson had despised his stepson, but for reasons unclear to Jensen. Jeff had been a kid at the time. What had Jeff done to earn the disdain of his stepfather? Did David hunt Jeff down to make sure he stayed dead? David had left Arizona several years ago and hadn't returned until now. Did he return only to rifle through his stepson's grave and frighten Kaylee? What was his connection to her? Kaylee held fast to her theory that David might be her biological father. Stone had put an APB out on him, and if they were lucky, he would be back at the precinct in no time.

The egotistical Michael Chambers was a shrewd businessman, but did he care enough about his daughter to take out her tormentor? Or did he kill Jeff to rid his family of the Swanson plague? What about his lover, Sara Hill, whom Jeff had blackmailed? Since Miss Hill's secret had come out, the blackmail angle didn't apply. Perhaps she wanted revenge against Jeff because he had ruined her reputation and friendship with Kaylee.

The game-changer would be proving that they knew Jeff was alive. As far as he could tell, except for the stepdad, who only suspected Jeff might still be alive, only Jeff's alleged, elusive mistress knew.

If Jeff's lover thought he still had feelings for Kaylee, she might've turned on him. Jensen only had a vague description and didn't know if the red-headed woman was Jeff's lover. Stone had called Bridget to find out the woman's name, but Bridget had refused to give it to her; she would only speak to Jensen.

Jensen knew he had screwed up. When Bridget called to get information about the plate, he yelled at her and told her to stay out of his investigation. She had called him an ass and hung up. He regretted his tone, but Kaylee had to be stopped. Her interference could jeopardize her safety and her life.

Jensen knew he would have to bite the bullet and call. Bridget would make him apologize and probably call him an ass again, but if he could get the name he needed, it would be worth it. He sent Blanchard an email notifying him of his intentions to contact his ex-girlfriend regarding the name of the victim's alleged lover.

While he waited for approvals and warrants, Jensen used his time to conduct searches and request more information. Someone had brazenly murdered Jeff, and he wondered if the killer would stop or if they would take revenge against them all.

Stone called to tell Jensen that Judge Bromin had refused to grant the exhumation until the body had been positively identified as Jeff Swanson and the VIN on the Mustang at the crime scene matched the VIN on Kaylee's car. Jensen had thought getting the order to exhume the body had been a slam dunk, but the judge must be friends with Michael Chambers and was playing it safe. He called Kaylee and notified her that they'd found her car, but the car thief had been killed, and he needed her to go to the morgue to see if she could identify him.

Jensen called the coroner to notify her that the victim's family would be there soon to ID the body. He received an email: Blanched approved him to call his ex. Bridget wasn't a morning person; he would call later. Jensen was already on her shit list.

*****

Jensen waited for the grief counselor to arrive. Most people don't do well at the morgue, but he expected this to be particularly distressing for Kaylee. She probably expected to see a stranger, but would be confronted with her ex-fiancé instead. Jensen had briefed the counselor that

206

the family didn't know they would be identifying a loved one, and he didn't generally do it this way, but this was the exception to the rule. The counselor advised him that he might be doing serious emotional harm and vehemently opposed not telling them.

Kaylee and Kyle arrived, and Jensen guided them, along with the counselor, to the identification room. After introductions, Jensen warned them that the car thief might be someone close to them. The counselor went over the procedure, instructed them to take their time, and said they could stop for any reason. She waited in the lobby in case they had any questions.

Jensen informed them that the deceased would be covered with a blue sheet, and the injury to his throat would be disturbing to see. He slid the picture toward them and said they could view it for as long as needed.

Kyle's hand hovered over the picture. "Are you ready?"

"Turn it over," Kaylee insisted.

Kyle flipped it over.

"What kind of sick joke are you trying to pull off? You said the guy in the morgue was the one who stole Kaylee's car." Kyle argued.

"Can you tell me the name of the man in the picture," Jensen asked?

"It's Jeff, but you don't really expect me to believe he stole my car. He's dead."

Jensen slid over another overturned picture. "Miss Chambers, can you identify the second picture?"

Kaylee grabbed it, turned it over, and stared. "I don't understand. Why am I being shown this picture again? I saw it months ago after Jeff fell."

"Why did you identify him back then?" Jensen asked.

"The picture was grotesque and hard to look at. They told me Jeff had his wallet with him, so I figured it was him."

"Who told you they found his wallet?"

"The counselor and his assistant; I don't remember their names."

"If you were to identify the person in the old photo now, would you say it's Jeff?"

"The old picture resembles Jeff, but there had been so much damage to his face. I can't be sure. What's going on—do you think the old picture isn't Jeff, but the new one is?"

"I'm afraid so. I don't know who's buried in his grave, but Jeff Swanson was definitely murdered last night."

Kyle tapped the picture of Jeff. "Murdered last night?"

"I believe Mr. Swanson faked his own death to stalk Miss Chambers, but someone must have found out and stopped him."

"I want to see him," Kaylee blurted out.

"It's not a good idea," Jensen advised.

"I was fooled once. I'm not going to let that happen again."

"Viewing someone you know in this condition can be extremely traumatic."

"Have you seen this?" She pointed to the old photo. "It's disgusting, and yet this is what they showed me. I can handle it. I would like to see him, and if I don't, I won't confirm it's Jeff."

Jensen escorted them down the hall. He knocked, went in alone, and spoke with the coroner. Jensen let them in, and the coroner pulled back the sheet, exposing the deceased's head and shoulders.

Jensen stepped back to give Kaylee room; she moved forward. He watched her consider the lifeless body and run one finger across the scar above his left eye. The wound on the deceased's throat didn't seem to faze her. He wondered why?

Kaylee continued examining the body. She paid close attention to a marking on the left shoulder and leaned closer to study it. "What's this?"

"It's a tattoo," the coroner noted, "and it appears fairly new."

"I never saw this. How new," Kaylee asked?

"Most of the dead skin had sloughed off, but I detected a minute area that's still scabbed. I'd say it was done about three weeks ago. It appears to be a list, possibly initials."

She took a closer look. "The first few letters could stand for Manara Thompson, Sara Hill, Bridget Carter, Stephanie Ortiz. K.C. could be mine, but I don't know anyone with the initials of W.T."

"You're positive this is Mr. Swanson?" Jensen asked?

Kaylee nodded. "It's him. I recognize the scar above his left eye. Do you think the letters represent the women Jeff wanted to date? Could W.T. be his lover?"

"Could be," Jensen replied. "I wonder how many of these women had sex with him."

"I didn't, but Stephanie did. I'm sure Bridget and Manara didn't sleep with him, and Sara was too busy screwing with my father." She pulled the sheet over Jeff's face and returned to the identification room.

Jensen and Kyle joined her. Kaylee looked up when they entered.

"Miss Chambers, are you all right?"

She massaged her temple.

"If you need to speak to the counselor, she's just outside the door."

"I'm fine."

"If you're sure—"

209

"Yes!"

"Jeff's death, his real one, has steered this investigation into a new direction, and I have more questions."

"I want answers, too. Have you found out how Jeff faked his death? What about David Swanson? Have you found him?" Kaylee asked.

"Until last night, no one but the killer knew Jeff was alive." Jensen surmised.

"Where's my car?"

"Your car is evidence; after we examine it, we might get some answers."

"His mistress could've killed him. Do you have any leads for her?" Kaylee asked.

"No—"

"Bridget can find out who she is. Just call her." Kaylee pulled out her phone and dialed. "Hey, it's Kaylee. Sorry to wake you, but Detective Jensen wants to talk to you." She handed Jensen her phone.

Jensen cleared his throat. He wasn't prepared to speak with her yet. "Bridget, I'm sorry to disturb you."

"What's going on, Randy?"

"I need the name of Cory's ex-girlfriend—the redhead."

"Why?"

"This is extremely important. What's her name?"

"It's Wendy Torrison; she's a nurse at one of the big hospitals, but I can't remember which one."

He hesitated. "We'll talk soon." Jensen handed Kaylee her phone.

"What did she say," Kyle asked?

"She said Cory's ex was a woman named Wendy Torrison. Do you know her?"

"It's the last set of initials from Jeff's tattoo," Kaylee stated.

"Are you sure the rest of them didn't sleep with him?"

"Except for Sara, I am one hundred percent positive. Do you really think Bridget would sleep with him?"

Jensen's stomach tightened at the thought. There was no way in hell Bridget would sleep with that womanizing psycho. "This may not be an appropriate time to give you this, but I did say I would look into it." Jensen handed her a card.

She read it and slid it into her purse.

"What is it," Kyle asked?

"It's the contact information for the state's leading DNA expert," Jensen stated.

"You're encouraging the ridiculous idea that Michael isn't her father?"

"Kaylee is the one who stated she believed she has a biological connection to David Swanson, and if there is a connection, and it affects the case, it is pertinent."

"She's being misled, and you know it."

"After seeing David, I believe they may be related."

"You saw him," Kaylee asked?

"He was questioned regarding another matter; I noticed something familiar about him but couldn't pinpoint it until you mentioned it."

"You let him go? What if he killed Jeff?" Kyle asked.

"He posted bail. We couldn't hold him any longer."

"Why were you questioning him," Kaylee asked?

Jensen had hoped to postpone the release of this information until he knew Jeff's stepfather's whereabouts. Still, he might be able to elicit genuine reactions and determine if either knew Jeff was alive.

"David was apprehended while desecrating his stepson's grave."

Kyle didn't blink or react. Instead, Jensen turned toward Kaylee when she blurted out her question.

"Why?"

"Kyle, can you answer her question?"

"How would I know?"

"Do you have any information regarding the defiling of Jeff Swanson's grave?"

"I don't know why he, or anyone else, would do that." Kyle snapped.

Jensen wondered what Kyle knew about the vandalism of Jeff's grave. "Maybe David thought he was alive and wanted to prove it?"

"You'll have to ask him."

"Kaylee seemed visibly surprised by the news, but not you. You didn't react at all."

"It's not in my nature to assume," Kyle stated curtly.

"Still, you aren't curious why he'd drive over a thousand miles just to dig up a grave?"

Kyle shrugged. "Maybe he's crazy?"

"Why are you drilling, Kyle? He doesn't know anything about this." She turned to him. "Do you?"

"Not specifically."

"What do you mean?" Kaylee asked.

"Rumors were going around that someone had seen Jeff after the date of his fall, but no one could corroborate his story, so your father squashed the rumors."

"Kyle, if you had shared this information with me, I could have interviewed the man to determine if he was telling the truth. Maybe if you did, Jeff wouldn't be dead."

Kaylee snatched her purse off the table and rushed out of the room.

"I didn't tell you because the man is a gambler and a liar. It wasn't a viable lead, or I would have told you. Your insinuation that Jeff's death was my fault was a cheap shot."

Chapter 21

Jensen returned to the morgue and spoke to the coroner. She informed him that it wasn't unusual for family members to misidentify a body. Jensen agreed, but by stating that Jeff's personal effects were found at the scene, someone had purposely led her to believe Jeff had died. Kaylee had no choice but to identify the body as her fiancé, and it saved her from the grim task of thoroughly examining the photo.

Now that Jensen had a positive ID on the victim, he could get the exhumation order for Jeff's grave and get a search warrant for the funeral director's properties. Jensen called Stone to have her retrieve the warrant, put an APB out on the director, and have the CSU team meet him at Heaven Star's funeral home.

Jensen weaved in and out of the lanes as he rushed to the funeral home. He wanted to surprise the director so he wouldn't have time to destroy evidence or bolt again. If the funeral director and Jeff were involved in fraud or identity theft, that could explain the large deposits in Jeff's accounts and could be the reason he faked his own death. But why kill Jeff now? Did he cross the line by stealing Kaylee's car, making him a liability?

He exited the 101, and as he drove down the access road, Jensen noticed two patrol cars at the funeral home's entrance. He parked by Stone's car; she was at the entrance speaking with the receptionist. Jensen approached and pulled her aside.

"What happened?" Jensen asked.

"Two employees arrived early and walked in on the director packing customer files. When he saw them, he grabbed some files, knocked the male employee to the ground, and ran. The receptionist called nine-one-one."

"Do they know which files he took?"

"The receptionist said it looked like the director only took his private ones. She thinks they're personal finance information; she never saw them, so it's only a guess."

"I need to speak to each of them; I'll talk to the male employee first. Watch for the CSU van, and keep everyone out of the office."

After speaking with employees, Jensen felt confident they weren't involved with whatever scam the funeral director had been perpetrating. The male employee, the mortuary cosmetologist, had no contact with the families or access to any documents. The receptionist helped customers make funeral arrangements and handled all payments, but she didn't have access to the director's private filing cabinet. She assumed it was his personal stuff and hadn't wanted to keep it at home. Both employees mentioned that the director had been nervous, even paranoid, for the past few weeks, but didn't know why.

The makeup artist had told Jensen he had always done the cosmetic work on all the deceased, but a couple of months ago, the director had insisted on handling a special case. Jensen pressed the issue, but the employee knew nothing about the body or how it came to the funeral home. Jensen asked about the key players in the investigation, and neither seemed to know nor have had dealings with them. Jensen got their contact information and let them go home.

Jensen instructed Stone to go with the CSU team to search the director's home and vehicles, then meet him back at the precinct.

*****

At the precinct, Jensen received a call about the DNA results from the baseball cap Kaylee had brought in. It matched David Swanson's. Did David follow his stepson's ex-fiancée while plotting revenge against her old

214

man for ruining his business and running him out of town? During the interview, David referred to Michael Chambers as the devil. Perhaps he felt it necessary to cleanse Kaylee of her father's sins. Jensen conceded David's behavior was bizarre–he had dug up a grave–but did that prove he had a mental defect?

Jensen spoke to Wendy Torrison's supervisor, Maggie Brown. She confirmed Wendy had worked three back-to-back twelve-hour shifts, from 6 p.m. to 6 a.m., starting on the day of Jeff's actual murder. Maggie said that Wendy worked in the NICU, which was tightly locked down, so it would be almost impossible for her to leave and return undetected.

Maggie told Jensen that Wendy was an excellent nurse who enjoyed her job and loved the babies and their mothers. However, recently, Wendy came in late and picked fights with the other nurses. The nursing supervisor had been about to fire Wendy, but she had straightened up and kept her job.

Jensen searched Wendy's social media accounts. She had an apparent affinity for expensive jewelry. Wendy would post all her new pieces. Her friends asked about the jewelry, and Wendy said that her new boyfriend had given it to her. Jensen couldn't find a single post from her alleged boyfriend, and he wasn't the only one to notice. A few of her friends begged to see his picture, but she had refused. When her friends gave her a hard time, Wendy would post snarky comments about them being jealous or haters. Her friend count plummeted. Unable to reach any of Wendy's friends, Jensen had left messages asking them to call him back.

Jensen ran a background check and confirmed that even though Wendy made a good salary, she couldn't afford the high-end jewelry she owned. Having expensive taste and red hair didn't prove she had been Jeff's mistress. It probably meant she had dated someone who had money.

Despite her healthy income, her credit cards were maxed and overdue. She had defaulted on a previous car loan, and due to bad credit, Jensen guessed he wouldn't find a lender who'd give her a car loan, and he was right. Her supervisor had seen her drive a red Lexus but had been told it wasn't Wendy's. Jensen located her Scottsdale apartment and planned to drop by later, unannounced.

Detective Housner called to confirm the fire had been arson. Jensen didn't have time to discuss whose car had gone up in smoke, so he thanked Housner for the information. Since Stone hadn't called, he figured the search was going well. He knew the real work would start once the evidence arrived at the lab.

Jensen received a call from Lopez, who verified that the cemetery owner, Roger Goldman, and Greg Goldman were related and that Roger and the funeral home director had been friends since college. If Roger participated in the scam, maybe Greg did too. Jensen had a feeling Greg was guilty, but of what?

Bridget called to notify Jensen that Kyle had picked up Kaylee from her house. Jensen had been preoccupied at the morgue, but had wondered where Kaylee had gone. Jensen hoped Bridget would forgive him for yelling at her and putting a damper on her workout schedule. Jensen knew Bridget wouldn't receive his next question well; she would be infuriated, and rightly so, but he had no choice.

"Bridget, you know I'm in the middle of an important investigation, and I wouldn't ask if it wasn't relevant." Jensen paused, not wanting to insult or anger her. "I already know the answer, but I have to ask. It's my job." He braced himself. "Have you ever dated or had sex with Jeff Swanson?"

It went quiet; Jensen hadn't heard a click; he guessed she was still on the line.

"You have some nerve—" Bridget snapped.

"So…your answer is no?"

"What's wrong with you?" She huffed. "Are you serious? Sleep with Jeff?"

Jensen imagined smoke fuming out of her head, her eyes turning a fiery red, and murderous thoughts of him dying a painful death over and over.

"I had to ask. This is a murder investigation."

An awkward and uncomfortable silence loomed.

"Your interview skills need some work. You owe me," Bridget paused. "Dinner at our old hangout."

"When I've made an arrest, I'll call you and set up a time—"

"We'll do it tonight."

*****

While Jensen waited for Bridget to arrive, he considered the significance of Jeff's tattoo. All but one of the women represented had rejected him. Perhaps Jeff tattooed their initials on his body to link them to him forever. Knowing the women would be freaked out by that might've satisfied his need for the perverse.

Jensen glanced around the café. The red benches intensified the grey of the chairs and brightened the room. The metal drop lights illuminated the table with a soft glow. It was where he and Bridget had had their first date. They'd loved to hike and would stop at the nearest café or restaurant when they were done, but this was where they had had their first sit-down, dress-up date.

He had chosen it because of its proximity to work and had been fortunate that it was a place he liked. He always ordered the New York Strip, and Bridget would get sushi or the kale and quinoa salad. The stunning view from the patio included Camelback Mountain. Still, he never really had time to enjoy it, and tonight would be no exception.

Jensen met Bridget on a hiking trail, and they had dated for three years, but Jensen hadn't seen her in over a year. After they broke up, making time for their friendship had been even more difficult. Bridget refused to tolerate his demanding schedule, and their relationship dwindled. He missed hiking with her; the regular exercise helped reduce his stress, and he missed exploring the mountains.

He hiked the same trails without her and ran into her friends. He awkwardly tried to explain why they broke up, but couldn't find a good reason. It had been Jensen's career. The long nights, the canceled dates, and leaving at a moment's notice were par for the course for him. The woman he dated had to accept those terms, or the relationship would end, and it had.

He checked his watch. As he pulled out his phone to call Bridget, she slid onto the bench. Her shoulder-length hair framed her oval face, emphasizing full lips and green eyes.

"Hello, Randy."

He looked up; her eyes twinkled. Damn, he missed her.

"I appreciate your help earlier, but I don't have much time."

She wore green, his favorite color. He smiled.

"You have to eat."

"True, but I could've eaten at the precinct while I worked." Jensen opened the menu.

"I called in our order so we'd have more time to talk. Besides, you can't live off of vending machine food."

"I agreed to meet with you tonight because I'm grateful for your help, but I don't have time to socialize; I have a homicide to solve." Randy looked up at the server.

The waitress said hello, warned them the plates were hot, and asked if they needed anything else. Jensen ordered another tea.

"Hearing your voice again stirred up memories, and I wanted to let you know that I feel guilty about our last night together. You have an important job; I should've been more patient. I guess what I'm trying to say is I miss you."

Jensen put his fork down. "What?"

"I want to try again."

The hint of butter and the spicy rub exploded on his tongue. Jensen didn't have much time; he was always one call away from an emergency, but wanted to savor this. He took several more bites and washed them down with the tea.

"I don't even have time for myself right now."

Bridget paused. "Once you solve this case, we can talk in-depth."

"There will always be another case and another and another."

Bridget smiled, "You should eat. You never know when duty will call."

Jensen cut up the last few pieces of his steak. "You haven't eaten much; are you feeling okay?"

"I weighed in this morning at my Zumba class. It wasn't pretty. Kaylee only stayed at my house for an hour and consumed more chocolate than I've had all year. And I'm the one gaining weight."

"How often do you work out," Jensen asked?

"I take Zumba three times a week; I've been going consistently for the past year."

"Don't get mad, but I'm going to break a cardinal rule. Okay?"

"Well," Bridget smiled. "This *is* a first."

"Ms. Ortiz, your Zumba instructor, is a person of interest in the Swanson case. I know this will throw a wrench into your workout, but I suggest you find another class until the investigation is closed."

Bridget set her glass down. "Why?"

"She knows I'm in charge of the case; I don't want her taking advantage of you. Worst-case scenario, I don't want her to hurt or use you as leverage against me."

She leaned forward, "She's dangerous?"

"Could be."

"Kaylee's life must be complicated right now."

"It would be fair to say she's been through the wringer."

Jensen's phone rang. He ignored it.

Bridget arched her brow, "Wow, another first. You didn't take a call from work."

"Just because I get a call doesn't mean it's work."

"It's always work."

His phone rang again.

"You'd better answer."

"Jensen."

"It's Stone. Get down to the trauma center at Scottsdale Osborn. Michael Chambers was attacked and isn't expected to make it."

"Damn. I'll call Miss Chambers, and I'm on my way."

"Is Kaylee okay? Is she hurt?" Bridget asked.

"It's about the case, I can't comment."

"But—"

"I have to go."

Bridget's shoulders slumped.

He could see the disappointment on her face. He was also entitled to a personal life, and sometimes, he resented giving it up.

"It's an emergency."

"It always is," Bridget said reluctantly.

"I want to be here with you. I miss you too, but you knew this could happen," Jensen leaned forward. "Hell, I knew it probably would happen, but if you want to try again, and I do, we both have to compromise. My job will always require sacrifice. Are you willing to do whatever it takes to make it work?"

Bridget shook her head. "How can we have a relationship if you're called away every time we get together?"

Jensen put his napkin on his plate and stood. "Bridget, you have to decide, once and for all, whether you support me and my career. Otherwise, tonight was a waste of time. I have to go." He brushed her lips with his and rushed to his car.

Jensen raced down the freeway; he phoned Kaylee and instructed her to meet him at the hospital. He hoped her old man would make it.

Chapter 22

Kaylee gripped the armrest in Kyle's car. Her throat constricted. Her mind raced with a dozen worst-case scenarios. Detective Jensen had been vague, but she could tell by the urgency in his voice that something horrible had happened. Did her father have a heart attack? Did he finally wreck his BMW? She wondered how badly he had been hurt and why Detective Jensen had been the one to call.

During rush hour on the 101, traffic moved at a snail's pace. Kyle exited the highway and took the side streets until he passed the jam. With each passing minute, Kaylee's heart pounded painfully in her chest. Michael was the only family she had left.

Finally, Kyle veered off the freeway again and pulled into the hospital lot. Kaylee leaped out of the car and ran straight for the emergency entrance. Her shoe fell to the floor, and she scrambled to put it on. What if her father had been fatally wounded? What would she do without him? She never had the chance to win his love or show him how much she needed him. She couldn't lose him, too.

She hurried to the information desk and was directed to the trauma unit. When the elevator door opened, she rushed to the nurse's station.

"'I'm Michael Chambers' daughter. I need to talk to someone about my father."

"He's in surgery," the nurse replied.

"What happened? How bad is it?"

"I don't have any information right now. Miss Chambers, please wait here."

The desk nurse rushed over to a nurse coming out of the OR.

Kaylee followed and asked the surgical nurse. "How's my father, Michael Chambers?"

The nurse brushed past, "Not now, Miss."

The surgical nurse stopped at the station, "We need more O negative."

"The MVA drained us. We're out." The desk nurse replied.

"Find some. Now!"

She rushed up to the desk. "I'm his daughter," Kaylee said. "I'm O negative."

The nurse looked her up and down. "Do you weigh more than 110 pounds, and are you in good health? Have you eaten recently?"

Kaylee's weight fluctuated constantly, but she was in good health. Had she eaten today? She hesitated. "Yes."

"Get her to the lab." The surgical nurse ordered.

The floor nurse took Kaylee down to the lab for the blood draw.

Her mind reeled. Kaylee had never given blood before–needles made her queasy. Growing up, getting shots had always filled her with anxiety and dread.

The nurse directed her to sit and recline the chair.

Kaylee's stomach churned. Her arms trembled. She could do this. Her father's life depended on it.

The nurse tied her right arm tightly and thumped the vein. She swabbed Kaylee's inner elbow with an antiseptic.

Kaylee turned away and took a couple of deep breaths. It stung as the needle pricked her skin. She winced and closed her eyes.

"You're doing fine, Miss, just relax. This only takes about ten minutes."

Each minute ticked by slowly. Kaylee felt a slight tugging where the needle was, and she believed she could feel the blood being extracted from her veins. The surgical nurse had demanded more blood; it sounded critical. Would her father still be alive in ten minutes?

Kaylee kept her eyes averted from the needle and the blood. She couldn't pass out, not now. She wanted to be waiting for her father when he came out of surgery. Kaylee started to feel light-headed, and her arms and legs went limp. Had she remembered to eat? It didn't matter. Helping Michael gave her purpose.

As a young adult, Kaylee had wondered to what extent she would go to help her father, and now she knew. If she needed him, would he be there for her?

Kaylee heard the nurse speaking, so she opened her eyes. Detective Jensen and Kyle tried to enter the room, but the nurse refused.

"How is he?" Kaylee asked?

"Your father lost a lot of blood," Jensen replied

"What happened?"

"Let's concentrate on helping him get better."

"I can give more. Michael needs more."

"I'm sorry, Miss. You need a break to replenish," The nurse insisted.

"Just one more pint. Don't let him die."

"Kaylee—" Kyle urged.

"Kyle, help me save my father."

"I'll be back in a few minutes." Kyle rushed out of the room.

Jensen moved closer. "Miss Chambers, endangering your health won't help."

"Detective, if your father were on his deathbed, wouldn't you do everything humanly possible to save him? If I get dizzy or even if I puke my guts out, I will do whatever it takes to save him."

Kyle pushed open the door. "Detective, Commander Blanchard is waiting for you at the nurse's station."

"Were you able to get approval for her to donate more blood," Jensen asked?

"The nurse feels Kaylee is a little underweight, but has agreed to let her donate one more pint. She is being transferred to the ICU, where she can be monitored."

Kaylee rested her head on the pillow.

Jensen hurried to meet Blanchard and ran into Stone.

"How the hell did this happen," Jensen asked?

"After responding to a stabbing in the Chambers' building parking lot, I found Mr. Chambers hunched over his car. He sustained several stab wounds to the chest and stomach; it appears that an artery was cut. He's lost a ton of blood."

"Did you canvas for witnesses?"

"I rode in the ambulance but left Lopez and Harrelson to canvas. Lopez called to tell me the CSU team had arrived."

Jensen ran his fingers through his hair and wondered if Chambers would make it and, if he didn't, if his daughter would survive. His phone rang.

Blanchard wanted to know Jensen's ETA and cautioned him to keep the media away from the hospital. Jensen sent Stone to monitor the entrance and notify the staff to keep all news personnel away from the family, warning them not to disclose any information under any circumstances.

The thought of this turning into a media circus filled Jensen with déjà vu. It was a horrible feeling, one that stuck to his insides. Since the case had been reopened, he had done everything he could to rebuild the confidence his commander once had in him. The media fiasco from Swanson's first murder investigation weighed heavily on his mind. Jensen felt that the out-of-control coverage of the first investigation, coupled with Mr. Chambers's intervention, led to a breakdown in procedure.

This time, the stakes were higher. Mr. Chambers was the victim, not the one calling the shots.

Lopez called to notify Jensen that the team had finished collecting evidence and processing the scene.

Based on the blood spatter, it seemed most of the fight occurred at the front driver's side of the vehicle. Chambers might have been getting back in his car when the assailant first attacked.

Jensen approached the nurse's desk. "Commander."

"What's his condition," Blanchard asked?

"Critical."

"What happened?"

"All we know right now is that Chambers was attacked on a side street behind his office. He fought back, but one of the blows cut an artery, and he went down."

"Did he have a meeting, or do we know why Chambers would park on the street?"

"Masters contacted Chambers' secretary; she's returning to the office to check his appointment book."

"Have Lopez meet her. I want her to check the appointment book and then get out. Call Judge Bromin, get a warrant, and have the CSU team return and tear the office apart. I have a few uncomfortable phone calls to make. I'll be at the office; call when you have an update." Blanchard instructed.

Jensen knew the news of Chambers' attack would guarantee an immediate warrant. Why was Chambers found behind his office and not in the parking garage? His job just got harder. He would have to protect Chambers and his daughter and keep the investigation rolling. Not an easy task. A murderer was on the loose, and if Chambers died, there could be two murderers on the run.

Jensen took the elevator to the first floor. He noticed Sara Hill sitting by the cafeteria window, hunched over a Formica table. He bought two coffees and handed her one.

"Miss Hill, did Detective Stone explain why I asked you here?"

"She told me Michael had been hurt, and you needed some information."

226

"That's correct. Do you know why Mr. Chambers was in the private alley behind his office?"

"He had a meeting, and it had been delayed, but he didn't tell me where."

"Who was he meeting?"

"Michael told me a woman named Wendy Toricksen, or something like that, had called him and wanted to meet.

"Wendy Torrison?

"Maybe."

"Had he done business with her before?"

"No, but she convinced him she knew who wanted to hurt Kaylee, and for a price, she would tell him where to find him."

"When did he arrange this meeting?"

"A couple of days ago. Michael wanted to check out her story, so he told her he couldn't meet until tonight."

"Do you know if he found out anything?"

"He just said he'd handle it. How is he?"

Sara looked worried and seemed to care about Chambers. She probably deserved an answer.

Jensen paused for a moment. "Sorry, I can only discuss his condition with family."

Chapter 23

The door to the interrogation room opened, and Jensen walked in. Wendy Torrison's lips curved up seductively as she lowered her lashes. He took a seat opposite her.

After Lopez had confirmed Mr. Chambers had scheduled a meeting with Miss Torrison, Jensen had put out an APB. They'd been lucky and had picked her up at her Scottsdale apartment.

"Ms. Torrison—"

"Wendy."

"Okay–Wendy, have you been read your rights, and do you understand them?"

"Yes."

"You are refusing an attorney, is that correct?"

"Yes."

"Ms. Torrison–Wendy, do you know Miss Kaylee Chambers?"

"No."

"You never met or bumped into her at a party?"

She twirled her red hair with her index finger. "I guess I may have. A year ago, she attended a birthday party for my boyfriend."

"Have you seen her since then?"

"No, I stopped seeing him."

"What is your ex-boyfriend's name?"

"Cory Carter."

"You dated Eric Carter's son?"

Jensen already knew that she dated Cory, and he didn't get worked up about most things, but the thought of a potential stalker and murderer dating Bridget's brother, Cory, troubled him. If Wendy could get to Cory, then she could get to Bridget.

"Why did you break up?"

"His bitchy sister didn't think I was good enough for him."

Jensen's lips thinned. Bridget's instincts were spot on. Getting Wendy out of Cory's life probably saved his life.

"When did you stop seeing Mr. Carter?"

"If you mean Cory, Eric is Mr. Carter, about eight months ago."

"Did you find a new boyfriend right away?"

"What difference does it make who I date?"

"I want to know if you ever met a Mr. Jeff Swanson."

"No."

"You never met or had a professional or personal relationship with him?"

"No."

"Maybe he didn't use his real name. He had blond hair and green eyes. He stood about six feet tall, medium build, and had a long, thin scar over his left eye."

"No."

"Are you sure?"

"Yes."

Jensen took a deep breath. "Do you know a Mr. Greg Goldman?"

She paused. "No."

"It appeared as if you recognized the name. He's a lawyer. Have you ever been to his office?"

She batted her lashes. "Why would I need a lawyer?"

Jensen knew the key to any good interrogation was pacing–keep the questions coming hard and fast and see if the perpetrator trips up. "Do you know a Miss Sara Hill?"

"Who is she?

"She is Miss Chambers' friend. Have you ever seen her or had any contact with her?"

229

"I don't hang out with Miss Chambers or her friends."

"Tell me how you know Mr. Michael Chambers."

"I don't." Wendy's sigh echoed throughout the room.

"Am I boring you," Jensen asked?

"I'm tired of answering the same questions over and over. I don't know the Chambers or any of their friends."

"Mr. Chambers was found stabbed near his office, and we found the alleged weapon covered in his blood in your apartment. Can you explain that?"

"Someone planted it."

"Why would someone break into your apartment and plant evidence?" Jensen asked?

"I leave my door unlocked all the time. Whoever came in didn't have to break in."

"Aren't you afraid of being the victim of a crime?"

"I wasn't until I found out someone put a bloody knife in my kitchen." She snickered.

Jensen wondered why she wouldn't lock her door unless she knew she was more dangerous than anyone trying to break in.

"I came from a small town where leaving your house unlocked is safe. When I moved to the big city, I should have known it would be different."

"Have you ever had anyone break in or come in uninvited?"

"People are always coming and going."

"Where were you last night between five and ten p.m.?"

"I wasn't feeling well, so I called my supervisor about three to say I wouldn't be in. I was home all night."

Jensen's stern gaze challenged her. "I called your supervisor, and she said you were off until Saturday. Try again."

Wendy scowled. "I took some medicine and went to sleep. I passed out cold until your men dragged me out of bed."

"Can anyone verify that?"

"I guess not." Her eyelashes fluttered.

"No one, a neighbor, a friend, or a boyfriend, can corroborate your story?"

"I was alone."

"Have you ever seen the alleged murder weapon before?"

"No."

"If you are not connected with Mr. Chambers or his daughter, why would someone plant the alleged murder weapon in your apartment?"

"How would I know?"

"The chances of this being totally random are microscopically improbable."

"So, what?" Wendy brushed a wayward strand out of her eyes.

"Are you claiming you never met Mr. Chambers, Mr. Jeff Swanson, or anyone connected to this case?"

"Yes."

"Wendy, what would you say if I told you I know you had an appointment to meet with Mr. Chambers last night at six–the same time his attacker brutally stabbed him?"

"I'd say you're mistaken."

"You were trying to extort money from him, and when he refused to pay, you viciously stabbed him."

"Why would I try to get money from him?"

"You dated his daughter's fiancé and caused them to break up. After Mr. Swanson faked his death and you realized he still wanted Miss Chambers, you were going to hand him over to Mr. Chambers on a silver platter, expecting the biggest payout of your life. But you didn't know Mr. Chambers doesn't give in to or pay extortionists.

You lost, so you stabbed him and stabbed him and stabbed him!"

"No! I've never met him."

"Bull!" Jensen slammed his fist on the table. "Do you think a jury is going to believe you?"

Jensen picked up the file and banged the door shut.

He couldn't take any more of her lies. Jensen knew Wendy had met with Mr. Chambers and brutally attacked him. The weapon had been found in her apartment, Chambers' records indicated he was scheduled to meet her, and she had a motive: money and revenge.

Something nagged at him. Why would Wendy make an appointment in her name, and why would she keep the knife? She wasn't stupid; she worked in a highly specialized field, and Jensen surmised her flirtatious behavior was just an act, using it as a distraction. He would let his accusations sink in and mix it up some more. Maybe she would slip up.

He returned with a water bottle and pushed it in front of her.

"When you were arrested, you wore an expensive diamond pendant and engagement ring. Where did you get them?"

Wendy's fingers quivered over her bare throat.

"They were gifts from my fiancé."

"What's his name?"

"Eddy Graham."

"Where can I reach him?"

"Are you going to drag him down here, too? He doesn't know the Chambers either."

"What's his address?"

"Find him yourself."

"Wendy—"

"Ms. Torrison."

Jensen drummed his fingers on the closed folder. He wanted to wait to show her the picture and introduce it at the right moment, but she started to shut down.

"Ms. Torrison, I'm going to show you a picture and ask you to tell me if you recognize the person in it. I have to warn you; it's a disturbing image."

"I'm a nurse. I can handle it. Is it a picture of Mr. Chambers?" She sneered.

"You tell me. Do you know the person in the photo?"

Jensen slid the photo toward her.

She flipped the picture over and gasped.

"Do you know him?"

As she gaped at the picture, her eyes darkened, and her hand shook.

"Ms. Torrison. Do you know him?"

She took a large drink of water. "No. Who is he?"

"It's Jeff Swanson. He had a burial a few months ago, but he was recently murdered."

She tightened her grip on the picture. "Who killed him?"

"I hoped you could tell me. Mr. Swanson's murderer was left-handed. Do you know of anyone who fits that description?"

"How would I know who killed him?"

"The deceased has a stepfather, David Swanson. Do you know him?"

"Do you think his stepfather killed him?"

"At this time, we do not have a suspect."

"I can't help you."

Jensen strummed his fingers on the table. Her hand shook, and her eyes widened when she saw the picture of the victim lying on the morgue table; he knew he had her.

"Ms. Torrison, I know you're lying. So, tell me what you know. It's for your own good."

"Detective, no matter how many times you ask me, I can't give you the answers you're looking for."

"You were in an intimate relationship with Jeff Swanson and plotted to kill Miss Chambers. When Mr. Swanson denied you the opportunity to kill your rival, you tried to cash in on her father's wealth. When Chambers wouldn't play ball, you saw the money slipping through your fingers. Everything you worked so hard for was going down the toilet. Miss Chambers was still alive, your boyfriend still loved her, and your ticket to the good life had vanished into thin air. You lost your temper and lashed out at Mr. Chambers, savagely attacking him. Isn't that true?" He watched her intently. "And when someone found out what you were doing, they sliced your lover's throat."

Wendy grimaced.

Jensen pounded on the table.

"Tell me!"

"I want a lawyer!"

Chapter 24

Kaylee woke up; her head throbbed, and she couldn't lift her arms. She hoped they were able to control her father's bleeding. Kaylee had done everything she could, and she prayed it was enough. An unpleasant odor emanated around her as she stared at the ceiling, waiting for news.

Disinfectants made Kaylee nauseous. The smell reminded her of when her mother had been in the hospital with breast cancer. Before deciding to go home to die, surrounded by those she loved, her mother had spent one month here. Kaylee had visited her twice daily and spent hours holding her mother's hand. The distinctive scent brought back a feeling of helplessness.

It amazed Kaylee, but didn't surprise her, how quickly she had come to her father's aid last night. She never really knew what she would do in that type of situation. She didn't know if her animosity toward her father would prevent her from doing the right thing. Without hesitation, Kaylee stepped up to help her father; her mother would have been proud.

She heard a moan and peeked over the side of the bed; Kyle was stretched out on a cot–a blanket twisted around his feet. His tangled hair didn't hide the dark circles encasing his eyes. He looked like Kaylee felt beat up and worn out.

A nurse came in and checked her tubes and vitals. The head nurse from last night had put her on an IV drip and said she would be observed for a couple of days. She felt woozy but didn't feel sick enough to be monitored. Kaylee guessed that giving blood without eating had caused her weakness. The nurse brought in a large bowl of grits, a sesame bagel, a tall glass of orange juice, and two dark chocolate candy bars. The nurse waited until she had started her enormous meal and then let Kaylee know she would be back with more juice and water.

She took a bite of the bagel and chewed. It was dry, so Kaylee broke off some of the chocolate, slid it between the bagel halves, and took a bite. It would be better if she could toast the bagel and melt the chocolate, but it wasn't bad. She took a large sip of the juice and continued eating. Kaylee decided to ditch the bagel and finished off the two candy bars. She had poked at the grits but chose not to try them. She wondered if she could have some coffee; Kaylee would ask the nurse when she returned.

Kyle stirred on the cot, and she watched as he ran his fingers through his hair and straightened his shirt. She bit back a laugh.

"Good morning, sleepyhead."

"You're chipper this morning. I didn't think the nurses would let you have coffee after donating."

Kaylee grinned. "They gave me chocolate."

"Great, more candy."

"Dark chocolate has iron."

"And a ton of fat. Eat a little at a time."

She shrugged. "Too late."

"You have to start eating better." Kyle examined her tray.

"I had half a bagel, and look, I'm drinking orange juice."

Kyle stretched. "I need a shower and a pot of coffee."

"Are you leaving?"

"No. I guess I'll settle for some coffee."

"Get me some too."

"You took a huge risk—"

"Have you heard anything about my father's condition?"

He rubbed the back of his neck. "I'll get coffee and check with the head nurse."

Kaylee turned on the TV and flipped through the channels. She wanted to watch a cooking show. They relaxed her, and she tried to rest in case her father needed more blood. Her choices were limited to the news and morning shows. Kaylee settled for the news and leaned back against the pillow. The reporter recapped the weather and morning traffic, then was interrupted by a breaking story.

The cameras zoomed in to show Commander Blanchard issuing a statement: We regret to confirm Mr. Michael Chambers, a prominent and beloved figure in Arizona, had been involved in an accident last night and died this morning from his injuries. Rest assured—

Kaylee dropped the remote. She thought she had saved him. Her chest tightened. He was the only person she had left. She grabbed the phone to call Kyle, but he wasn't answering. She hit the emergency buzzer, but no one came. She pressed it again and didn't let go. Kaylee used the hospital phone to call the nurse's station, but no one answered. She still had her finger on the buzzer and tried to swing her legs over the bed, but couldn't.

A nurse rushed in.

"Is it true?"

"Miss, I'm sorry."

"I don't believe you!"

"Miss…I'm sorry."

Kyle came in, and the nurse closed the door on the way out.

"Why are you yelling?" Kyle asked.

"He can't be dead."

"Michael?"

"The news showed the police making a statement that my father died this morning."

"I'll find out what's going on."

"I'm coming."

"I'll take care of this."

If she didn't believe it, why was this wave of doom sweeping over her? Kaylee's entire life had been built around trying to earn his love. Sometimes, she felt like she walked a tightrope, unsure of her footing. Her one wish, to be loved by the man who gave her life, may never come true. If he died, not only would she lose her only living relative, but she would never know if he loved her?

Why hadn't Kyle returned? If her father were alive, wouldn't Kyle be back by now? Wouldn't he rush in with the good news and say they were mistaken? Kyle had been gone for a while; it felt like a lifetime.

If Kaylee weren't so weak, she would climb out of bed and go straight to the nurse's station. Someone there should know something about her father. She tried Kyle's phone again; it went straight to voicemail. She texted and asked him to return to the room. Just as her finger hit the call button, Kyle returned with Detective Jensen.

Kaylee feared the worst. Her chest tightened. Her breathing increased, and she squinted, trying to focus. Why was Detective Jensen here—to give an official statement?

She sat up. "Is it true?"

Kyle closed and locked the door.

"Tell me."

"Kaylee," Jensen began, "Do you give me permission to speak in front of Kyle?"

He used their first names; would familiarity lessen the blow?

"About my father–of course."

"What I'm about to tell you can't leave this room. I trust you can handle it. You must trust Kyle to keep this secret as well. Understand?"

She leaned forward. "Yes."

"Your father was the victim of a brutal attack—"

She bit back a whimper. Kaylee would've never dreamed of using Michael Chambers and victim in the same sentence. As a child, and even now, he seemed invincible.

"His condition is critical, and until we find out who's responsible, I'm posting an officer outside your room."

She knew Jensen had a job to do. Still, she couldn't live in fear, afraid to go anywhere, or constantly worried about what was around the corner.

Kaylee blew out a long, painful breath. Her father had survived the attack; she had to concentrate on him. "I want to see him," she whispered.

"No visitors; his life could still be in danger."

"Does he need more blood?"

"You're in no condition to give blood," Kyle interjected.

"Does the nursing staff know," Kaylee asked?

"The governor has sent over a couple of top-notch private nurses to care for him. The regular staff has been told it's an out-of-town dignitary, and they don't have clearance to enter the room."

"Do you know who attacked him?"

"We are going through his possessions and trying to piece together what happened."

"He hates it when other people go through his private belongings. I hope they're being careful."

Kaylee stifled a giggle. Her father was alive, and he would be mad.

*****

The nurse brought in dinner and checked her vitals.

Kaylee managed a weak smile. "I'm sorry about before."

"Losing a loved one is hard. We were all praying for him."

"Thank you."

She looked over at Kyle; he nodded.

Kaylee didn't want anyone calling to offer their condolences, especially when her father wasn't dead, so she turned off her phone. It would be easier that way, and she wouldn't have to worry about slipping up.

Kyle's phone rang; he frowned and closed the door behind him.

She finished her orange juice and waited for him to return. She should tell him to turn off his phone; he could use a break from the constant interruptions.

Growing up, Kaylee didn't remember him being chatty. Their talk by the pool made her realize she had neglected him as a friend. She had made a mess of things; she couldn't change what had happened, and second-guessing her decisions would be futile. Life was a balancing act, learning from the past while not wasting time regretting one's mistakes.

Kyle closed the door and slid the phone into his pocket.

"Who called?"

"The police notified Sara that Michael didn't make it."

"The police called her to keep up the pretense; do they suspect her?" Kaylee asked.

"Everyone's a suspect until cleared. She wants to see you."

Kaylee shook her head and instantly regretted it. "I can't."

"I let her know you weren't allowed visitors."

"Good. Sara broke the code. Fathers are off-limits. Besides, I need some rest and to get out of here." Kaylee shifted in the bed. "When do I get to leave?"

"If you don't start eating better, never. The nurse said that your levels are dangerously low, and they won't release you until they're up."

"That's not a problem. Have the nurse bring me more dark chocolate; it should help get my iron up."

"You should eat fortified cereal, dark green, leafy vegetables, lean meats, chicken, and fish."

"The chocolate is the only edible food, and it probably came from a vending machine."

"If you'd eat something other than sugar-coated everything, you'd appreciate real food."

Kaylee wasn't about to leave her father, but she wanted to get out of the hospital gown and out of the room. Ever since she gave blood, she felt extremely weak and, at times, dizzy. Kyle might be on to something; her diet was atrocious.

She closed her eyes and tried to sleep, but realized the person who attacked her father could've killed Jeff. Would they come after her, and why did Jeff fake his own death? Did he want to kill her? Kaylee rolled over, started to hum, and tried to drown out the disruptive questions plaguing her.

"What are you humming?" Kyle asked.

"Mom used to sing me this song. It relaxes me so I can sleep."

"Can you hum it for me?"

"I can't perform on the spot; besides, it's private–something I hum while in bed."

"What about when we're sharing a bed? Will you do it then?"

"We're going to share a bed?"

"Why wouldn't we?"

"You implied we'd never be together as a couple."

"I didn't want to give Detective Jensen any more reasons to suspect me, and we shouldn't do anything until you're safe."

"Shouldn't or won't?"

He leaned against the bed. "Let's say we shouldn't and leave it at that."

241

Chapter 25

The overhead page blared. Kyle jumped off the cot; Kaylee bolted upright. The voice over the loudspeaker repeated "Code Blue" six or seven times. She watched as nurses clad in multi-colored scrubs ran past her room.

This was another reason why she didn't like hospitals. Patients came here hoping to get better, but sometimes they would die.

"What's going on," she asked?

"I'll check."

Kaylee wondered if her father needed help. She grabbed the railing and swung her legs over the edge. She eased herself down; her feet made contact with the tile. She crumbled. She lay sprawled on the floor. The gown rolled up above her waist. Kaylee tugged it down and maneuvered onto her hands and knees. Her head felt heavy. She inched her way to the wall to lean against it.

Kyle returned to find Kaylee on the floor. "What the hell are you doing?"

"I wanted to make sure my father—"

"What if I didn't come back for an hour or two? What would you have done then?"

"Help me up." Kaylee extended her arms. "What's going on?"

Kyle closed and locked the door.

She hadn't noticed his appearance before, but now his facial expression spoke volumes, and the look on his face scared her.

"Is it my father?"

"Michael went into cardiac arrest, but they were able to stabilize him."

She pulled the sheet to her chest and rested her head on the pillow. "He doesn't have a heart condition."

"The doctor said extensive trauma and bleeding could cause it."

"But he's going to live, right? He's going to be okay?"

Kyle rubbed his temple. "It's too soon to tell."

She rolled over and stared out the window. Kaylee thought her father was out of danger. Yet his critical condition required constant care. Why had she assumed he would bounce right back? Because the Invincible Michael Chambers would have.

As a child, she had thought her father seemed larger than life and could do no wrong. As an adult, his business partners had used that nickname frequently. Kaylee had thought it had been an inside joke, but his ability to always come out on top reaffirmed why he was called invincible. Now, as Michael fought for his life, Kaylee had to believe he would succeed because she had no other choice. After everything that had happened and all she hoped to achieve, losing him now would devastate her. If he failed, so would she.

She said a silent prayer. For the first time, Kaylee was thankful her father had money and status. He would receive the best the world could offer, even if the doctor had to be flown in.

During high school, when Jeff's mother became ill, she had to miss months of work, which jeopardized her job, her home, and her security. She had been passed around from doctor to doctor. They ran tests her insurance wouldn't cover, and she couldn't afford. Some of them didn't or couldn't diagnose or solve the problem. After several months, Jeff's mom's condition had worsened, and she had been too sick to travel and had been forced to see the doctor nearest her home. Proximity did not guarantee quality. If she had received better care, would she have lived longer?

Kaylee started to appreciate the value of money, not for the material things it could buy, but for the intangibles, like security and quality of life.

Her arm tingled, and she rolled onto her back. She glanced over at Kyle sitting on the cot; his clothes were wrinkled, and his face had a thin layer of stubble. Even in dim lighting, Kaylee could see the dark lines under his eyes. She felt terrible; he hadn't showered and had only eaten cafeteria food. Even though she could tell he needed a break, he refused to leave her.

She angled herself to see his face without straining her neck or putting any weight on her arm.

"What's bothering you?" Kaylee asked.

He leaned against the wall. "Jeff and I had been best friends since grade school. I don't know why he did what he did, but I have to wonder if my feelings for you had caused it."

Kaylee jolted forward. "Are you blaming me for what Jeff did?"

He shook his head. "I want to understand what happened to the boy I met in third grade. How did things get so messed up?"

"You think I'm responsible?"

"What if we pushed him past his limits?"

Kyle's insensitive words cut deep. She gasped.

"I mean… sometimes, I wonder if we'd never met you, would he still be alive?"

"Get out!"

"Kaylee—"

The officer at the door peeked in. "Miss Chambers, are you all right?"

"Please escort Kyle out."

The officer entered the room and waited for him to gather his stuff.

For a long time, Kaylee had tried to blame Jeff for the demise of their relationship. She had finally admitted, at least to herself, that she had been partially responsible. Kaylee had chosen Jeff when she wanted Kyle, because Jeff needed her.

Kaylee regretted her choice; it might have led to Jeff's downward spiral and his death. Ultimately, Jeff had to be accountable for his actions. Kaylee would never apologize for meeting them–their friendships strengthened her by helping her face her fears. They helped her grow as an independent woman by making her realize her successes would not be defined by her failed relationships.

The nurse returned with Kaylee's breakfast, checked her vitals, and hung another bag on the IV pole. She told Kaylee that starving herself wouldn't bring her father back; she needed to concentrate on getting healthy. On her way out, the nurse suggested she look under the napkin. Kaylee's face was stiff from dried tears, and her smile didn't reach her eyes. She peeked under the napkin. Chocolate.

She poked the food on her plate and pushed it around with the fork. Kyle's questions had hurt. Did he wish he could travel back in time and choose not to be Kaylee's friend? Would he throw away their future for a man who tormented her? If he blamed her for Jeff's death, could she ever love him?

She skipped the rest of the breakfast and took a bite of a chocolate bar, chewing slowly. It didn't have the expected effect of temporary euphoria, but it would do.

The nurse's gesture had been kind, and she would thank her next time she came in. Kaylee longed to get out of bed and stretch her legs. A short walk would do wonders for her legs and mood, but she felt weak and shaky. She must be having a reaction. The nurse had been right. She needed to eat more.

She bit into a piece of crispy bacon and then downed some orange juice. Her throat felt raw, and swallowing was difficult. After a few bites, her stomach turned. She spewed her breakfast all over the blanket. The officer at the door came in and then called for assistance.

Two nurses rushed in; one helped Kaylee onto the cot while the other cleaned up. Her regular nurse helped her into a new gown and back into bed; she gave Kaylee a water bottle. The cold water soothed her throat. If she didn't feel so sick, Kaylee would be embarrassed about wearing nothing but underwear and a flimsy gown in front of the officer. Now she knew why the hospital put limits on how much blood a person could give at one time, but her father would live, and that was all that mattered.

Her throat still hurt, but at least she could swallow without much pain. She took a few deep breaths.

The hard, quick taps on the door startled her. She sat up.

"Kaylee, it's Detective Jensen. May I come in?"

"Sure."

Jensen looked around the room. "Where's Kyle?"

"I don't know?"

"I'm here." Kyle hurried in and dumped a duffel bag on the cot.

"What are you doing here?" She asked.

"Kaylee, I asked him to join us. If I could postpone this, I would, but in light of what's happened in the last twenty-four hours, I can't take the chance and have someone else get hurt. My questions aren't meant to hurt you; I'm just trying to gather information."

That sounded ominous. Kaylee hoped her stomach had calmed down. She didn't want a repeat of what happened earlier.

"Is it possible your father was doing business with or dating Wendy Torrison?"

"Seriously?"

"I warned you these questions would be difficult."

"I don't want to sound pretentious, but I doubt he'd date someone who wasn't in his social or financial circles."

"He's dating Sara Hill."

"She graduated top of her class and is a respected attorney at a prominent firm in California. She may not have money, but she does have credentials."

"There are other reasons for a man to date a woman, and they have nothing to do with her pedigree."

"What makes you think he even knew her?"

"Your father's secretary confirmed that Wendy Torrison was the one he planned to meet."

Kaylee pounded her fist on the bed. "Just because Michael had an appointment with her doesn't mean he dated her. She probably tried to blackmail him and, when that didn't work, tried to kill him."

"I'm sure he didn't realize how dangerous she could be, or he wouldn't have agreed to meet her. I must know if he had a legitimate reason to meet her."

"Since we can't ask my father, why don't you ask her?"

"Currently, she is nowhere to be found."

"Did that horrible woman attack my father?"

"I'm trying to locate her; she may have pertinent information and may be the only person besides your father who knows what happened to him. If you run across her, consider her dangerous; do not approach her under any circumstances, and call me as soon as possible."

"It appears I'm going to be stuck in the hospital for a while, so unless she strolls past the officer at the door, I guess I'm safe."

"I've instructed Detective Lopez to notify me when you are scheduled to be released. I will make sure you have a team protecting you."

"Thank you."

"I know you're not feeling well, but the sooner I get more information, the quicker I can put an end to the violence."

Kaylee nodded.

Jensen began, "Someone else was murdered—"

She gripped the railing. "Is it someone I know?"

"Please look at this picture and tell me if you know who this is."

She reached for the photo; she recognized the familiar chin. "It's the man in the parking garage. The man you said was David Swanson."

"Are you sure," Jensen asked?

"Yes." She leaned forward to give the picture back, but changed her mind. She hadn't noticed David's hair before; the cap had covered it, but his neck wound made her do a double-take.

"David's wound, the thin, deep slice, looks similar to Jeff's, except David's is going the opposite way."

"Very good. Anything else," Jensen asked?

"I am still convinced we have the same chin."

She held the picture to her face. "We both have triangular-shaped faces."

She watched as Jensen examined the picture.

"It's a diamond shape, but just because you have similar chins—"

"It's identical, and not just the chin. The eyes. You can't see them now, but when I saw him in the parking garage, he'd lifted his cap, and I looked directly into them. It freaked me out."

"Perhaps you were frightened because a stranger was following you," Jensen said.

"I know what I saw."

"Do you honestly believe that David might be your dad?" Kyle asked. "Is that what you're getting at?"

"I just want to know why he looks like me."

Jensen motioned for the picture to be returned. "It's said that everyone has a doppelganger, a counterpart, who has similar features."

"My ex-fiancé's stepdad is my look-a-like; what are the chances," Kaylee asked? That sounded lame even to her.

"I want you to look at this last photo. I need to know if you can identify the people in it. Don't take it out of the plastic bag."

Kaylee picked up the photo, instantly recognized the woman sitting on the park bench and the small child clinging to her leg, and clutched the picture to her chest.

"It's Mom, and that's me. Where did you get this?"

"May I have it back?"

"This was the picture I had in my room as a child. It went missing, and I never knew what happened to it. It's mine."

Jensen extended his arm. "I'm going to have to insist; it's evidence."

Kaylee stroked her mother's face through the plastic.

"If it's yours, you can arrange to get it back," Jensen assured her.

"If it will help him catch a killer, isn't it worth it?"

She glared at Kyle and squeezed the picture tighter. Kyle pried the photo from her fingers and handed it back to Jensen.

"Miss Chambers, I know you're hurting right now."

"Do you?" She tugged on the sheet.

"Do you know who took the picture?"

"No."

"Could it have been David Swanson," Jensen asked?

"I was six." Kaylee's lips turned down wistfully.

"Do you know why David had this picture in his apartment?"

She leaned forward. "David had my picture?"

"When officers responded to a disturbance at a Tempe apartment complex, they found Mr. Swanson dead, clutching this picture."

She closed her eyes and swallowed.

"Do you need to stop?"

She felt nauseous but shook her head no.

"We found your license plate. It's in evidence and will be tested, but it looks like it might be the weapon that killed Jeff and David Swanson."

"Someone used my plate to kill two people?"

"It was next to David's body, covered in what appeared to be his blood, and the dimensions are consistent with the coroner's findings for Jeff's murder weapon. We'll know more after the lab tests are done."

"Were you able to collect any information from Kaylee's car?" Kyle asked.

"We're running some fingerprints, but Kaylee's and Jeff's prints are the only ones we've positively identified."

"Do you have any leads on Wendy? Did she have a motive to kill David?" Kyle asked.

"All I can tell you is we're doing everything we can. I've got to get back to the precinct." He shook their hands and left.

Kaylee thought she would feel better by now, but instead she felt worse. She could barely lift her head or move; if she moved, she would get dizzy. Her head pounded loudly, and her thoughts were muddled. All she wanted to do was sleep.

She swallowed the last of the water.

"Have you eaten anything today?" Kyle asked.

"I ate breakfast and heaved, but I had nothing else. Will you get me some aspirin and more water?"

She heard voices and looked up. Kyle and her nurse were hovering near the door.

"Can I have some water?"

The nurse came over, looked into her eyes, and pinched Kaylee's arm."

"Ow."

The nurse turned to Kyle. "I'll be back in a minute."

"Why did she pinch me? Where's my water?"

"The nurse needs to run a test first."

"For what?"

"She's going to test for dehydration and hypoglycemia."

The nurse returned and drew blood. "I'll order this stat. We should have the results shortly, but in the meantime, she needs to drink everything I brought her. I'll be back to check on her.

"Can I get some aspirin?"

"I'm sorry. You can't have anything for forty-eight hours. If we can get you hydrated, your headache should go away."

"Why are you here?" Kaylee asked Kyle.

"Detective Jensen called to say he had more bad news. I wanted to be here in case you needed me."

Kaylee wrung her hands. "I thought you wished you had never met me."

"I'm sorry. I didn't mean to hurt you. It was my clumsy and painful way to deal with my guilt."

"Do you honestly believe things would have turned out differently if you two had never met me?"

Kyle moved to her side. "What's wrong?"

"Wrong?"

"I'm going to get the nurse."

The room was spinning. *What now?*

The nurse came closer and smiled. She pulled out a large needle and jabbed it forcefully into Kaylee's arm.

Chapter 26

Jensen made sure the lights were turned up in the interrogation room. He could feel their heat and hoped the intense brightness would have the desired effect. James Fuller, the elusive funeral director, flinched under Jensen's glare. Fuller had been apprehended trying to cross over into Mexico. The man sweated profusely; he probably never dreamt his white-collar crime would morph into murder.

"Mr. Fuller, have you been read your rights, and are you giving up your right to an attorney?"

"Yes, but I want a deal?"

Jensen scowled. "Why would I cut you a deal?"

"I didn't kill anyone."

"You and Roger Goldman have been defrauding families for years. Jeff Swanson found out and tried to blackmail you. Instead of paying him off, you made him a partner. He wanted revenge against his ex-fiancée, so you faked his death and used the body of Charles Pierce as a substitute for his. Still, when his obsession with Miss Chambers became a liability and threatened your livelihood, you killed him."

Fuller sat tall. "I didn't kill him. He was crazy. After his phony funeral, he followed her everywhere and set her car on fire. What kind of lunatic starts a fire in Arizona? He could have burnt down the whole damn area."

"Your concern for the state's welfare is touching, but what about all those grieving families you swindled?"

Jensen had a hunch his altruism toward Arizona had a narcissistic twist, just like everything else about him. He opened the file, checked the address, and closed it.

"You don't care about Arizona or its residents. It appears you live in the Biltmore Fashion Square area, and if Mr. Swanson had torched it, your million-dollar home would have gone up in smoke."

"Anyone who owned a home or business in the area would have a motive to kill him. He was a danger to everyone."

"If that area had burnt down, your family would have been in danger, so if you weren't previously motivated to get rid of him, the immediate threat to your family pushed you over the edge and forced you to commit the ultimate act of savagery."

He shook his head vigorously, "I could never take a life, even one as demented as his."

Jensen paused. "Earlier, you asked about a deal. What information do you have that would entice me to give you a break?"

"Jeff Swanson's killer."

"You killed Jeff Swanson?"

"Don't be ridiculous, but I know who did."

"Really? Who?" Jensen asked.

"Not until I get a deal, in writing, approved by a judge."

"To get a sweet deal like that, you must give me the name of the murderer, the name of a credible witness; you'd have to testify and come clean on all the crimes you ever committed. You must agree to everything, or I won't consider taking this to a judge."

Jensen had this jerk pegged as one of the top three for killing Jeff Swanson, but running elevated him to number one. If Jensen could get him to spill, he wouldn't need a deal, and justice would be fully served.

"I figured swindling your customers would be a full-time job. When did you have time to babysit Jeff and miraculously come across his killer?"

"He came to me."

"You expect me to believe the killer came to you and confessed to murdering Jeff, just like that, for no reason?"

Fuller wrung his hands together. "No, he terrorized me."

"You're such an upstanding citizen; why would he threaten you?" Jensen sneered.

"I never did anything as crazy or messed up as he did."

"Someone thought so, or he wouldn't have taken time to visit you after he murdered Jeff. He could have been long gone, but instead, a cold-blooded, vengeance-seeking killer took the time to try and put you on the straight and narrow. Talk about crazy."

"Both he and his stepson were insane, birds of a feather—"

Jensen arched his brow. "David killed his stepson?"

"He'd been pestering my staff for days, trying to get information on Jeff. He stopped coming around, so I thought he'd gotten what he wanted. But Thursday, he came to my house all hyped up and demanded I turn myself in. I refused and called him a demented fool, and he showed me how dangerous he was."

"Did he assault you," Jensen asked?

"Worse, he showed me a bloody license plate and said his stepson had committed a grave injustice to Kaylee Chambers and had paid the ultimate price. He promised me that if I would make amends to those I'd hurt, I wouldn't have to pay the same."

"What did his stepson do to Miss Chambers?"

"Who cares? A lunatic with a bloody weapon was standing on my porch." Fuller wiped the sweat from his brow.

"You promised to be a good boy, and he just let you walk?"

"I don't care why he left–he just did."

"So, you ran?"

"Hell yeah."

"Which hand did he use: right or left?" Jensen demanded.

"I don't remember."

"Think!"

The funeral director ran his fingers through his hair. "Left."

"You sure."

"After I promised to go straight, he made me shake on it. He extended his left hand, and he used his left hand to open his truck door."

Jensen stood and headed toward the door.

"What about my deal?"

Jensen shrugged, "Sorry."

"But you said—"

"I said I'd think about taking it to a judge, but after careful consideration, I've changed my mind."

Jensen slammed the door.

In Stone's office, he said, "Hold Fuller for the full seventy-two hours, then charge him with fraud, forgery, money laundering, tax evasion, and falsifying records. Throw the whole damn book at him, and don't let him slip through the cracks as Wendy Torrison did. Make certain the prosecutor knows he's a flight risk and tell her he's an accessory after the fact."

Rage filled Jensen's being. He could feel the heat radiating throughout his entire body. What kind of man runs and leaves his family unprotected when he knows a killer has his home address?

Jensen poured himself some coffee and headed back to his office. If he were to be autopsied right now, he would have more caffeine in his veins than blood. This case was beating him down; when he thought he had a handle on the situation, another twist led him in a different direction. He examined the picture of Mrs. Chambers and Kaylee and wondered why David had had it and why he would hug it

255

close in his last moments on earth. Did he have a connection to the Chambers, and was it biological?

Kaylee had been adamant that David looked like her. Mrs. Chambers must have spent many hours alone. Had she fallen for an attentive man and borne his child? An affair might explain the eerie similarities. What other connections could the Chambers and Swansons have?

His left-handed stepfather had killed Jeff, and David had been killed by a right-handed person with the same weapon that was possibly used to kill his stepson. Did David's killer know he killed his stepson? And why did Wendy want to meet with Michael Chambers the night he was attacked?

Jensen asked his secretary to call Wendy's public defender. She had probably skipped town, but he had to try. While reviewing David Swanson's file, Lopez called to notify him that Kaylee was missing. Jensen pounded his fist on the desk and asked how she could have gotten past Officer Ryan at the door. Lopez stated that she had become ill, and when Kyle and Ryan returned with a nurse, they found an empty syringe on the floor and Kaylee gone. A witness had described the nurse who had been seen with Kaylee. The description sent chills down Jensen's spine.

Jensen had Lopez secure Mr. Chambers' room and put an extra guard at the door. He warned him to keep a close eye on Kyle. He yelled for Stone to follow him, and they sped down the road. Dispatch called to confirm that the hospital administrator had locked down the hospital and that an APB had been put out for Kaylee and Wendy. He knew if Wendy had kidnapped Kaylee, she would be dead soon.

Wendy would need a gurney or wheelchair to get Kaylee out of the hospital, and taking the stairs would be impossible. Wendy worked at the hospital; she must have used her badge to gain access. No one had questioned Wendy as she walked down the hall, entered the room, and drugged Kaylee. Wendy knew she would go unnoticed in a sea of scrubs, and when Wendy saw Ryan and Kyle leave the room unattended, she pounced on Kaylee.

They parked in the emergency room entrance, flashed their badges to the security guard, and took the staff elevator to the ICU. Kyle leaned against the wall near Kaylee's room. His usually tan face had paled, and he looked as though the life had been sucked from his body. Lopez paced, waiting for instructions. Down the hall, three well-dressed and highly skilled officers stood watch in front of Michael Chambers' room.

Jensen spoke to the head nurse, who directed him downstairs to the morgue. The brightly lit basement had large steel chambers stacked three high, covering two walls. The aluminum autopsy tables were haphazardly shoved against the wall. Stone checked the compartments while Jensen confirmed the other rooms were empty and hadn't been disturbed. Jensen returned to the morgue and noticed a small office in a corner and, next to it, a door. It led to a private parking lot used by funeral homes and hadn't been included in the lockdown.

The lot was empty.

A knot tightened in Jensen's stomach: the odds of finding Kaylee alive had just plummeted.

Jensen called the FBI Phoenix Division and found out that Blanchard had requested assistance in the search for Kaylee–an agent would be arriving at the precinct within minutes. On Jensen's way back, his secretary notified him that Wendy's lawyer had one address for her, the address where Jeff had been killed. He had no idea what vehicle she had; her last two cars had been repossessed. Jensen remembered her supervisor had seen her in a red Lexus; maybe it was registered to her alleged fiancé, Eddy Graham. He would have Stone check and get back with him.

Wendy's apartment and Kaylee's house were continuously under surveillance; they weren't there. Jensen instructed Lopez to check out the subdivision where Jeff had been killed. Jensen headed back to the precinct to meet with the FBI. He knew he hadn't given the agent much time, but he had hoped she had information on Kaylee and Wendy's whereabouts.

The sinking feeling in his gut tightened. Kaylee didn't have much time. Blanchard informed Jensen that the governor wanted to hold a press conference about Kaylee's disappearance, but Jensen vehemently opposed it: making Wendy a target could cause her to panic. If spooked, she wouldn't hesitate to kill Kaylee, and Jensen couldn't let that happen. Kaylee counted on him to bring her home safely; this was his chance to redeem himself, to his dad, and to his brothers in blue.

*****

In the ICU, Jensen listened to a message from Stone indicating that the red Lexus belonged to Eddy Graham, Wendy's fiancé, and that the Scottsdale address listed was Wendy's apartment. On his way to Kaylee's old room, he spoke with the head nurse to see if Wendy had checked in and to verify there were no issues with Mr. Chambers. Jensen dug in his pocket for the house key and walked over to Kyle.

Trying to reassure a victim's family that he would do everything he could to bring their loved one home took patience and finesse, both of which were currently in short supply. Kyle looked up when Jensen came over, but didn't speak. He might be afraid to ask. Jensen knew how difficult it could be, waiting to hear about a loved one–he had seen it a thousand times.

"Have you found her?"

"No."

Kyle pinched his nasal bone and closed his eyes.

"Don't give up."

Kyle ground out. "Either she's already dead, or she's alive and being butchered by a psycho!"

"I know this is difficult—"

"Save your pep talk. I need to know that Kaylee is safe."

"Then help me find her. You were friends with Jeff for a long time; tell me everything you know about his stepdad. How does he know the Chambers, and why did he have their picture when he died?"

"How's this going to help Kaylee," Kyle asked?

"Anything I learn about him may give me insight into finding her."

"Jeff's mom didn't have much money, and he refused to have friends at his house; we spent most of our free time at mine. As a teenager, I only met David once or twice. I don't remember him."

"Did he ever mention his stepfather abusing him?"

"You think David abused Jeff?"

"Sometimes kids say they're embarrassed by their home, when in reality, they're afraid to go home."

Kyle shook his head. "No, I would've known."

"Did he mention hearing from David again? What about his biological father?"

"He never knew his real father and never spoke of David after he left."

"While you two were growing up, did you notice anything that may explain why he behaved the way he did?"

"You mean other than me loving his fiancée?" Kyle balled his fist.

Jensen ignored his sarcasm. "Yes."

"His two fathers abandoned him. He couldn't deal with the rejection." Kyle slumped against the wall. "Why aren't you out looking for Kaylee?"

259

Jensen's phone rang. "Stone, did you find anything?"

"No," Stone responded, "But the man who called in Jeff's murder flagged me down to tell me he saw a red Lexus with two women in it. He thought they might stop at the crime scene house, but when the driver saw him, she sped away."

"Did he see what direction they went?"

"Out the main exit, but he couldn't see which way they turned."

"Get every available car out there to scour the neighborhood and update the APB. At least we know what she's driving."

"Someone spotted her," Kyle asked.

"Yes. Does Kaylee know anyone near 57th and Northern?"

"I can check her phone and her home office."

"Here's the key. When you're done, lock up, return to the hospital, and wait for me. Call me immediately if you find anything."

Kyle hurried to the elevator.

Jenson called Commander Blanchard. "We need a chopper."

Chapter 27

Kaylee lay on her back, arms at her sides, palms touching the sheet. She couldn't lift her head, and her eyelids felt heavy. When she tried to sit up, nausea flooded her; Kaylee thought she might hurl and knew if she did, she would probably choke on her own vomit. She remembered feeling a searing pain rush through her upper torso, then a pain in her arm. Kaylee had caught a glimpse of a nurse's hair and name tag. She had then seen the wicked smile on Wendy Torrison's face as she had thrust the needle into her arm. The drug had already taken effect, and she had blacked out.

She didn't know where she was, but she wasn't about to die on a stranger's bed. She would fight to stay alive despite her non-responsive limbs. Kaylee was a Chambers, and if her father could do it, so could she. She had his blood flowing through her veins, had his tenacity, determination, and strength. Kaylee wondered why she had ever doubted her lineage. She was, and would always be, her father's daughter.

Unfortunately, Kaylee still couldn't move and had no idea how long the drug would take to wear off. The only weapon available to her would be to connect with Wendy. She had experience in the art of communication, and it helped her excel at her job. Kaylee could proficiently appease difficult and anxious clients, but convincing her abductor to keep her alive would be the most significant challenge Kaylee had ever faced. If she knew what motivated Wendy, it might make connecting easier. Traditional approaches wouldn't work if Wendy wanted revenge. There were dozens of ways to exact revenge; all could be extremely painful or frightening. Kaylee had another hurdle to overcome; she felt numb; speaking would be difficult.

Kaylee wondered why Wendy hadn't come in to taunt her. Had Wendy dumped her off in an abandoned house to starve or overdose? Why kidnap her to let her die alone?

She slid her hand slowly across the bedding, hoping to find her purse or phone, but all Kaylee found were dust bunnies. Her health had deteriorated since she had donated blood, and she prayed she wouldn't get worse without water, food, or a clean environment.

A person can only survive without water for three days, but she didn't have three days. She felt already dehydrated. Kaylee had to outsmart Wendy to avoid arousing suspicion. If Wendy figured it out, she would make sure Kaylee paid if she lived that long. And if she never showed up, Kaylee would die alone.

She struggled to sit up, but her body refused. Her hope of defeating Wendy backfired. A nurse by profession, Wendy knew how sick Kaylee was. Wendy wouldn't have to do anything; she only had to do nothing. Wendy could be watching from another location, getting her kicks while Kaylee fought to survive.

Her swollen tongue ached, and she couldn't breathe. She might be having a panic attack. She tried to slow her breathing, but her chest hurt. A slow, steady darkness ascended upon her, and she felt as if Wendy had already won.

*****

Kaylee slowly opened her eyes. The barren room was devoid of light, and her skin beaded with sweat. She couldn't feel or hear the air conditioner. She couldn't gauge how long she had been out, but it had to be late evening. Arizona summer days were long, not getting dark until nine o'clock.

Kaylee flexed her toes and balled her fist. Eventually, she might even be able to walk, but how much time did she have? She knew a victim's chances of survival decreased with each passing hour. She had never considered herself a victim, even when Jeff had assaulted her. It didn't matter; Kaylee would probably have a heart attack worrying about whether or not Wendy would show up.

Jeff had brought Wendy into their lives, and it was his fault she lay on this bed in a creepy, abandoned house, too weak to escape. While they were dating, Kaylee had always defended Jeff. She couldn't understand why so many people had disliked him, but she had chosen Jeff and had stood by him.

During their time together, Kaylee had noticed certain tendencies that had made her wonder if Jeff really loved her or if, like some people, he had been enthralled with the Chambers' money. He had seemed to enjoy, a little too much, the attention he received by being her boyfriend. It had worried her, but then Jeff had vowed to commit fully to their future as a couple and promised to stop using the Chamber's name to advance his goals, and she had let it go.

Hot, stagnant air seared her throat. Kaylee lifted her arm, causing an explosion of pain to shoot through her entire body. She moaned.

"You should try to stay still."

Wendy. Her oppressor. Her savior.

"Nurse, may I have some water?" Kaylee hoped that appealing to her professional, nurturing side might establish a favorable connection.

"I think you should wait a while before you try to drink anything."

Kaylee didn't know how long she would make it without water, but if Wendy wanted her to wait. She would wait.

It went quiet, and Kaylee didn't know how she missed it before, but she could hear Wendy breathing. Her breaths were quick and shallow.

"How do you like your accommodations?" Wendy mocked.

"They're fine."

Wendy hit the end of the bed, shaking the mattress and jarring Kaylee.

"Don't lie to me bitch! I know your kind; nothing is ever good enough, not even a hardworking man who did everything he could to make you happy."

She winced. If Wendy's tone indicated how much she despised her, Kaylee was in for the fight of her life.

"Jeff treated me well, but he didn't love me."

Wendy's tone softened, "He loved me."

Kaylee tried to sound remorseful. "I know, and it hurt."

"Because you couldn't wrap him around your finger like you did everyone else? It hurt because you couldn't be the center of his universe?"

"When you promise to marry someone, you're supposed to love them."

She shouldn't have mentioned marriage. Kaylee inched closer to the wall and waited for the assault to begin, but it didn't. The silence frightened her. Was Wendy planning painful ways to hurt her, or had she grown tired of the conversation?

"You promised to marry Jeff. Did you love him," Wendy asked?

Kaylee wished she had changed the subject. Talking about Jeff could be dangerous. "We were friends, and when he asked me to marry him, I couldn't say no. I didn't want to hurt him."

"Did you love him?"

"I didn't mean to mislead him."

"Then say it!"

264

"No," Kaylee said quietly.

"Next time, answer honestly if you want to survive."

Kaylee writhed.

"It doesn't really matter; he never loved you. You were just a means to an end." Wendy laughed.

"If he used me, why does it matter how I felt about him?"

"Just because you come from money, you think you can take anything you want."

"I didn't mean to," Kaylee asserted.

"You just accidentally accepted his proposal and accidentally wore his ring, but wouldn't have sex with him?"

"Jeff told you?" Kaylee lifted her head; pain shot throughout her entire body. She wanted to see Wendy's face when she answered.

"We'd shared everything. Jeff knew my flaws, and I knew his."

Kaylee's head plopped down on the pillow. It sounded like Wendy had started planning a future with Jeff. This turn of events just made surviving more difficult.

"It's hard admitting your shortcomings."

"Only if you think you're perfect," Wendy paused. "Do you think you're perfect?"

"No."

"Seriously? You think you can have anyone you want, even if you don't want them."

"Jeff obviously hadn't told you the truth."

Wendy slammed her fist against the wall. "You're the liar."

Kaylee swallowed hard.

"Sleep tight…"

When the door slammed, Kaylee panicked. She needed to get out before Wendy came back. Kaylee scanned the room for a weapon, but all she could see were shadows. And if, by some miracle, she could see better, she didn't have her strength–Wendy had made sure of that. Kaylee knew trying to connect with Wendy had been a long shot, but it seemed like her only chance.

What would her father do? Or Kyle? They wouldn't just wait for death to knock on their door; they'd fight. Kyle once told her that the best defense was a good offense. She didn't understand until now, but why let your opponent have the advantage? Attack first. She had to get Wendy back in the room.

Kaylee could distract her just long enough to get the jump on her. A key component of any great plan was execution; since she could barely move, physically overpowering Wendy would be a problem.

She called out to her, "Wendy?" She waited a moment. "Wendy?" Still nothing. "I need to see you."

Kaylee didn't know if Wendy had left. She tried again.

"Wendy, are you here?"

How was she supposed to subdue a killer hyped up on adrenaline when she already lacked the energy to make a simple request?

"Please come back?"

The door swung open and slammed against the wall.

"Do you want me to kill you now?"

She took a deep breath. "Can I have some coffee?"

"Coffee will only aggravate your condition."

Kaylee choked back a laugh. What a touching sentiment; she didn't want to kill a sick person. "I know it sounds weird because it contains so much caffeine, but coffee has always had a calming effect on me."

"What possibly could keep you up at night?" Wendy demanded. "Growing up, did you ever go to sleep hungry or wonder if you'd get to finish school or be stuck on a farm for the rest of your life?"

"My father hates me. I'm his only failure, and he never lets me forget it. I lie awake at night trying to think of ways to make him proud, but it's useless."

"You live in a big house with a nice car and rich friends. You get to eat every day, and your only issue in life is that your father hates you," Wendy taunted.

Kaylee had it better than most, and she tried to give back by volunteering and sharing what she had with others, but she valued love more than money. "Do you have a good relationship with your father?"

Wendy crumpled onto the chair and looked straight past Kaylee. She whispered, and her voice trembled. "Every night, he'd sneak into my room, and as he screwed me, he'd tell me how much he loved me."

What kind of monster would molest a child? Kaylee knew that children were abused, but it sickened her. Did abuse turn Wendy against the world?

"I'm so sorry."

"You're not sorry. I know you don't care about me or anyone else."

"Seriously? How would you know?"

Wendy smirked. "Jeff never loved you. He wanted your money and what it could do for him, for us. We were both tired of working hard and being trampled on because our families were poor. We connected in a way that you are incapable of. He never cheated on me. I gave him everything he needed: love, inspiration, and sex."

Kaylee knew she should have trusted her instincts about Jeff, but she kept making excuses for him. And despite what Wendy and Jeff had done to her, what had happened to Wendy as a child was horrific.

"Your father did despicable things to you. No child should be betrayed by someone who's supposed to love and protect them."

"I don't want your sympathy. I want the same opportunities you've had. I'd worked hard on my father's

267

farm every morning, and if he woke up happy, he let me go to school. If he were angry, I'd work all day with chickens and pigs–disgusting animals. Then I'd get to shovel manure. It would take days to get the stench out of my clothes. At the end of the day, my hands were raw and bleeding. And if I were a *good* girl, Daddy wouldn't come to my room; he'd let me sleep so I could work hard again the next day. I had no choice; he exploited me for free labor and used me as a sex pawn. The ways he violated my body…"

Wendy moved to the window and stared out into the darkness.

Kaylee didn't know how to respond. Wendy's childhood had been wrought with immeasurable torment, and saying 'I'm sorry' again would sound insincere.

"You survived and overcame your tragic childhood."

"I didn't get to be a child!"

Kaylee recoiled from Wendy's anger but couldn't let her see it affected her.

"Don't pity me," Wendy blurted out.

"I don't."

"You're treating me like a victim. Well, I'm not. You're the one lying in bed wondering what I'm going to do to you; you're the one who's going to die."

Kaylee didn't want to die; she hoped Wendy would confide in her so they could bond, but Wendy twisted everything she said. Things were going from bad to worse.

"I can't change what happened to you, but I am sorry you suffered at the hands of your father."

"He violated my body, attacked my self-esteem, and infected my way of thinking. I couldn't cope with his brutality or his betrayal. My romantic relationships were doomed from the start." Wendy faltered, her words fading to a whisper. "Jeff understood. He knew how it felt to be betrayed by a parent, to be a child at the mercy of heartless adults. He helped me love me again."

Kaylee remembered how supportive Jeff had been after her mother died. He had been able to comfort her when no one else could. Jeff had sat with her for hours. He truly understood her loss. Since both his biological and stepfather had abandoned him, he knew the ache of losing not just one but two parents. Jeff's loss had been amplified by his guilt of never being good enough. Kaylee knew how devastating that felt, and they'd bonded. This feeling of kinship had been exactly what she needed, and it appears Wendy had too.

She realized her connection to Jeff had been one of shared trauma, not true love, and their shared perceived flaws had made up their entire relationship. He had become reliant on her and her family's money. Jeff hadn't developed the skills needed to thrive on his own, and Kaylee hadn't learned to interact with men romantically.

She knew how destructive it could be to try to please someone and constantly fail. Kaylee wasted valuable time trying to please her father when she could have been making memories with her mother and friends. She had decided where to live, what car to buy, and where to work based on her need to earn his love. Kaylee finally accepted that he would always have other priorities, which had nothing to do with a lack of love for her. His obsession with overcoming his childhood poverty would always come first.

"It sounds like Jeff had been more than just your lover."

"He helped me realize I deserved more. And I wanted something concrete to show for all my hard work and sacrifice, but I didn't get it. Jeff tried to give me a nice home, a car, and a secure future. But you took him from me. You destroyed him–he couldn't let his revenge go—"

"He didn't love me. How did I ruin him?"

269

"Because you ruin everything!"

Kaylee shrank back. Wendy blamed her for Jeff's plight. Jeff had been the one using Kaylee; Wendy couldn't see it or didn't care.

Chapter 28

Kaylee felt weaker. Sparring with Wendy was taking its toll. She had to get her strength up, or she would die.

"I don't want to be a burden, but I'd appreciate a cup of coffee."

"Black?"

"Lots of sugar. Please."

"I guess one wouldn't hurt, but you need to lay off the sugar."

There she goes again, trying to be nice and acting as if she cared. It must be difficult being a nurse *and* a lunatic.

While Kaylee waited for Wendy to return, Kyle's words echoed in her head. He had said she would have to cut down on sugar and coffee. She would gladly promise to give them both up if it meant she would make it out alive. Kaylee continued to survey the room, looking for an escape.

Wendy seemed to be taking her time making the coffee. Did she only agree to tease Kaylee and get her hopes up to crush them? Or rather than making coffee, Wendy decided to mix up some deadly concoction to end her life?

Wendy returned with two cups of fragrant coffee, which smelled heavenly. She put the mugs down, went to the window, and angled the blinds just enough to illuminate the room softly. Wendy came to the bed and loomed over Kaylee, standing there for a few minutes. Then, she bent down and put her hands on either side of Kaylee's head. Wendy fluffed the pillow, leaned it against the headboard, and helped Kaylee sit up. She handed Kaylee a mug and took a seat by the door.

Kaylee inhaled the sweet, nutty aroma, and her mouth watered in anticipation. She took a sip and swallowed it carefully. It was hot, just the way she liked it. She took a few more sips and felt a surge in confidence and strength.

"This is the best cup of coffee I've ever had." Kaylee took another sip; she needed to keep her talking. Maybe Wendy would reveal a secret, a way to end this nightmare.

"Why did you become a nurse?"

"I have a way with needles." She grinned.

Kaylee frowned.

"Jeff said you were a stick in the mud."

"I can take a joke," Kaylee said defensively. "If Jeff never wanted to be with me, then he never got to know the real me. He used me."

"It doesn't matter. Jeff's gone, and it's your fault," Wendy hissed.

If Kaylee didn't want to enrage Wendy, she would have to stop trying to defend herself at Jeff's expense. Did Wendy want to trip her up, to give her a legitimate reason to hurt her?

"I help with babies. They're hanging on by a thread, and each breath they take could be their last. They need a lot of love."

For a moment, Kaylee saw a side of Wendy she hadn't expected to see, a caring nurse and human being.

"Did your childhood trauma make you want to help children?"

Wendy shook her head yes. "Kids need to be protected at all costs."

Kaylee couldn't imagine the horror Wendy went through while her father brutalized her. Why hadn't her mother helped her?

"This doesn't change anything." Wendy's eyes darkened; she put her mug down.

They stared at each other. Kaylee's momentary wave of confidence dived.

"Is everything all right?" Kaylee asked.

"I'm trying to figure you out."

"What exactly did Jeff say about me?"

"You're a liar—"

"I don't—"

"Lie? Everybody lies, but some are honest enough to admit it."

Kaylee knew she had to tread lightly, or she would go down a dangerous path, but if Wendy wanted honesty, here she goes. "I made a mistake by dating Jeff, but that doesn't mean I deliberately lied."

"He said you wanted his best friend."

Kaylee shook her head. "The truth was, I didn't know who I wanted."

"So, you thought you could string Jeff along while you made up your mind?"

"I cared for them both."

"Jeff said you loved Kyle; everybody knew it."

"I didn't *know* I loved Kyle—"

"Save your confession for someone who cares," Wendy jeered.

"My father built his business from the ground up; I won't apologize for his efforts to give us a good life. We have money, but that doesn't mean I'm not a good person."

"What have you done to consider yourself a good person?"

Before Kaylee took another sip, she peered into the bottom of her mug. She knew she couldn't make the remaining coffee last through another heated conversation. Kaylee started to ask for more, but something struck the wall below the bedroom window.

"Jeez!" Kaylee bolted up.

"Stay put."

Wendy turned to leave but then looked back. "Don't think about screaming, or I'll slit your throat too."

She could hear Wendy running down the hall and opening and closing the front door. It sounded like a scuffle, a high-pitched screech, then something hitting the ground. It went quiet, and she heard shuffling or scraping but couldn't figure out what had happened. During the few minutes before Wendy came back, Kaylee had time to digest what she had said when she left, *slit your throat too.*

Kaylee never imagined that not only had Wendy attacked her father, but it dawned on her that she must have killed Jeff or David or both. Detective Jensen said that one was killed by a right-handed person and the other by a left-handed person; which was she? But why would Wendy kill Jeff?

Kaylee pretended to be sipping her coffee when Wendy returned. Instead of drinking, she had been calculating how many feet from the bedroom to the front door. Wendy ran and had made it in about five seconds—twenty feet? Kaylee could barely walk, so running was out of the question. Maybe the window would be better.

"What crashed into the wall?"

Wendy shrugged. "A cat in heat got stuck in the bushes."

"Were you able to free it?"

A grin flashed across her face. "I freed it."

A knot tightened in Kaylee's stomach.

Kaylee lifted the cup to her lips and frowned.

"What's the matter?"

"I drank all my coffee. May I have another cup?"

"I don't know," Wendy hesitated, then took the cups and went down the hall.

Kaylee started to feel like her old self, more alert, and she could lift her arms and legs without wincing. If she could convince Wendy to keep the coffee coming, she might be as good as new.

Wendy handed Kaylee a cup, and Kaylee inhaled it a few times before taking a sip.

"What kind is this?"

Wendy shrugged. "I just found it in the cupboard."

"This isn't your house?"

"It's my ex-boyfriend's."

"This is Jeff's house?" Kaylee could've kicked herself.

"No, Jeff's tastes were more refined; he liked modern architecture and furniture. It's Cory's."

"Cory Carter?"

"It's a rental; he lets me use it when I need a place to crash."

"Hmmm." Kaylee forced a weak smile.

Wendy smirked. "I knew your true colors would come out if we talked long enough. You don't think I'm good enough for Cory, and neither did his bitch sister. He likes me because I'm fun and sexy."

"It's not my place to judge."

"You're right. It's not."

The conversation veered off into dangerous territory. Men, including fathers, friends, money, status, and animals, were all topics she should avoid. Kaylee figured it would be safer not to say anything for a while.

Wendy drank her coffee and glared at Kaylee.

"What are you afraid of," Wendy asked?

Besides sitting here with you, with no clothes on, and waiting for you to lose your temper, flip out, and slit my throat?

"What?" Kaylee asked?

"What strikes fear into your whole being?"

Kaylee didn't want to share her deepest fear with a murderer. What if she used her fear against her? Yet, if she stopped sharing, Wendy would leave, which would mean certain death for Kaylee.

"I'm afraid of water."

"Water?"

"I can't swim."

Wendy burst out laughing.

Kaylee couldn't help herself. She glared at Wendy.

"It's not funny! When I was seven, I almost drowned."

Wendy grew quiet.

Kaylee regretted her outburst. She had worked so hard to gain Wendy's trust, and in an instant, it could've been blown to hell. Kaylee mentally prepared for a fight. She had a weapon, her only weapon, her mug. She could smash it over her head, scream, and try to make it out the front door. Or she could throw the hot coffee in her face, grab the chair, and use it to keep Wendy from attacking her. She might wake the neighbors if she screamed loud enough, and they could call for help. Kaylee wondered why Wendy hadn't pounced on her yet. She couldn't possibly think that Kaylee might win a fight.

"Where were your parents?" Wendy asked.

"Parents?"

"Why weren't they watching you?"

"My dad took a business call and went inside. He couldn't see me from there, and I slipped and hit my head on the side of the pool."

"What were you thinking when you thought you were dying?"

"I wasn't. I kicked and splashed and tried to get out."

"I almost died once," Wendy said somberly.

Kaylee cringed; she assumed this would be another topic better left unexplored. "What happened?"

"Why should I tell you?"

"You don't have to."

Wendy kicked something; it hit the wall. She moved her chair closer to the bed. "When I was twelve, I lived in Kansas. My brother and I were racing around the barn. I ducked under the clothesline, fell, and hit the

276

ground. I landed on a garden hoe; it stuck in my side, and I wondered if I'd died, would I go to heaven?

Kaylee's words stuck in her throat. "Who saved you?"

"My father put me in the truck and drove to the hospital with that damn thing still inside me. They took me to surgery and stitched me up. About six months later, my father started visiting me at night." Wendy glared down at Kaylee.

Kaylee closed her eyes; she didn't want Wendy to relive the most traumatic event of her life. The one that probably sent her spiraling out of control.

"I wanted to know why he would do that to me. He said he had to show me how to satisfy a man. He said I would be coming of age soon, and he needed to prepare me for when I got married. He would have started sooner if I hadn't been in the accident. What do you think about that?"

"I think your father was a sick bastard."

"Jeff told me you never cussed. I guess he didn't know you very well."

"No. He didn't."

Chapter 29

The air search proved a waste of time and money. The pilot had searched a fifty-mile radius but could not locate the red Lexus. Jensen had every available unit going door-to-door. It seemed the women had vanished.

After leaving the hospital, Jensen hurried back to the precinct to regroup with the FBI. He already knew the FBI didn't typically intercede in kidnapping cases unless the suspect and victim crossed state lines. The governor and a few other high-ranking politicians asked the FBI to join the search for their esteemed friend's daughter. The agent seemed more interested in the money laundering, mortgage fraud, and identity theft that Jeff and the funeral director had been involved in than in the kidnapping. Jensen tried to convince the agent that there'd be no ransom demand and that the victim had been abducted for the sole purpose of taking her life. The agent had to follow procedure, and Jensen knew each agency had its priorities, but his top priority was life.

Jensen realized his prior feelings of guilt over his absence during a pivotal case had been unwarranted. Despite Blanchard's disappointment, Jensen had done what any other person would have done. Jensen's father had instilled in him a strong sense of duty. Still, somewhere along the line, Jensen's devotion to his career had taken over his entire life. He had sacrificed his relationship with Bridget and most of his free time to carry on the family tradition. He recognized that social and professional lives were equally important. He knew now might not be the exact moment to start planning his future, but he would call Bridget later and ask her to go hiking; they needed to talk.

Keeping Kaylee alive had to be Jensen's primary objective; any other outcome would be unacceptable. He would prove to those who doubted his commitment that he was dedicated to public safety and upholding the rule of law.

Jensen tried to introduce the serial killer element. Still, he couldn't prove the kidnapping suspect was the same person who killed Jeff and David Swanson or that she had killed before. The only identifiable prints at the Jeff Swanson crime scene were from Kaylee, Jeff, and David Swanson. David's prints had been found on the bumper and plate frame. Wendy's prints were nowhere to be found on the car or at the crime scene; David must have tried to steal the plate and had been caught by Jeff. Or he had deliberately used it to kill Jeff and tried to frame Kaylee.

The serial killer theory had been a bust, and Jensen's attempt to entice more interest in the kidnapping case had failed miserably. If he didn't bring Kaylee home, she would die, but not before enduring agonizing pain. Desperation engulfed him.

The mound of paperwork on his desk kept getting higher. Jensen had asked for all the files on the Swanson case; he thumbed through them, hoping something new would catch his eye, but it proved useless. Jensen had read each of the files thoroughly. His eyes grew tired. He had hoped it wouldn't come to this, but it appeared that he would have to call Bridget's brother, Cory. He had dated Wendy and might have pertinent information. He hated involving his friends in the investigation, but Kaylee's life hung in the balance. He dialed Cory's number.

"Cory, It's Detective Jensen—"

"Hey, Rand. What's up?"

"I need your help."

"Help," Cory asked?

"I'm working a case, and you need to tell me everything you know about Wendy Torrison."

Cory didn't respond. Jensen wondered whether he had clammed up because he was afraid to talk about her, or if he had tried to squash down his memories of Wendy altogether.

"Cory, please, this is urgent."

"Rand, she's crazy. She's relentless, aggressive, and erratic. She has a nasty temper. One day, while we were at the mall, she assaulted a customer in a jewelry store because she wanted to try on a diamond bracelet. She's scary, dude."

"Who ended it," Jensen asked?

"Last May, she'd called and told me I wasn't good enough for her, and she'd found a real man."

"Could it have been Jeff Swanson?"

"Don't know. Believe me, bro, I didn't care."

"If Wendy felt scared, where would she go?"

"I don't know where she'd go, but nothing scares her."

Cory confirmed Jenson's previous findings: Wendy had a history of greed and violence. Jensen had spoken to her family in Kansas, and they all but denied her existence. Had she hurt someone before? She had no criminal background and no traffic violations. Her only vice seemed to be spending; did she flunk math or deliberately run up credit card debt she had no intention of paying off? Right now, money wasn't the issue. Jensen suspected Wendy must've viewed Jeff as her ticket to Easy Street. Now that he was dead, she lashed out at the person she held responsible: Kaylee.

Wendy's limited social circle made it nearly impossible to pinpoint specific areas she might use to lay low. On the advice of Wendy's former friend, Jensen and Stone visited Scottsdale's Old Town restaurants and bars. Two men who had reacted to Wendy's picture were adamant they'd never seen her. No matter how Jensen tried to spin it, he couldn't get either of the men to admit they knew or dated her. The trip was a total wash.

Jensen tried to identify places where Wendy would go if she felt vulnerable. She could hide in hundreds of abandoned buildings or unfinished subdivisions in Phoenix alone. All would provide shelter, but could be detrimental to Kaylee's condition. She had been in a precarious state before she had been kidnapped.

He checked in with the officers canvassing door-to-door and the FBI; both had struck out. Jensen ran his fingers through his hair. His hand shook. He hadn't eaten in two days and hadn't slept in three. He went to the lounge, poured himself a cup of coffee, bought a bag of pretzel M&Ms, and returned to his office.

At his desk, he reviewed the toxicology report on the water given to Kaylee in the hospital. The empty bottles had been tested, and the results showed large quantities of Rohypnol, the date rape drug, present. It must have been crushed and diluted in the water bottles. A hole that appeared to have been made with a small-gauge hypodermic needle had been found in the lids.

Immediately after Kaylee had been kidnapped, Kyle seemed agitated, and he had verbally lashed out at Lopez. Jensen had asked Kyle to help, to keep him busy and out of the investigation. When Kyle called to report back, Jensen requested that he meet at the precinct.

When Kyle arrived, it appeared his mood hadn't improved.

"Have you heard anything?" He asked.

"No—"

"What about the FBI," Kyle asked?

"I've met with them, but they have no leads."

"How hard is it to find a red Lexus?"

"Harder than you might think," Jensen replied.

"Kaylee is going to die a horrible death, so don't—"

Jensen answered his phone.

He couldn't believe it. Goldman had been stabbed, and he had found Kaylee.

He motioned for Kyle to follow him, and they rushed to his car.

"Who was that," Kyle asked?

"Stephanie Ortiz. She said Wendy had stabbed Greg Goldman, and he knows where Kaylee is."

Jensen called Lopez and instructed him to go to St. Luke's Medical Center and meet him in the ER. Jensen hit the lights and siren and sped down 16th Street.

At St. Luke's, they hurried to the nurse's station. Jensen identified himself and demanded to see Goldman; a nurse showed them to the stall. Jensen whipped back the curtain, and Greg turned white.

Kyle rushed to the bed, grabbed Greg's shoulders, and shook, "Where is she?"

Jensen and Lopez pulled him off.

"Let me handle this," Jensen ordered.

"Stephanie told me Wendy stabbed you, and you know where Kaylee is."

"I don't know what you're talking about," Greg insisted. He rubbed his shoulder.

"Don't play games. Tell me where Kaylee is," Jensen snapped.

"Where's my doctor?"

"Where is she?!" Kyle lunged toward him.

"Get him away from me!"

Lopez pulled him back and stood between Kyle and Greg.

"If you tell me where she is, I will find out what's keeping your doctor."

Greg glared at Kyle. "Keep that Neanderthal away from me."

"Get him out of here," Jensen demanded.

Lopez escorted Kyle out and closed the curtain.

Jensen approached the bed and leaned over Greg, "Where is she?"

"If I did happen to drive by the house where Kaylee was being held, and I tried to rescue her, you're not going to charge me, are you?"

"I don't care why you were there; I need to know where she is."

Greg licked his lips. "16th Street and Portland. The Lexus is parked in the drive."

"What's the address?"

"It was too dark to see, but it's the fourth house from the corner, south side."

Jensen called Stone and had her block off the street to keep everyone away from the crime scene.

He turned to leave. "Why didn't you call the police?"

"I couldn't protect her from Jeff, but I had to try to save her from his psycho girlfriend."

Chapter 30

When Wendy entered the room, Kaylee kept her eyes closed. She hadn't been sleeping but replaying her escape route over and over. Kaylee had no idea if help would arrive, so her fate rested in her hands. She prayed she had the strength to get outside.

"It's time," Wendy gleamed.

Kaylee opened her eyes and yawned.

"Time?"

"Maybe under different circumstances, we could've been friends, but—"

Kaylee had been preparing for this all night. She was as ready as she would ever be.

"I'm going to give you a choice." A smirk hovered on Wendy's lips.

"Choice?"

"Before I tell you, do you know why you're here?"

Kaylee was getting sick of this. She could tell by the look on her face that Wendy enjoyed watching Kaylee squirm. "You're mad that Jeff never got over me, and you can't handle it."

"Wrong, bitch! You were his meal ticket–nothing more." Wendy loomed at the foot of the bed.

"Whatever gets you through the night." Kaylee's words dripped with sarcasm.

"I should kill you now." She rounded the bed and towered over Kaylee.

Stop stalling. "Go ahead…"

Wendy glared.

"Jeff felt sorry for you. He said you didn't have a clue that his best friend loved you. He thought you were naïve, but I think you're just stupid."

"What difference does it make? I'm going to die."

"Don't you want to know why?"

Kaylee didn't want to give her the satisfaction.

Wendy placed her hands on the pillow on either side of Kaylee's face and leaned in. "I'm tired of working my ass off while rich, lazy people have nice things and all the fun. I want to show the world that money can't save you from violence—"

Wendy's proximity startled her. "You're going to kill me to make a statement?" Kaylee asked.

She straightened up as if she had been fluffing the pillow. "If that were true, then killing any wealthy person would have done the trick. You stole my future with Jeff, so you don't get one. You get to choose between possible death and certain death."

Wendy left the room, returned with a breakfast tray, and set it on the nightstand.

Kaylee watched as Wendy meticulously cleaned and dried each blade, then held up a long, thin blade and watched it glisten in the light.

Kaylee wondered what Wendy had planned.

"If I were you, I'd choose certain death."

"I'd like to hear my options."

Wendy disappeared again. When she returned, she brought a tall glass of water and set it next to the tray.

Kaylee's eyes followed her every move. Was she going to torture her before killing her?

Wendy scowled. "Since I can't have kids with the man I love, neither should you."

Kaylee's throat went dry. "What do you mean?"

"I can give you a hysterectomy, which would be my first attempt at surgery, and you'd probably bleed to death, or you can go for a swim in Cory's pool."

Either way, her death would be painful. Butchered by a psychotic nurse or asphyxia caused by drowning. She remembered the water burning her chest as she sank to the bottom of the pool. The fear she had been keeping at bay erupted like a volcano. Spewing its poison through her

285

body and holding her prisoner in its vice-like grip. Bile shot up her throat, choking her. Panic swelled inside her, clouding her vision. She made a grave error in telling Wendy about her fear of water.

"You'll never get away with this."

"That's not the point, is it?"

"You killed Jeff; why are you punishing me?"

"Why would I kill Jeff?"

Several reasons popped into Kaylee's head. "You tell me."

"I didn't kill him; his good-for-nothing stepfather did."

"David?"

"He said it just happened, that he was only trying to protect you, but I didn't believe him."

"Did he say why? Did he know my mother?"

"I didn't give him the chance to explain."

It took a moment, but it finally dawned on Kaylee what Wendy meant: she had killed David and, in a few minutes, would kill her.

"This is a big decision, so I'll be back in a minute. You can give me your answer then."

Fear built in her core. "Can I have some coffee?"

"No." Wendy took the tray and left.

The door slammed, and Kaylee could hear the handle jiggling as if it were locked. Now, she had no chance to run and didn't have a weapon to use against Wendy. Kaylee had hoped she could convince Wendy to let her go, but Wendy had other plans that did not include letting Kaylee live. Kaylee had spent the entire time alone in this desolate room, preparing for a fight just in case, and it looked like the worst-case scenario would play out. She glanced around the room one last time, looking for anything she could use to ward off an attack, but the room was empty.

Wendy opened the door, replaced the tray on the nightstand, and stared at the blades. She carefully ran her fingers over them, then picked up a long, serrated blade and the glass of water. She displayed both so that Kaylee could see them clearly.

"What's your poison," Wendy asked?

Kaylee focused on escaping.

"Times up! What's it going to be?"

"Go to hell!"

Kaylee jumped up and shoved Wendy into the wall. She ran toward the door. Wendy pushed her down.

She scrambled to get up, but Wendy grabbed her legs and dragged her down the hall.

Her skin slid across the hot tile, and she started to panic. They were heading to the pool.

Wendy's nails tore Kaylee's skin.

Kaylee grabbed the table leg and tried to hang on, but it was ripped from her grip.

Wendy dropped her legs to open the patio door. Kaylee kicked her in the stomach, forcing her outside. Kaylee fumbled with the lock. Wendy grabbed her arms, yanked her up, and swung her toward the pool.

Kaylee rolled toward the grass, wobbling as she stood.

Wendy charged her; they smacked the water's surface. Fluid filled Kaylee's lungs. She thrashed about, striking Wendy in the face, and Wendy went under.

Kaylee gasped for air. Chlorine stung her eyes and throat. She struggled to get control–to push down the panic. She knew if she gave in to fear, she would never see Kyle or her father again. She pushed off the tile through the water. Wendy grabbed her hair and pulled her under. Kaylee swung and kicked wildly, trying to free herself. She made contact with Wendy's leg, and Wendy sank to the bottom.

Kaylee splashed through the water.

She headed for the stairs.

Freedom was only steps away.

She grabbed the railing.

Wendy slashed Kaylee's foot with the blade.

Kaylee dropped to her knees and kicked hard. She grabbed the rail and pulled. Stumbling up the steps, she fell flat on the wet tile, gasping for air.

A loud pop echoed in Kaylee's ears.

Chapter 31

Kaylee sipped her salted caramel mocha while relaxing on Kyle's scallop-backed sofa. She had tried to convince Kyle that coffee had helped her because, without it, she wouldn't have had the strength to fight. Kyle had told her it had been an adrenaline rush, and she had said he could believe whatever he wanted. Truth be told, her anger had helped, too. She resented her father's lifelong indifference toward her and was disappointed with her inability to recognize her love for Kyle.

When Detective Jensen arrived at Kyle's, Kaylee noticed he had a large manila envelope.

"Kaylee, I hope you're feeling better."

She smiled, "Much. Thank you."

"I know you've been put through hell these past few weeks, but I need to tie up some loose ends and get answers to complete my report." He sat next to Kyle. "I learned that Wendy drugged you and took you out through the basement. Can you tell me what happened after that?"

"I remember waking up in a strange bed and thinking about dying and going to heaven to be with my mom, but then Wendy arrived and began taunting me."

"Did she say anything about your father or David before the attack?"

"Wendy had mentioned she'd confronted David about Jeff. David had tried to tell her Jeff's death had been an accident, but she'd killed him anyway."

"You're a courageous woman," Jensen said.

Kaylee gripped her mug. "I didn't know if I would make it out alive."

"Bravery is about doing what needs to be done; sometimes, that means doing nothing until the time is right."

"So, adrenaline gave me the strength to survive," Kaylee asked?

"Afraid so," Jensen agreed.

"In the pool, Wendy had let go; why did you shoot her?"

"She refused to drop the weapon. It was all by the book."

"She kidnapped you and would have killed you," Kyle said, squeezing Kaylee's hand. "I'm glad she's gone."

Kyle's painfully honest words hung in the air. She knew exactly how he felt. When it seemed that Wendy would win, Kaylee blamed Jeff for their failed relationship, missing out on Kyle's friendship and love, and her tenuous situation with her father. Jeff had hurt her, and he had done horrible things to a lot of people. She knew he didn't deserve all the blame, but it had made her feel better at the time.

Jensen handed Kaylee an envelope.

"What's this?"

"These are David's personal belongings. I'm sorry for your loss."

"Loss," Kaylee asked?

"David was your mom's twin brother," Kyle answered.

"That can't be; Mom told me her brother had died in the hospital."

"We found clippings in David's possessions indicating he'd been kidnapped by a nurse who'd worked at the hospital where your grandmother had given birth. We're not sure who uncovered the decades-old crime, but we guess that's why David left Arkansas."

Kaylee felt an immediate and overwhelming sense of sadness. It would have been wonderful to meet her mother's twin. She would've loved to ask him about his life and what made him happy. She would wait to open the envelope later when she could view its contents in private.

290

Kaylee hugged it close, just as she imagined David had done when he took his last breath, clutching the picture of her and her mother.

"Why did he leave Arizona?" Kaylee asked.

"Ask your father," Jensen replied.

"My father?"

"It would be best if your father explains his role, if any, in David's departure."

"How did David and Jeff's mom get together," Kyle asked?

"Unfortunately, we don't have all the answers."

Kaylee's mother had known her twin brother had survived, so why didn't she tell her, and why didn't Kaylee get to meet him? She would have to sort through David's items to see if she could put the pieces together.

"I'm charging Greg Goldman with obstruction," Jensen stated.

"What about Manara?" Kaylee asked?

"Greg planned to get closer to you, and he used Manara. She didn't betray you or your trust. You can rest easy now. The investigation into Jeff's death is officially closed."

"Were you able to find out why Wendy attacked my father?"

"Until Mr. Chambers can make a statement, I can only speculate that Wendy either thought your father killed Jeff or she wanted to get revenge on you by killing him."

"What about my boss, James Canon; did Jeff murder him?"

"The results were inconclusive, so his death remains undetermined."

"But his friend, Larry, needs closure."

"Mr. Lawson should concentrate on their lifelong friendship and not on how he died."

Kaylee knew memories and regrets sometimes go hand in hand, and staying focused on the happy times could be difficult. Jeff had been her friend, and she would try to remember his good qualities and let go of the monster he had become. Kaylee would have to accept that some questions would never be answered and be content with knowing she had an uncle who loved her and sacrificed his life for her.

"When can I bury David?"

"His body will be released to you in a couple of days."

Kaylee smiled at Jensen. "I appreciate all that you did for my father and me."

Jensen nodded and extended his arm. "I have the paperwork for your car."

She waved it away. "I don't want it. Too many bad memories."

As a child, she had honestly believed she could earn her father's love by working hard to show him how alike they were, but it hadn't worked. She had sacrificed so much of her life trying to please a man who couldn't be pleased. She had hoped their shared love of cars would help them bond, but this, too, had failed. She realized she had done all she could to build a relationship with him. She loved him, and that would have to be enough.

Jensen stood to leave. Kaylee asked, "If you and Bridget get back together, can I call you Randy?"

For the first time since the case had been reopened, Jensen smiled. "Will, see."

*****

Later that afternoon, lounging on Kyle's sofa, Kaylee sifted through David's personal items. She removed the picture from the plastic bag, the one of her with her mother at Chaparral Park. Kaylee had just been a child, and her mother looked so happy. She traced her mother's chin and smiled when she thought about who took it. It must have been David.

The envelope contained pictures of her mom, newspaper articles about the kidnapping, car keys, a driver's license, and one baby picture. They looked so much alike; she couldn't tell if it was her mom or David. Had David discarded all mementos from his other family? She guessed he had been angry at them for robbing him of a life with his real family. She was mad, too.

Her mother had repeatedly expressed an emptiness caused by the loss of her twin. And now they were both gone. Kaylee missed her mom and her unfailing support, and she wished she had the opportunity to get to know her uncle. He had sacrificed so much and died trying to protect her. It warmed Kaylee's heart to know that David had been reunited with her mom. The twins were finally together and at peace.

Was her father jealous of David? Is that why they had a tumultuous relationship? Did Michael envy the relationship her mom wanted with her twin? A relationship that Michael would never be a part of? Kaylee would ask Michael later, but his pride and need for privacy meant he probably wouldn't tell her.

She reverently replaced the items. Kaylee frowned knowing that all David had left, a few pictures and his car keys, fit into one envelope. His whole life had been reduced to a few meager belongings. A knot of regret formed in Kaylee's stomach. She would grieve his loss and hoped one day she could understand the senseless violence that swept through her life.

She put the envelope on the table and headed to the kitchen.

Kyle's phone rang. He walked toward her, a smile tugging at the corner of his mouth.

"Who is it?" Kaylee asked.

"Your dad's awake, and he's asking for you."

"Really?"

She followed Kyle into the garage, and he opened the car door.

Kaylee turned toward Kyle; her heart raced. "We're taking the Viper?"

He handed her the keys; she got in and buckled up.

She pressed the start button and revved up the engine. Kyle tugged on his seatbelt a second time. It was the same thrill she used to get from driving her Mustang. Kaylee gripped the steering wheel tightly and felt the power rumble beneath her hands. She pulled onto the 101, lightly tapped the gas, and glanced over. Kyle shrugged; she pressed the gas and shifted. They sped down the road.

In the elevator, on their way to the ICU, she wondered why her father suddenly wanted to see her. People don't change overnight, and she was finally ready to accept that they may never be a close-knit family. His obsession with power and wealth would always come between them. She had done all she could to repair their relationship and knew her mother would be proud of her. She could live with that.

The End

www.ingramcontent.com/pod-product-compliance
Lightning Source LLC
Chambersburg PA
CBHW070309260626
47160CB00003B/782